Praise

The Broken Hearts Bakery

"Carla Laureano can do no wrong in my eyes. *The Broken Hearts Bakery* is a delectable treat oozing with hope, heart, and the power of home. I'm rarely more content as a reader than when I'm getting lost in one of Carla's stories."
—BETHANY TURNER, BESTSELLING AUTHOR OF *THE DO-OVER*

"A Carla Laureano novel never disappoints me. A skilled storyteller, Laureano pulls you into the imaginary lives of characters she's crafted, page by page. *The Broken Hearts Bakery* is a perfect blend of romance, hope, and the satisfaction of coming home, all written in Laureano's distinctive style. After reading this book, I'd love to spend some time in Haven Ridge, which I'll do again with the eagerly anticipated next novel in the series."
—BETH K. VOGT, CHRISTY AWARD-WINNING AUTHOR

"In *The Broken Hearts Bakery*, Carla Laureano delivers a completely heartwarming and romantic tale fit for a Hallmark movie. Authentic characters struggling with real-life issues had me cheering them on through my tears. A little bit of magic, a lot of yummy baked goods, and a deliciously satisfying ending makes this novel an absolute winner!"
—HEIDI CHIAVAROLI, CAROL AWARD-WINNING AUTHOR OF *THE ORCHARD HOUSE* AND *HOPE BEYOND THE WAVES*

The MacDonald Family Trilogy

"*Five Days in Skye* swept me away to Scotland! Laureano's voice is deft, seamless, and wonderfully accomplished. An exciting newcomer to the world of Christian fiction."
—BECKY WADE, CHRISTY AWARD HALL OF FAME INDUCTEE

"Another captivating story! *London Tides* is as compelling and engaging as Laureano's award-winning *Five Days in Skye*. It's deliciously romantic and filled with tension, wonderful characters, and vivid scenery. A must-read this summer!"
—KATHERINE REAY, AUTHOR OF *THE LONDON HOUSE* AND *A SHADOW IN MOSCOW*

"Solid characters, brilliant dialogue, believable conflict, a setting you can taste—and, always, breath-stealing love scenes. No one writes a romantic hero like Laureano! *Under Scottish Stars* takes us back to Skye to explore poignant truths of single parenthood, family loyalty, the pursuit of dreams—and faith. A satisfying and stellar finish to the MacDonald Family trilogy."
—CANDACE CALVERT, BESTSELLING AUTHOR

The Saturday Night Supper Club

"You don't have to be a foodie to enjoy *The Saturday Night Supper Club*, but if you are, you're in for an extra treat. Carla Laureano has written a delicious romance you'll want to devour in one sitting. Filled with sugar and spice, *The Saturday Night Supper Club* will leave you hungry for more from this talented author."
—IRENE HANNON, BESTSELLING AUTHOR AND THREE-TIME RITA® AWARD WINNER

The
LARKSPUR
House

Books by Carla Laureano

MacDonald Family Trilogy
Five Days in Skye
London Tides
Under Scottish Stars

Supper Club Series
The Saturday Night Supper Club
Brunch at Bittersweet Cafe
The Solid Grounds Coffee Company

Discovered by Love Series
Jilted (novella)
Starstruck (novella)
Snowbound (novella)
Sunswept (novella)

Haven Ridge Series
The Brick House Cafe (novella)
The Broken Hearts Bakery
The Beacon Street Bookshop
The Larkspur House

The Song of Seare Trilogy
Oath of the Brotherhood
Beneath the Forsaken City
The Sword and the Song

Provenance

The
LARKSPUR

House

CARLA LAUREANO

LAUREANO
CREATIVE MEDIA

Published by Laureano Creative Media LLC
P.O. Box 460241
Aurora, CO 80046, U.S.A.
laureanocreativemedia.com

Cover design by Hillary Manton Lodge Design. Images from Dreamstime and Adobe Stock.
Copyedited by Denise Harmer

ISBN 978-1-960079-06-0 (sc)
ISBN 978-1-960079-05-3 (e-book)
Library of Congress Control Number: 2024910084   062424

ACKNOWLEDGMENTS

I seem to think that writing books should be easy, but every time I look at past acknowledgment pages, I realize that's anything but the truth. But it's clear that I'm blessed with a wonderful group of family, friends, and publishing professionals who are with me every step of the way. I'm immensely grateful for all of you!

First, thank you to my wonderful Haven Ridge Beta Team—Meaghan Ahlbrand, Jessica Baker, Elisabeth Callahan, Leslie Florea, Amy Parrish, and Hope Thacker—for their astute yet kind feedback. You're my first line of defense in the editing process, and you're so amazingly smart and insightful that you leave very little for my editors to do!

More thanks to my lovely Facebook Reader Room crew, who were so encouraging when I was considering deleting the entire book and starting over from scratch. That didn't turn out to be necessary, but it feels good to know you have my back. Thanks, my friends!

A special shout-out to my copyeditor, Denise Harmer, and my wildly talented cover designer, Hillary Manton Lodge. You two helped me create a book that I could be proud of—couldn't have done it without you!

A big round of applause for my literary agent, Steve Laube, who has been in my corner for a full decade and has stuck with me no matter which path I've chosen on this publishing journey.

And last, lots of love to my family who always pretend to be interested in what I'm writing even if they're not, feed me when I'm working late, and act like I'm not actually a giant weirdo who lives in her head most of the time. I love you all!

CHAPTER ONE

When Rose Cameron was young, she'd thought novels that began with the heroine metaphorically limping into town with all her possessions packed in the back of her beat-up car were dramatic and romantic. Just because she was a defended dissertation short of a PhD in nineteenth-century American Literature didn't mean that she was immune to the lure of commercial fiction. In fact, she loved it for its promise: no matter how bad things looked for the main character, the author practically guaranteed that everything would work out in the end.

Until, of course, she found herself in that very scenario. Now it just felt pathetic.

At least she wasn't crawling back *home*. That really *would* have been pathetic. Her parents had offered, of course, but the only thing worse than listening to your parents say *I told you so* at twenty-eight was doing it post-divorce with your reputation in tatters, a cautionary tale for how intelligent women were often the stupidest when it came to love.

No, this wasn't a *coming home* story. This was a

running away story, and in her experience, those had the potential to be so much more interesting.

At least that's what she told herself as she bumped up the rutted Colorado road in the aging Volvo she'd purchased with her last three thousand dollars just before she left Wisconsin—another depressingly cliche detail in her personal tragedy. Gravel flew up behind her tires and pinged the pitted frame, probably adding more "character" to the already rusted-out undercarriage. She pulled closer to the shoulder, which sloped down into a gully, as a battered pick-up truck roared down the road the other direction. The guy behind the wheel was wearing a trucker hat, and he lifted a finger off the steering wheel in a salute as he passed. She gave a half-hearted wave before navigating the car safely back into the lane.

We're not in Wisconsin anymore, Toto.

The thought brought a smile to Rose's lips, perhaps her first one since this whole nightmare had begun, and despite herself, her spirits lifted. She rolled down the window and sucked in a deep breath of clear high-altitude air before the choking cloud of road dust sifted in. She hurriedly rolled the window back up and turned on the rattling fan inside instead.

There hadn't been any exterior photos in the online ad for the temporary position at the quaintly named Larkspur House in the equally quaintly named Haven Ridge, Colorado—just a picture of the charming guest room that would be her digs for the duration of the job and a stock photo of the nearby Arkansas River—but she'd assumed that she was coming to the land of snow-capped mountains and expansive groves of spruce and aspen. She hadn't understood that Haven Ridge was actually close to New Mexico, the landscape rougher and more arid than her visions of evergreen ski areas. The mountains were craggy and painted in a dry June's shades of brown, the landscape dotted with cactus and piñon. Beautiful in a high-desert sort of way, but far more forlorn and barren than she'd visualized.

Oddly appropriate, given it reflected how she currently felt about her life.

After what felt like an eternity, the GPS on the phone suction-cupped to the dash chimed, and a robotic female voice announced, "You have arrived."

Rose braked in the middle of the dirt road and looked around. She'd arrived? There was nothing here but untouched landscape, and if she squinted, the thin Morse code of the highway in the distance, sparsely punctuated by the dots of cars and dashes of eighteen-wheelers.

And then she saw a break in the clutch of piñon pine, a stake holding a rickety wooden sign that proclaimed in faded letters: *Larkspur House.*

Her stomach clenched. She'd thought this was a romance or some high-concept women's fiction, but now she was wondering if it were actually a horror novel.

But there was nothing to do but to find out. Carefully, she pressed down on the gas pedal, spinning her rear wheels on the gravel as she turned down the poorly marked lane.

As soon as her tires touched faded asphalt, she let out her breath. Okay, so maybe this wasn't quite as isolated as she'd thought. The wild landscape gave way to signs of human cultivation: the lane was lined with American elms, a tree she knew most definitely was not native to Colorado. Some scraggly foliage clung to a derelict wood-and-wire fence that backed the trees on both sides; it took her a few seconds to figure out they were neglected grapevines.

The road took a dip and a turn, and Rose was so startled that she slammed on her brakes, eliciting a disturbing mechanical creak. The description had said that Larkspur House was a private Tudor-style home that had been completed in 1906 but had been only intermittently inhabited since 1930. She'd expected something modest that blended into the landscape, suitable for an early wealthy settler who had wanted to be closer to his mining or railroad interests.

This was a castle. A literal castle.

When Rose regained her senses, she pressed down on the accelerator and crept the last hundred yards to the house, taking in her temporary home. Tucked into a niche formed by the jagged separation of two rocky cliffs, it rose in four stories of red stone blocks, its crenelated roofline contributing to the castle feeling, the dozens of arch-topped windows on each level explaining the Tudor manor reference. One side of the house was rounded like a turret, the rectangular section of the building nestled up beside it. As unexpected as it was, its red stone and dark trim blended into the landscape, almost as if it had sprung fully-formed from the earth at the hand of some architecturally inclined force of nature.

It was nothing short of spectacular.

As she neared it, however, she began to see the telltale signs of neglect: trim missing or splintered by dry-rot, a missing pane of antique glass replaced by plywood, the mill's stamp clearly visible. Beyond the arches of what could have either been a bridge or a retaining wall stood what must have once been an impressive rose garden, now choked with weeds and native grasses, the occasional bright streak of blooms struggling upward through the chaos.

Not for the first time in the last year, Rose wondered what in the world she had gotten herself into.

But she was here, her bank account was in the low triple digits, and however neglected, the castle offered shelter and a job. She couldn't get picky now. She pulled up the drive and slowed to a stop at a paved section just to the left of the entrance, into what she presumed was a parking space.

She twisted the key in the ignition and the car shuddered to silence with an ominous cough that made her think it might not start up again. That was not helping the horror movie vibes. Rose pushed open the driver's door and stepped onto the bed of gravel with a crunch, where she was hit by the simultaneous sensations of burning-hot sun and a cool breeze, without a hint of the wetness that characterized a Midwestern summer. She could almost feel her pale Irish skin charring to a crisp—the drawback of being a true redhead. She reached for her ever-present SPF50 Chapstick in the front pocket of her jeans and swiped a coating over her lips.

Now or never.

Before Rose could get even halfway to the front steps, the massive oak door creaked open. She halted, suddenly gripped by the memory of too many Gothic novels, wondering if she'd be met by a brooding owner or a snarling caretaker who didn't want Rose to find out their dark secrets.

And then the figure stepped into the slanted sunlight. Rose let out a startled laugh at how quickly her own imagination had run away with her.

"Hi! You must be Rose!" The woman who strode toward her was young, petite and lithe with a shining cap of dark hair cut into a pixie style. Rose had barely registered what was happening before the woman moved straight up to her and pressed her into a quick hug.

"Uh, hi. You'd be Erin?"

The woman nodded and stepped back, her wide smile lighting her face. Up close, Rose realized she'd

been wrong about her assessment—Erin was older than
she looked, perhaps somewhere in her late thirties, the
lines around her eyes and mouth giving her away. But
there was a sparkle about her that was irresistible, and
Rose instantly liked her.

"I am Erin, yes. Long drive, was it? You didn't do it
all the way through from Milwaukee, did you?"

"Uh, no. I stayed over in Omaha."

"Oh, that's smart. Shall we grab your bags?"

Rose nodded, swept along by Erin's enthusiasm, and
followed the woman to the trunk of her car. The button
beneath the lip of the trunk turned out not to work—
another unpleasant discovery about her already sketchy
purchase—and she had to go back to the driver's side to
release the catch. But through it all, Erin stayed as perky
and upbeat as ever, the smile never leaving her lips.

And people called Rose pathologically cheerful.

Between the two of them, they managed to hoist
Rose's two large suitcases out of the back, Erin politely
ignoring the small scattering of boxes with sad labels
like *College Stuff* and one that had said *Wedding* before
she'd aggressively scribbled it out with black Sharpie. In
the numerous phone and email conversations they'd had
over the past couple of weeks, they hadn't discussed
what had brought Rose halfway across the country, but
what other reason was there for a woman to hide out in
the middle of the Colorado mountains if not something
to do with a man?

But while she was musing, Erin was already
chattering away, dragging the larger suitcase with a rocky
hiss through the gravel up to the front door. "You'll be
staying on the fourth floor next to me." Erin paused and
threw her a concerned look. "I hope that's okay. I know
you were looking for a little solitude."

Rose looked around the property, only the rustle of

the wind and the faint buzz and chirp of insects breaking the deep silence. "I think I'll find quite enough solitude here, no matter where I stay."

Erin's smile broke free. "I'm so glad. I have to admit, the house is a little big for one person, and I was finding it lonely. Parts of it were modernized sometime in the seventies, but the bedrooms in the family wing are still quite old-fashioned. I thought you might like that better anyway. Did you say you studied Victorian literature or something like that?"

"Realist literature, actually. Henry James, Edith Wharton . . . you know, women trapped by unfeeling social forces and the consequences of moral corruption."

Erin paused in her process of hefting the suitcase up the first step and looked Rose up and down, taking in her simple jeans, T-shirt, and rolled-sleeve blazer. "I suppose that tracks. So, no madness or wives in the attic for you?"

Rose flushed, wondering if that was a hint of disappointment in Erin's gaze. Whenever people heard she had been a literature PhD candidate, they seemed to expect her to either be whimsical and bohemian or dressed head to toe in tweed. Her Brooks Brothers wardrobe just threw everyone off. She offered a slight smile. "Not so much. Please tell me there are no secret wives in the attic here. Is there an attic?"

The shadows disappeared, and Erin laughed. "No wives, just a lot of dust and maybe some old furniture. I haven't been up there yet. I thought I might need some moral support." She leaned on the lever-style door handle and pushed the heavy door open, waving Rose in behind her.

Rose stepped into the foyer and stopped in her tracks, gaping up at the two-story entryway. From the exterior, she'd expected something faithful to its Tudor references. But inside, the castle was warm and welcoming, with parquet floors and wood paneling and walls washed in an inviting shade of cream. Paintings and tapestries hung everywhere she looked, evoking more of a Craftsman vibe than a castle. If it looked like a monument from the outside, from the inside, it was clear that the Larkspur House had once been a family home.

As if following Rose's thoughts, Erin smiled and said, "It's pretty, isn't it? It was a nice place to grow up. My twin brother and I lived here with our grandparents until we went off to college."

"Oh, you have a twin?" That was something that Erin hadn't mentioned.

"Yeah, but he rarely comes here. He was never quite as attached to the place as I was."

There was a volume of information in those words and that tone, but Rose had just gotten here, and there was no way she was going to pry into the owner's personal business. Instead, she turned her attention to the wide flight of stairs in front of her, which crawled however many stories through the core of the house. "You don't happen to have an elevator, do you?"

Erin laughed. "Unfortunately not. We're going to have to carry these up ourselves."

Rose groaned. Erin laughed again, and somehow the solidarity lifted her spirits. She'd been wondering what she'd gotten herself into, agreeing to help empty this behemoth and prepare it for sale—probably the reason Erin hadn't actually posted pictures—but she liked her employer. Normal, probably with some family drama, but positive and upbeat. There were worse places to hide out when your life fell apart. And based on the square footage here, she might be here longer than she'd thought.

After huffing and puffing their way up three flights

of stairs, they finally emerged into a wide sunny hallway, courtesy of the arched windows that Rose had noticed from outside. Erin led the way down the hall, the wheels of Rose's suitcase bunching up the antique runner beneath them, and then stopped at the second door from the end on the right side.

"I thought we'd put you in here," she said. "It has the nicest view of the grounds, and I'm right next door if you need anything."

Whatever Rose was going to say next disappeared when Erin pushed the door open for her. She wandered into the room and turned in a slow circle to take it in. "Wow."

Erin beamed. "I thought you would like it. I cleaned it up for you. It was pretty dusty."

Rose wouldn't have cared if it was covered in a layer of soot. The space was absolutely gorgeous. Wood-paneled walls—unusual in private spaces, which would usually have had cheaper, painted paneling—stretched down to aged parquet floors, antique rugs spread nearly corner to corner. On one end of the room was a carved four-poster bed covered with fresh white linens and a down comforter; on the other was an old-fashioned blue velvet settee set in the niche below one of the large, arched windows. Heavy brocade draperies could be closed against the cold and light, and the original gas lamps appeared to have been converted to electric around the room.

Rose wandered over to the window beside the settee and drew the curtains back to peer out the window. It had a view of the backside of the house, what had no doubt once been rolling, manicured lawns but had now largely gone wild, overtaken by weeds and grasses. In the middle of it all was a rock-bordered pond, surrounded by the tangled, neglected rose garden. It was utterly charming.

She turned to Erin, who was still waiting just inside

the door with a look of pained anticipation. "It's perfect."

Erin clapped her hands together in delight. "Oh, I'm so glad. How about I leave this here"—she indicated the other suitcase, still by the door—"and let you wash up and rest for a bit? And when you're ready, just knock next door and I'll show you around the place."

"That sounds great, thank you." Rose crossed the room to grab her suitcase at the same time that Erin reached for the handle. Their hands collided and they both pulled back with self-conscious laughs. As Erin snatched back her arm, the long sleeve of her blouse rode up, revealing a ropy white scar running vertically inside her wrist.

Rose froze in place, but Erin didn't seem to notice, already turning back to the door. "Rest well. I hope you'll be happy here."

"Thanks," Rose said faintly, not moving, even after Erin shut the door behind her.

The scar was old and long-healed, but there was no mistaking what it was from.

Once, a long time ago, Erin Parker had tried to kill herself.

CHAPTER TWO

AFTER ERIN LEFT THE ROOM, Rose explored her new digs a little further. Clearly, there had been updates made to the castle since it was built around the turn of the century—she doubted that the large walk-in closet or the en suite bath had been original construction. Or maybe it had. It wasn't as if indoor plumbing had been unheard of in that time period for wealthy houses, and it was clear that there was nothing rural or backwards about this castle.

She unpacked her suitcases, shaking the wrinkles out of her clothing and hanging them on some of the hangers that had been helpfully provided in the closet, then packed away her T-shirts and nightclothes and underthings in the drawers of an antique highboy situated across from the bed. Then she went into the bathroom where an old-fashioned claw-foot tub stood and turned the taps as hot as they would go. The faucet spluttered and spit for several seconds—a sure sign Rose was the first person to use this bathroom in some time—but eventually clear water poured out.

And some time after that, it actually turned hot.

When Rose had soaked away the aches from her last two days in the car, she dried herself with one of the slightly threadbare towels provided and slipped on a pair of pajama shorts and a tank top. Then she padded back into the bedroom, slipped between the clean sheets, and promptly fell into a deep, dreamless sleep.

When she woke again, the light slanting through the window had changed to a deep gold, the shadows falling in a different direction through the room. Rose sat up, disoriented and disheveled, casting about for a clock—there wasn't one. She jumped out of bed and raced back to the bathroom, where she'd left her phone, and stared at the face in disbelief. Six o'clock? She'd slept an entire four hours? She was just supposed to rest and then get a rundown of her duties.

Rose wiped her face with her hands and groaned. This was not the impression she'd wanted to make on her employer. She stumbled into the closet and pulled out a fresh pair of jeans and a short-sleeved blouse, then thrust her feet into rubber-soled clogs that should suffice for any kind of mess that they might encounter.

Only then did she hear what she should have noticed sooner—the clear, moody strains of a cello playing somewhere deep within the house.

Ignoring the Gothic vibes that the resonating C-string set into her bones, Rose moved out of her room and followed the sound. It seemed to be coming from the floor below, so she slowly descended the stairs, relying on her ears to guide her down the hallway. The sound led her to the second door on the right, a sliver of light coming through the crack between the door and the frame.

Feeling like she was intruding—which she was—Rose carefully pushed the door inward and peered into the room. It was a library, or at least it had been; the tall shelves were mostly empty, making what should be a warm and inviting space feel somewhat forlorn. And over by the window, seated in a stiff-looking antique chair, sat Erin with a stunning cello, coaxing from it the most beautiful and mournful notes that Rose had ever heard.

Even knowing she was interrupting something private, Rose couldn't tear herself away, held by the music and the look of furrowed concentration on Erin's face as she played. The mournful sound changed into a frantic, angry tone and then melted again into what Rose could only call despair. It was the most emotional piece she had ever heard, and she couldn't help but think back to the scar on Erin's wrist, wonder if it could only be played by someone who had known that kind of anguish. Tears gathered on Rose's lashes at the sheer feeling in the music.

When at last the final notes faded and Erin put down her bow, Rose hesitated by the door, undecided on how to make her presence known. But as Erin rose and placed her cello in the open case beside her, she asked, "Do you play an instrument?"

Rose jolted at the idea her presence hadn't gone unnoticed, but she took the question as an invitation to venture farther into the room. "No, unfortunately. But that was lovely. And sad. What was it?"

"Fauré's Élégie, opus 24." Erin threw her a melancholy smile. "About the time period you study, I'd think. It was written in 1880."

"You're a professional then?" It seemed silly to think otherwise, after what she'd just witnessed, but Erin had said nothing about being a massively talented musician in all their online conversations about this job. They were in the middle of the southern Colorado mountains—where could someone of her talent actually find to play professionally?

But Erin answered that too in her next breath. "I'm on leave from the Chicago Symphony right now. Principal cellist. At least, I was."

The statement, like her playing, was loaded with meaning, the context for which Rose knew she was missing. But before she could find a way to ask any of the wildly inappropriate questions that were flitting through her mind, Erin straightened with a bright smile, the haunted look of moments ago vanishing so quickly that Rose wondered if she'd just imagined it. "Do you feel up to a tour now?"

"Of course!" Rose stepped back from the doorway to let Erin pass, noting that she left her cello case lying open on the antique rug by the window, and followed her back into the hallway.

"So, you've already more or less seen the upper floor. There are six bedrooms upstairs, and they're pretty much the same, though only the three on our end have en suite baths. The other three at the other end of the hall share one. Don't ask me why." Erin threw an amused look at Rose. "There was probably a logical structural reason for it, but my grandparents always used to say that sharing a bathroom built character. I think they just didn't want us to have a reason to never leave our bedrooms when we were young."

"They probably didn't want to set you up for unrealistic expectations as an adult. Who can afford to live alone these days, and with two bathrooms?"

Erin smiled. "Easier in Haven Ridge than you might think. This is not exactly a tourist destination. Though," she added after a moment's thought, "that seems to be changing. I'll show you the town later and you'll see what I mean. I thought we'd eat dinner out later."

"Sounds good," Rose said, but once more, there were plenty of things that were flying over her head. She shouldn't be surprised. The entire situation—a lone woman hiring her to help clean up a historic castle for sale in the middle of nowhere—reeked of subtext that she didn't quite understand, and why shouldn't that extend to the town as well? For that matter, she still couldn't quite say how she'd come across the online job listing in the first place. She'd been searching in entirely different states, figuring that Colorado would be too expensive, and yet this listing had come up as a match for her searches in Oklahoma.

Erin was going on, though, and Rose realized she was missing part of the tour. ". . . used to be the library, but it had water damage and my brother sold off a lot of the books last year." She made a face, clearly not happy with that decision. "I understand why he did it, though. There's been plenty of damage from all the utilities being turned off. The floors in particular haven't fared well." Erin toed a gap in the parquet floor, clearly a response to extreme temperatures. "That's partly why I need you here. We need to assess the damage before . . . well, we just need to see what we're working with."

Another hint that there was something going on here that she didn't understand, but Rose didn't press. Erin went on anyway, opening and closing doors just long enough to briefly peer inside. On the third floor there were two more studies, both filled with antique furniture, a room that was outfitted as a bedroom but probably had been something else at some time, and two completely vacant rooms, devoid of everything but the painted paneling and light fixtures. It was indeed far too big of a house for a single person; too big for most families, in fact.

On the second floor, there were more rooms being used as storage for furniture and boxes and what looked like an office. "My brother uses this when he's here,"

Erin explained, though it could just as easily have been empty since the house was built, for all the signs of life inside. "He's an accountant."

Rose smiled. It was almost a twin cliche. The responsible brother had gone into accounting, and his polar opposite twin had pursued music. No wonder he wasn't as enamored with the house as Erin. He probably looked at this place and just saw dollar signs. For that matter, Rose wasn't even an accountant and that's what she saw. There were grand details, of course—beautiful plaster and wood moldings, detailed paneling, stunning floors, antique furnishings—but also cracks in the walls, signs of previous water damage, a chill that seemed to linger even during the middle of summer. So far, she wasn't seeing what she could do here, besides begin removing the half-century worth of grime that had accumulated in the unused rooms.

But there was dignity in hard work of any kind, so she told herself to keep an open mind as Erin led her back down to the ground floor.

"Here's where we spent a lot of our time," Erin said, pushing open a swinging door to the kitchen.

It was. . .enormous. It reminded her of the period kitchens from shows like *Downton Abbey*, with its huge, wide-open spaces, massive freestanding wood island, and a fireplace that looked large enough to fit an entire tree trunk inside. Rose was sure that the cabinets were original, painted in an off-white color and sporting old-fashioned clasp-style hardware. But there was a newer commercial stainless-steel refrigerator and freezer set into the wall on one end, and a massive eight-burner range that had probably cost as much as Rose's first condo.

"Wow." It was all she could think of to say.

"I know." Erin laughed. "Kind of a shame that I mostly eat takeout or in town while I'm here."

Rose threw her a look. "You don't cook?"

"Never learned," Erin said, perfectly unperturbed. "I spend my life in rehearsal halls and most nights by the time I get home, I'm too tired to do anything but scramble eggs or microwave something."

"Oh, we're going to change that," Rose said, mentally rubbing her hands together. She wouldn't say she was a gourmet cook, but she'd always made dinner at home, even though Jordan had insisted they had enough money to eat out or even hire a cook. Now that she knew where all that money had come from, she was glad that she'd refused. On different grounds, of course, but at least she'd only been minimally dragged into his profligacy.

She threw off that thought and the dark corridors it led to and refocused on the kitchen in front of her. She moved to the refrigerator and opened it, finding only a case of Topo Chico mineral water and a half-eaten package of strawberries. She looked to Erin, who just shrugged.

"I told you."

The freezer was only a little better, stacked with a handful of frozen pizzas and a few cartons of an ice cream brand she didn't recognize. Rose started to make a mental grocery list as she circled the rest of the room. "We definitely need to make a stop at the store. It's time that you ate some home-cooked meals."

"As long as you don't make me cook them," Erin said with a laugh. "How about I pay for the ingredients and you make them into something edible?"

It might have seemed like an uneven trade, but right now Rose had far more time than money, so it seemed fair to her. "Deal. Maybe when we go out to dinner tonight?"

Erin flashed her a brilliant smile that made Rose think maybe she was here for company as much as labor, and she didn't hate the idea. No matter her troubled past, the woman seemed easygoing and forthright.

That was exactly what Rose needed. A retreat, free of complications and drama. She'd had enough of that in the last three years to last a lifetime.

As if the kitchen wasn't impressive enough. Erin led her to the back of the house and through a set of French doors. Rose ground to a stop. "Wow."

"Yeah, it's beautiful, isn't it? I read or play my cello out here when the weather is nice."

Rose could only call the room a conservatory. It was clearly an outdoor space, with a fitted stone floor, but the entire thing—walls, ceiling—was completely made out of glass panels. A scattering of old-fashioned wicker furniture occupied the space, but it didn't take much imagination to see it like it was probably intended—filled with delicate tropical plants and potted fruit trees. She couldn't entirely understand the sudden itch for a matched pair of lemon and lime trees to flank the glass doors that led out onto the neglected grounds, but she wanted them all the same.

This isn't your house, she reminded herself. Her job was to take away, not to add, to help make it appealing for a future buyer.

If they appeal to me, they'd appeal to someone else, that inner voice said, completely oblivious to the fact that actual fruit trees were not in the same class as say, a record player or a book collection.

She stepped up to the wall of windows on the far side and looked out on the grounds, turned golden by the slowly setting sun, a flaming jewel in a brilliant orange and blue setting on the horizon. And despite the fact that this was supposed to be a short-term gig and she had no reason to feel this way, she couldn't throw off the recognition that for the first time since leaving South Carolina ten years ago, this was the first place that actually felt like home.

CHAPTER THREE

There were a few more stops on the tour—all boring but necessary, like the fuse box, the water main, and other utilities in the house—but when they were finished, Erin clapped her hands together excitedly. "So. What do you think? You want to see the town now?"

"Sure." What Rose really wanted to do was take a book into any one of the beautifully decorated rooms and read until nightfall, but that wasn't what she was here for, and besides, she'd probably end up sneezing from all the dust within ten minutes. Besides, it would be useful to get a town tour from a local so she knew where to go, where to avoid, and generally how to not look like a clueless tourist.

Erin led her back out the door of the kitchen and started down a small slope to what the woman identified as the carriage house. When she unlocked the padlock on the double barn doors and pulled one open, it revealed a cavernous space fragrant with wood shavings, the only occupant a blue 1950s farm truck.

"Wow," Rose said. "Does that thing really run?"

"Of course," Erin said with a grin. "This beast will

probably outlast us." She went back to pull the other door open, then fished an old key out of her pocket. She climbed into the driver's seat, inserted it into the ignition, and gave it a twist. The old truck coughed as it started, but then turned over with a throaty rumble.

Rose smiled, and at Erin's gesture, climbed through the passenger door onto the bench seat. Despite the fact the night was chilly, she rolled down the window and propped her arm on the sill. This was just feeding into the secret Hallmark movie fantasies she had harbored since childhood. All they needed was snowfall and a Christmas tree in the back of the truck to be complete.

Well, and a flannel-wearing small-town lumberjack.

She grinned at the thought as Erin pulled out of the carriage house, then jumped out to close the doors behind them. Then they bumped up the gravel road toward the highway, the cloud of dust immediately reminding Rose why it was a bad idea to have the window down.

"So what do you know about Haven Ridge?" Erin asked conversationally as they turned onto the highway. The rattle of the unpaved road turned to the smooth hum of rubber on asphalt.

"Only what you put in the job listing. Isn't it an old mining town or something?"

"Not exactly. Kind of an anti-mining town, actually. It was founded by a woman named Elizabeth Strong who wanted a safe haven for her own children and women with no place to go, and it kind of expanded from there. From what Mallory has uncovered, it looks like the Strong Supply Depot was the first woman-owned business in the region, which is pretty impressive."

Rose threw her a quizzical look. "Mallory?"

"The town historian. She's writing a book and everything on us. You'll probably meet her. She co-owns the cafe in town."

It truly was a small town when the town historian was also the cafe owner. Rose grinned, enjoying the contrast from the metropolitan area she'd just left. "What else should I know?"

"Well, the fact that the town is magic."

Rose blinked. "Come again?"

Erin laughed. "Oh, I don't know if it's really true. It's an old legend. Something about the town drawing people to it who needed a haven. And if you look at the history, it certainly seems true. The place wouldn't even be here if it weren't for a long string of coincidences that feel a little *too* coincidental, if you know what I mean."

Rose really didn't, but she was charmed by the idea, so she just nodded. "It seems to be true for me. Your listing literally showed up when I was despairing of what I was going to do next. I had to be out of my house in a week. That's part of the reason I jumped on it."

"You know, you never did say exactly why you're here."

There was a reason for that. The whole story was too sordid to spill to a stranger, and it cast her in the worst, most naive light. "Nasty divorce. Let's just say that my husband wasn't who I thought he was. No, let's not even give him that much credit. He hid that he was an awful person and he tried to pin the blame for his own actions on me. His family is still convinced I was the bad apple who dragged him into temptation."

Erin grimaced. "Ouch. And you let them get away with that?"

"I'm just a nobody. If I told you their last name, you'd know why that would be an exercise in futility. They own half of Milwaukee and a good chunk of Chicago."

Erin threw her a sympathetic look. "I'm really sorry. It does sound like this came along at just the right time."

It was better than being out on the street with her pathetic handful of boxes, that was for sure. Though

Rose still wasn't sure where she was going from here. This was just a stopover. A respite. A haven, if she wanted to get poetic about it.

"Well, if you need a good divorce lawyer, we have one of the best." Erin grinned at her. "She also happens to be the owner of the greatest and only bakery in town."

Rose laughed at yet another mash-up, hoping she'd have the chance to see the bakery herself when Erin navigated into town a few minutes later. Haven Ridge proper was just as charming as she had imagined, streets lined with orange brick buildings trimmed out with white gingerbread or painted in pastel shades. She could tell that it had fallen on hard times—here and there, she saw boarded up windows and peeling paint or lots surrounded by chain link fence and littered with weeds.

But there were also signs of revival—newly painted storefronts and freshly whitewashed brick and dumpsters on the street speaking to renovations. Maybe it was just that she needed to believe in second chances, but a feeling of hope radiated from this old downtown. Like a reminder that even old battered things could come back to life again given enough love and patience.

"Hey, look right there." Erin pointed at a block of buildings, all of which seemed vacant except the white one in the middle, which had warm Edison lights in the windows and a charming blue sign out front declaring *The Beacon Street Bookshop*. "Our family trust owns that building. The bookshop just opened last year. I'm sure you'll want to visit it. The owner used to be a New York book editor."

"Sounds great." Rose certainly would want to visit it, though she wasn't sure she'd have a ton of time, given the size of the job she had apparently undertaken. Still, she had to have some time off sometime, didn't she?

Erin made a turn down what seemed to be a main street—the sign called it Dogwood Street—and here it seemed like most buildings were filled with a mix of touristy and practical: a laundromat here, an herbalist there, an old-fashioned-looking five-and-dime with new-fashioned items like iPhone chargers in the window. Rose saw the bakery before Erin pointed it out—a corner brick building with a whimsical design of hearts and vines on the glass, beautifully decorated cakes on display. The window declared it the Broken Hearts Bakery.

Rose smiled. Now she understood the divorce lawyer/baker connection. She made a note to stop in when she made a trip to the bookstore. That was definitely a place she'd be spending some time.

And then they were at the end of the street and the mostly deserted lane was suddenly crowded with cars parked along the curb. Bright light spilled from plate glass windows, illuminating the interior of a diner packed with patrons at booths and tables. Erin whipped into an open parking spot just past the diner and smiled. "Some places have bars and coffee shops. We have the Brick House Cafe."

Rose followed Erin over the curb and up the sidewalk, through a glass door with a jingle of harness bells to announce them. They were immediately hit with warmth and conversation and the heavenly aroma of delicious-smelling food.

Almost as soon as they entered, a beautiful dark-haired woman circled the counter with two menus in her hand. "Erin!" She gave the other woman a warm hug and then turned brilliant emerald eyes on Rose. "Hi! I don't think we've met. I'm Mallory."

"Rose Cameron." Rose offered a tentative smile and was rewarded with a warm one in return. "I'm working up at Larkspur House with Erin."

Mallory's expression shifted a degree, the sudden knowing light in her eyes making Rose feel like she was missing something important. "Well, let's get you a seat. The counter is available now, or we're clearing a table in the corner if you want to wait."

"We'll wait," Erin said immediately and drew Rose out of the way of a new party coming in.

"Does pretty brisk business," Rose said, watching the newcomers take the few open seats at the counter.

"It's been an institution for about as long as the town has existed. It almost closed after the owner died, but his grandson, Thomas, came back and revived it. You'll meet him eventually. He also happens to be the town mayor. Mallory is his wife."

"Does everyone have multiple jobs around here?"

"Everyone except for me," Erin said cheerily, but there was a shadow beneath her words that belied the tone. Before Rose could respond, Erin said, "Look, Mallory is ready for us."

The owner gestured to them and they followed her to a small table near the back window, where she set water and menus in front of them before disappearing. Rose perused her menu for a moment. "What's good?"

"Everything. The meatloaf is their specialty, but they also make a pretty mean burger. The Reuben is good, too, and the French fries are to die for . . ."

Rose laughed. "Got it." She quickly settled on the burger—she hadn't had one of those in *ages* considering that Jordan thought that sort of stuff was too lowbrow and unhealthy—and on a whim ordered a strawberry milkshake to go along with it.

"I like your style," Erin said with a satisfied nod when Rose ordered from Mallory a few minutes later. "I'll have that too."

As soon as Mallory moved away, Erin folded her arms

on the table and leaned over them. "Fair warning. At some point before we leave this diner, we're going to be accosted."

Rose went still, studying her host's face for any sign she was kidding. "Accosted how? By who exactly?"

But Erin didn't answer, just sat back in her seat with a smug look and nodded toward the entrance. "See for yourself. I swear she has some sort of radar."

Winding directly toward them like a heat-seeking missle was an older lady wearing a jean jacket, cropped black pants, and a pair of black-and-white Air Jordans. Even from this distance, Rose could see that the ends of her silver bob were colored a bright blue. She glanced back at Erin. "Seriously?"

"Oh yeah. Either she really does have some weird sixth sense or she has the place bugged. Anyone new walks into the Brick House Cafe and she's here to greet them within twenty minutes. Every time."

Rose didn't have much time to consider how that was possible—and which was more plausible, spy gear or magic—because the woman was upon them, looking down at them with a sparkle in her eye and a knowing look on her wrinkled face. "Well, hello there. Are you going to introduce me to your friend, Erin?"

Erin just lifted an eyebrow as if to say *see?* "Granny Pearl, this is Rose Cameron. I've hired her to help up at Larkspur House for a bit. Rose, this is Pearl Anderson, but everyone calls her Granny Pearl."

"Nice to meet you," Rose said, immediately offering her hand. "I love your hair."

Granny took her hand with a surprisingly firm grip and shot a look at Erin. "I like this one."

"Yes, I think she'll fit in nicely," Erin said with a laugh. "She's a literature PhD."

"*Almost* PhD," Rose corrected.

"There seems to be a lot of that going around." Rose couldn't tell if Pearl meant it as an observation or a criticism. Either way, she was still holding Rose's hand. When she finally dropped it, she looked directly into her eyes. "Welcome to Haven Ridge. I think you're exactly where you need to be."

And then she smiled at both of them. "Enjoy your meals, young ladies." With that, she turned and flounced off.

Rose watched her go and then turned to Erin, baffled. She wasn't even sure what to ask.

"I know," Erin said. "She's something. She tends to give the men the third degree, but somehow with the women, she just knows."

"Knows what?"

Erin shrugged. "Whatever it is she wants to find out, I guess. You'll see her around. She knows everything that happens here—and practically every-thing that's happened since the beginning of the town—so if you need anything, just head over to her gift shop on Beacon Street."

"Is she . . . a psychic?"

Erin considered. "I don't know if psychics exist, but I don't think so. I just think she's a busybody who has cultivated her sources. And she's the descendant of Elizabeth Strong, so maybe she's just trying to look out for the town."

"I see." Rose figured the words were just meant to add a bit of local color to her experience, but inwardly, she felt unsettled. It was as if Granny Pearl could see straight into those things she was still hiding from everyone, the things she was hoping no one would find out. Because she had a feeling if the old lady knew her secret, it was just a matter of time before *everyone* knew her secret.

And then she could kiss her fresh start goodbye.

CHAPTER FOUR

By the time they rattled back down the dirt road to the Larkspur House, Rose was unaccountably exhausted. She supposed she shouldn't be surprised, given that she'd driven nearly twenty hours in two days, but she couldn't help but think some of it had to be from overwhelm.

When she'd taken the job, she'd been thinking more about the distance from her current situation. She hadn't taken into account the fact that newcomers stuck out like sore thumbs in a small town, that everyone would want to know her story.

Now, she could only hope that they didn't dig too deeply. It wasn't like she had anything to be ashamed of, but she also didn't want to get into details about why her name came up connected with one of the biggest recent scandals in Chicago—a city that was used to scandals. It was the very reason that she'd escaped the Great Lakes region in favor of a place where no one knew her name or likeness.

"So what do you think?" Erin asked as she backed the truck into the carriage house and turned off the ignition.

"The town is charming," Rose said honestly. "I think I'm going to like it."

"Good. Me too. I've missed it." She threw Rose a wry look. "I didn't love it when I was a teenager and everyone was in my business, but it's nice to go back where people know you, to not have to constantly explain your past."

Rose made a vaguely non-committal noise and climbed out of the truck. "So, what do you think? Hit the grocery store tomorrow morning before we get started on the work here?"

"Sounds good. I'm sorry I forgot about it tonight. I got wrapped up in being back in town. I've only been back a few days myself."

Rose threw Erin a surprised look. She hadn't realized that when they'd talked. Then again, she hadn't asked for too many details. She'd wanted to book the position and get out of Milwaukee as quickly as possible. But now all sorts of questions surfaced. Had Erin taken leave from her symphony position to come out here and settle the house? Or had she come out here because she'd taken—or been forced to take—leave from the symphony?

No, it wasn't her business. No matter how friendly Erin might be, Rose was still an employee. Her only concern was to do her job well—even if she was still somewhat murky on what that job entailed—so she didn't have to go back to a place where she was subject to whispers and speculation every time she walked into her grocery store or her hair salon.

They left the truck in the carriage house, padlocked the doors—somewhat unnecessarily, Rose thought—and then climbed up the short trail to the back door of the kitchen. Rose frowned when they stepped inside. She could have sworn that they'd turned off all the wall fixtures, but the light from the hallway spilled through the cracks around the kitchen door, giving them enough illumination to navigate by. She dismissed the thought—after all, hadn't she decided that she was *not* in a Gothic novel?—and started up the first of several flights of stairs to their bedrooms, Erin right behind her.

When they hit the top floor, Rose gave a sleepy wave and suppressed a yawn. "I promise, I will be up bright and early and ready to work."

"That makes one of us," Erin said with a grin before returning the wave. "Sleep well."

"Thanks, I'm sure I will." Rose placed a hand on her door, just before Erin reached the switch at the end of the hall and plunged them into darkness.

Rose pushed into her room and fumbled for the light switch, which she knew had to be somewhere on the entry wall, but her fingers only touched the ridged surface of the paneling. The window didn't offer any light either, the moon hidden by clouds. She sighed. She'd planned on going straight to the bathroom to brush her teeth, but now the prospect of stumbling across the room in the dark felt like too much to deal with. Instead she headed for the dark shape of the bed, toeing off her shoes as she went, sliding her jeans down her legs. She climbed into bed in only her T-shirt and panties and pulled the covers up to her chin, enjoying the feel of cool sheets against her skin. And then she stretched out . . .

. . . and her fingertips touched warm, bare skin.

Rose jerked away with a strangled yelp and scrambled out of the bed, taking half the covers with her. A flurry of movement on the other side was followed by a crash, and then suddenly, the room was flooded with bright yellow light.

On the other side of the bed stood a bare-chested man, his wide-eyed, freaked-out expression mirroring exactly what she imagined her own to be.

"Who are you?" Rose managed to ask, just as he demanded at the same time, "What are you doing in my bed?"

"Who am I?" he answered at the same moment she responded, "*Your* bed? It's supposed to be *my* bed."

They blinked at each other, and then the man held up a hand. "No, you first."

But before Rose could even manage to put words to this situation, the door burst open to reveal Erin, holding a baseball bat. She looked between the two of them, then lowered her makeshift weapon. "Will?"

The man visibly relaxed. "I should have known you were behind this. I was going to tell you I was here in the morning. I thought you were already asleep."

"I didn't even know you were going to be here! Why didn't you tell me you were coming?"

Rose watched the two—the *twins*—work out the unexpected arrival, completely nonplussed by the situation. Only then did she realize she was standing in front of two virtual strangers in her underwear, half-covered by the bedspread clutched to her body.

"I'm just going to . . ." Rose bent down to pick up her jeans and started to creep around the twins, the bedspread now wrapped more securely around her waist. Will and Erin both turned to her as if they'd forgotten she was even in the room.

Erin blinked. Then, as if Rose and Will weren't both half-naked, she said, "I'm sorry, I should introduce you. Rose, this is my brother, Will. Will, this is our new house assistant, Rose Cameron."

It was only then that it seemed to sink in that he was standing with a stranger—and new employee—wearing only a set of cotton pajama pants that rode dangerously low on his hips, because color suddenly flushed his cheeks. He snatched a T-shirt from the floor and dragged it on over his head. But rather than offering the greeting that Rose expected, he instead turned on his sister with lifted eyebrows. "House assistant? When exactly did we agree to hire a house assistant?"

Rose's stomach dropped. She'd sensed something fishy and now she knew why. But she would much prefer to have this conversation while wearing pants. "It seems like we all have a lot to discuss, but I would really like to get dressed. So if you wouldn't mind leaving my room so I can do that, I'll meet you outside."

A flash of something approaching humor lit the man's eyes before it disappeared beneath a scowl. "Technically, it's my room, but I get your point."

"Since when is it your room?" Erin asked. "Your room is across the hall."

Will gripped Erin's arm and gently but firmly steered her toward the door. "Since the tree branch broke the window in there and we boarded it up . . ."

He reached back to close the door behind him and their voices faded as they walked down the hallway. Rose let out a long breath, though her heart was still beating frantically in her chest. That had been the longest three minutes of her life. She wasn't even sure how to begin processing the situation. She should probably start with the fact that Erin had hired her without the approval of her brother, who presumably should have had a say in the matter.

But instead she was thinking about how absolutely off base she'd been in her imaginings of the man. When Erin had said he was an accountant, she'd expected a small, slightly stretched version of Erin. There was no way she could have pictured this tall, dark-haired, dark-eyed specimen with the body of an endurance athlete and the face of a J. Crew model. Had it been any other time in her life and in any other situation, she would probably have enjoyed her eyeful of shirtless Will Parker.

Instead, she could only think about how this would probably be her *last* night at the Larkspur House. Because if she'd learned one thing about men over the years, it was that they didn't like surprises. If she'd learned a second, it was that they rarely liked ideas that weren't their own.

Rose finally let go of her death grip on the coverlet and instead pulled on her jeans. Thank God she didn't sleep naked. It was bad enough that he'd probably gotten a glimpse of her legs—it was no more than he would have seen in a swimsuit.

No, that wasn't even the half of it. Thank God *he* didn't sleep naked. Because her fingers had very definitely touched bare skin, and at least she could be sure that it hadn't been in an inappropriate place. Even if her slight shiver at the recollection was definitely inappropriate.

Or maybe it was just because this house got *cold* at night. The temperature had dropped rapidly as soon as the sun went down, and any vestiges of heat had disappeared with the light. She went to the closet, grabbed a sweatshirt to throw on over her top, and then shoved her feet back into her shoes.

It was time to face the music. If this was going to be her last night here, she wanted to know.

Rose pushed open the door, wishing that she'd asked them where she should meet them. In a four-story house, there was almost no limit to where they could be waiting. But as soon as she stepped out into the hallway, she heard the strains of raised voices.

Ugh. The last thing she wanted to get involved in was a family squabble. But considering they were probably arguing over her, she figured she had the right to at least hear what was being said. Slowly, she walked down the hall and rounded the corner to one of the bedrooms that Erin had mentioned. As she got closer, the voices resolved into actual words.

"I know you do," Will was saying, his voice tight but not angry. "But you know that we don't have the money to make the necessary repairs, let alone *hire* someone to do it."

"I wouldn't have had to hire someone to help me if you'd been willing to come back. I've been asking you for a year, and you've been saying no. What are we going to do? Let it rot away? Fall down around us?"

"You know what I want to do with it."

"I do. And you know why I don't want to do it."

Rose had heard enough. Any more and she would be intentionally eavesdropping. She knocked lightly and the conversation stopped immediately. Erin opened the door and gave a smile, though it lacked her usual ease. "Rose, come in."

Rose stepped inside cautiously, momentarily distracted by the surroundings. This room, unlike the ones on the other end of the corridor, was smaller and scaled for a child: instead of a huge four-poster bed, there was a low, modern-looking full. The dressers were similarly small and clean-lined, like something you'd get from IKEA. And while there were no signs of childish designs or toys, the navy-and-gray color scheme seemed custom-made for a teenage boy. If she wasn't mistaken, this was Will's childhood room.

Except nostalgia didn't seem to be softening him any. He was standing behind Erin, his arms crossed over his chest, his expression implacable. Had she not heard his patient, level tone just moments before, she would be sure that he was angry.

Or maybe he just looked like that because he was staring at her and not his sister.

Rose opened her mouth, but before she could actually say anything, Will took a step forward. "I'm sorry for what happened tonight. It was a series of misunderstandings. I'm Will Parker."

Rose stared at his outstretched hand for a long moment before she convinced herself to reach for it. The warm, firm grip that enveloped her hand definitely didn't belong to her image of an accountant—but hadn't she already determined that he wasn't the typical bean counter? She finally found her voice, but it came out croaky. She cleared her throat and tried again. "Rose Cameron."

His brown eyes—almost more golden than brown, she noticed now—held her gaze for a long moment, but there was no falling into their depths. Instead, she felt pinned in place, like a butterfly on a board. When he finally let go, she realized she'd been holding her breath.

Well shoot. What did she do now? The longer she held her breath, the more light-headed she became, but she was a second away from gasping for air like a fish out of water . . .

And then he turned back to his sister, and she sucked in oxygen as surreptitiously as she could. As if she needed any more embarrassment in front of this man.

Why do you even care? her inner feminist, which sounded suspiciously like her mother, fired back.

Because I want him to let me stay, she responded, even though it wasn't anywhere close to the truth. *Okay, fine, because he's unexpectedly, inexplicably hot.*

If her inner voice had actually been another entity, it probably would have sighed in exasperation.

"Rose, I'm afraid that Erin overstepped here. I don't know what she told you about our situation, but we can't—"

"—make this decision in the middle of the night," Erin finished, shooting him a death glare. "So why don't we all go back to bed and we can discuss this in the morning."

Rose stared between the two of them, nonplussed. Will had been just about to tell her she didn't have a job or a place to stay. Did Erin actually think she was going to change his mind in the next eight hours?

Still, it was a stay of execution, and it did Rose no good to push the issue. But there was a more pressing one at hand. "Apparently, I don't have a room."

Will actually looked embarrassed. "Stay where you are, of course. I'll sleep in here. Just . . . let me grab my things first." He brushed by her, not meeting her eyes, and slipped out the door.

Rose turned to Erin. "What on earth is going on here?"

Erin's grimace looked so much like her brother's, it was suddenly easier to see the family resemblance. "I have a confession to make. I didn't exactly hire you to help me get the house ready to sell."

"I gathered that much. But why did you lie?"

"Because I needed plausible deniability." The little twist of amusement in Erin's smile failed to reassure her. "This house is technically owned by a trust, and Will is the trustee. He insists that the trust can't afford the upkeep any longer, and he wants us to sell."

"And clearly, you don't."

"No. This was our family home, and I think our grandparents would roll over in their graves if they knew we were thinking of selling it. Will only looks at the numbers. He doesn't have a single sentimental bone in his body. I don't even know how we're related."

Split down the middle, Rose thought to herself. *Will got the practicality and Erin got the whimsy.* Because she had a feeling the buttoned-up Will Parker would never dream of pulling a bait-and-switch on an employee. Right now, she actually thought she might be on his side.

"Then why did you hire me, if not to help you get it ready for sale?"

Erin peered past her to make sure that Will wasn't yet returning. "I really did need your help sorting through this place and clearing it out. Will wasn't supposed to be here for another month. I was banking on us finding something of real value we could sell in order to pay for the house repairs. To convince him to keep it." Erin ran her fingers through her short hair, making it stick up in tufts. "I figured we could put together some sort of plan to save the place, and given your very impressive history of organization and planning and management, I thought you were the right person to help."

It was a flattering assessment, if not exactly the truth, but it still didn't earn her a place to stay. "So what happens now?"

"I try to convince or wheedle or threaten Will into letting you stay, give us some time."

"And do you think you'll be successful?"

Erin shrugged, but there was a mischievous look in her eye when she said, "We'll see." Clearly, she was confident in her ability to manipulate her brother.

Before Rose could ask for specifics, Will appeared in the doorway, dragging a compact roller case behind him. "The room is all yours. It's probably time for all of us to get some sleep."

Rose didn't wait around to see if Erin would argue. She just slipped out the door and walked down the hallway, her heart thudding with unease. She'd always known that coming here was a risk, but she hadn't expected to land in the middle of a sibling squabble.

Once more, it seemed that she'd made a decision without having all the information. And once more, it looked like she'd chosen wrong.

CHAPTER FIVE

He was going to kill his sister.

Oh, William Parker loved his twin. How could he not? But only she would pull something like this, a scenario from a bad soap opera or one of the comic operas she played for. Hiring a woman they didn't know, for a job that didn't exist, to save a house they couldn't afford to keep.

And then having her sleep in *his* bed.

He almost groaned at the recollection. If he was going to have to work with this Rose Cameron, he would have preferred that they'd met in the daytime with all their clothes on, not half-naked across a bed. Now every time he looked at her, he was going to have the image of long red hair curling over creamy bare skin and—if he hadn't been mistaken—hiding a pretty little rose tattoo on one shoulder.

Wait, what was he saying? Of course he wasn't going to work with her. He just hadn't wanted to kick her out into the cold late at night in what was admittedly the middle of nowhere. They could discuss Rose's next moves in the morning. They just wouldn't be here.

He hated the fact that he had to be the bad guy again. That was always the dynamic between Erin and him, though, and it hadn't changed in thirty-six years. She got to be the fun one, the artist, the creative. He had to be the responsible one, the voice of reason, the stick in the mud. Once, when they were teenagers, he'd overheard Erin's friends talking while she was out of the room.

"He's cute," one of them had said, "or he would be if he'd ever lighten up."

At the time, it had struck him as unfair. As if he didn't want to be out there, acting vaguely irresponsible like all of his friends? But that had never been his lot in life. He was the older twin—even if it was only by eight minutes—the stable one, while Erin was the fragile one. It had been his job to look after her. It still was.

So he was going to save Erin the embarrassment of having to fire the woman she'd hired and they'd move on. Because no matter what his sister thought, they were not keeping the house. They couldn't. He was the one who managed the trust, knew the numbers. And all it would take was one big disaster—not counting the forty-thousand-dollar roof the place needed—and the trust would be bankrupt. There was no magic in the world that would change that fact.

"Earth to Will. . .?" Erin's voice broke through his reverie, reminding him that while Rose had exited his bedroom—his old bedroom, and one he wished he hadn't automatically retreated to, given all the memories it held—his sister still remained, staring.

He rubbed his forehead wearily. "Really, Erin. What did you think you were going to accomplish here? You do realize that I'm not doing this to hurt you, right?"

Her mulish expression melted into one of embarrassment or maybe shame. He so rarely saw that expression from his irrepressible sister that he didn't immediately recognize it. "I was just trying to buy time," she said finally. "I thought if we could go through the house before you got here, maybe we'd find something that would make it worth keeping. Or something worth selling, at least. You never *did* say why you were here so early, by the way. You said you'd be in Chicago for at least another month!"

It was a dodge, and not even a subtle one, but he let it go. He didn't want to argue with Erin, not when he was already going to have to break her heart. "Plaintiff settled out of court, so I wasn't needed, and we're still waiting for all the documents from our next client."

"Anything interesting?"

He shrugged. "Embezzlement. I haven't looked into it too much since it was Arlene who closed the deal."

"Leave it to you to work as a forensic accountant in *Chicago* and you still haven't come across an interesting mob case!"

Now he laughed. "That's a good thing. Divorces and petty theft and embezzlement are a lot easier. Besides, companies that just want their cash back pay a lot better than law enforcement." He narrowed his eyes at her. "Don't think I don't realize what you're doing."

"What?" she asked innocently.

"You think if you divert me for long enough, I'll give in and let Rose stay."

"Why can't she stay?"

"Did we not just go over the bank account situation?"

"Listen, the bulk of her pay is room and board. She just needed a place to go. She recently got divorced and it sounds like she barely got the clothes on her back in the settlement. There's probably room to negotiate."

Except that would make him the guy who took advantage of a destitute woman. If she had any money, she could have afforded a good lawyer and she probably wouldn't even be here.

And if you kick her out with nowhere to go? What does that make you?

The conflict must have shown on his face, because Erin's hangdog expression was slowly transforming into triumph. "A couple of weeks. I'll explain the situation to her, maybe she'll be willing to work for room and board while she's looking for something else. If we don't find anything, we don't find anything, but if we do . . . ."

"Yeah, it's that *if* that worries me."

Erin gave him a brilliant, confident smile. "You promise to make a logical, reasonable assessment of the facts."

And there it was. He was always telling her that she needed to be more logical and reasonable, act less on whim and feelings. And now it was coming around to bite him. He rubbed his forehead again, but what exactly was he going to say to that?

"Fine. You have two weeks. And if there's nothing but a bunch of useless junk here, she goes and I hire a Realtor as planned."

Erin thrust out her hand to him, and they shook on it, but the triumphant look in her eyes made him think that she'd gotten exactly what she wanted . . . and somehow it wasn't going to work in his favor.

After Erin finally left his room, Will climbed under the slightly dusty blankets in his childhood bed and squeezed his eyes shut. Not surprisingly, sleep didn't come. It wasn't simply that his adrenaline was still pumping after the unexpected awakening and conflict, a mere hour after he'd climbed in bed. But he'd underestimated the memories still present in this place.

They're not all bad, he told himself, and truly, they

weren't. Given their rocky start in life, being abandoned first by their father and then their mother before they even turned a year old, he and Erin had had a relatively happy childhood with their grandparents here in Larkspur House. They'd been too young to remember a falling-down apartment in a sketchy part of Colorado Springs; his earliest memory was playing with Matchbox cars on the parquet floor in a spill of sunlight from one of the tall, arched windows. As places to grow up went, Larkspur House was pretty great.

And yet he'd avoided it for his entire adult life, trying to hold onto those early memories and let go of the later ones. He still couldn't go into the third-floor bathroom without a horrifying flash of memory: Erin's lifeless body draped over the side of the tub, the water stained red.

He shook off the image, but even now he welcomed the knife twist in his stomach, sharper than the one she'd used to slit her wrists at the age of fifteen. It was a reminder of why he was here, why he let Erin get her way so often. She was more fragile than she looked. The fact she was here on leave from the symphony seemed to be an indication that things hadn't changed all that much in the last two decades. If his twin wanted to reassure herself that they'd done everything possible to save their childhood home, then he'd indulge her. She'd be a lot less likely to give into feelings of regret and shame if she had these two weeks with an objective helper.

Heck, maybe Rose would even put things into perspective for Erin. It sounded like the young woman had suffered a big loss and was taking active—if unconventional—steps to move on. Despite their rough start, her coming here could turn out to be a good thing.

And if not, it was only two weeks. He could survive anything for two weeks.

The countdown started now.

* * *

Will slept fitfully and woke before dawn, feeling like he hadn't rested at all. Still, he pried himself out of bed, showered in the bathroom next door, and shaved in front of the foggy mirror. Then he pulled on a pair of dark wash blue jeans and a T-shirt, threw a V-neck sweater on over top of it—it would be hours before it warmed up in Haven Ridge, even in early July—and headed down the three flights of stairs to the kitchen. The house was still and quiet, an indication that he was the first person up this morning, so he slipped out the front door and into his rental SUV. If he hadn't parked on the side of the house last night instead of on the concrete pad, he might not have ended up in bed with a stranger. Then again, he probably should have questioned why Erin was driving an unfamiliar Volvo. Without thinking about it, he turned it toward town and within twenty minutes was parked in front of the Brick House Cafe.

The minute he pushed through the front door with a jingle of bells, the dark-haired, bearded man behind the counter broke into a smile. Will felt his spirits lift at the first sight of his high school friend. He hadn't been sure Thomas would be here today, given his additional duties as the somewhat-recently elected mayor of Haven Ridge.

Thomas greeted him with a bright smile. "Will! Hey!"

"Thomas." Will slid onto the seat at the long counter and clasped hands with the other man. "How's it going?"

"Good! I didn't know you were going to be in town. Erin came in last night and she didn't say anything to Mallory."

Will chuckled ruefully. "That's because she didn't know."

Thomas immediately followed the direction of his thoughts. "I take it you got a big surprise up at the house?"

"In my bed." Will related the incidents of the previous night, and Thomas threw his head back in a hearty laugh.

"Well that would have been a surprise. What did she do?"

Will thought about it. Rose had been composed. Impressively so, given what a shock it must have been for her and the weirdness that had ensued between him and Erin. "Took it rather well, all things considered."

"What are you going to do?"

"About what?"

"About the fact that Erin hired someone without your okay?"

He grimaced. "What do you think I'm going to do?"

Thomas swiveled away to grab a mug and the coffee pot and poured a cup in front of him without asking. "You know, your sister isn't made of glass. She can deal with disappointment."

It was a nice thought, but Will still wasn't so sure that was the case. He couldn't be sure what would trigger one of her episodes. She had clearly already been in an anxiety spiral if she'd taken leave and come here—principal cello with a major symphony had been her goal since she was a little girl. But as soon as she'd gotten the position, her anxiety had gotten so bad she'd started missing rehearsals. He wasn't judging, or at least he wasn't blaming her. But Thomas's view of Erin's stability wasn't based in experience. Will's was.

"This is kind of a big one. She's been against selling the house from the start, and it's not like I'm thrilled about it, but I'm not going to let it take the entire trust down." He took his responsibility as trustee seriously. The point of the trust, as his grandfather had explained to him, wasn't to preserve the house itself, but to preserve Andrew Bixby's legacy in Haven Ridge and help support Erin. And that could quite possibly be better served by handing Larkspur House over to someone who could restore it to its previous glory. They still had the block of historic buildings on Beacon Street—one of which was currently occupied by a bookshop and another that he was negotiating a lease for—that would remain within the trust. The money from the mansion could go to restoring and renovating the entire block, which would do far more for the good of Haven Ridge than retaining a big, crumbling mansion up on a hill ever could.

But that was treading dangerously close to another topic he didn't want to touch, so he pivoted. "How is Mallory, anyway?"

"Good! Finished with her PhD finally, so she's not sorry she doesn't have to drive to Colorado Springs several days a week. Liv is helping her edit her dissertation into a more commercially appealing format, which she'll publish toward the end of the year. I know her expectations for sales aren't high, but I imagine visitors will want to pick up copies of the Haven Ridge history in the bookshop and gift shop."

"That's great!" Will genuinely meant it, though he had to ignore the little pinprick of pain at Liv's name. If anyone deserved happiness, it was Thomas and Mallory. Thomas had lost his wife to cancer five years earlier, and he'd only been married to Mallory for a little over a year, but it was like the light that had gone out after Estella's death had come back in full force. Mallory hadn't had it that easy herself, but she'd made herself a place in Haven Ridge, and now it felt like the town had never existed without her.

"Thanks. I'm proud of her. I've seen how hard she had to work to catch up."

Will was trying so hard not to ask the question that was on his lips, but it spilled out anyway. "And Liv?"

"You really haven't talked to her since last year?"

He shook his head. "Not since the bookstore opened. I called to congratulate her, but. . . ."

"Well, it looks like you're going to have the opportunity to ask her yourself."

Will twisted on his seat, following Thomas's gaze to the window. A pretty blonde wearing jeans and a flowered blouse was striding confidently toward the main door of the cafe. His heart slid into his stomach, heat rising to his face. "I should go."

But there was nowhere to go, and his ego wouldn't let him slip out the back door like he had something to be ashamed of. He had to hold his head high, look her in the eye, and pretend that she hadn't broken his heart.

Oh, don't be so dramatic. It had been a minor disappointment, not a broken heart. It wasn't as if they'd ever dated. She had been married to his best friend, who had died tragically in a plane crash almost four years ago. He and Liv had looked to each other for comfort, and along the way, Will had started to wonder if they couldn't be more. Except he'd let his sense of responsibility toward Jason—and Jason's daughter— override his instincts to make a move. She'd fallen in love with someone else before he ever could.

He just wished he hadn't been the one to introduce them.

Thomas was moving away from the counter, a menu

in hand, to greet Liv when she walked through the door. Will swiveled on the stool and took a moment to look her over without her notice.

She was as beautiful as ever, with her willowy build and cascade of wavy blonde hair, but he was pleased to find that the grip that she'd once had on his heart had eased to a mild pang. He put on a welcoming smile as Liv's gaze slid away from Thomas and hit him at the counter.

Her eyebrows flew up. "Will?"

He hopped off his seat and took a couple of steps toward her. "Hi, Liv."

She blinked at him, but she accepted his quick hug before stepping back. "When did you get back in town?"

"Just last night. I finished a case early and flew back to surprise Erin. Operative word, *surprise*."

Liv laughed, a sound that he'd once loved—still loved, who was he kidding?—but the delight that crossed her face was real. "Well, it's good to have you back, however it happened. But why?"

"Have to deal with the house," he said, and Liv's smile slid into a grimace.

"I'm sorry. I know that's not going to be easy. You've decided to sell then?"

"Unfortunately. I don't see any other way, even though it's going to crush Erin. She's talked me into a two-week stay of execution. She's hoping she'll find something amazing we can sell to help fund the repairs."

"I hope she does then. I know you don't want to sell any more than she does."

That was not entirely the case, but letting her think that painted him in a better light than the truth, so he just nodded. "Thanks."

"It was really good to see you. Maybe we can catch up

later. I'm going to go grab a table." Liv reached up to push a strand of hair back behind her ear, and only then did he see the sparkle of a diamond on her left hand.

A modest diamond, to be sure, but it was unmistakably an engagement ring.

Will's heart fell to his stomach for the second time. "It, uh, looks like congratulations are in order?"

Liv froze, looking for all the world like a trapped animal, and that alone was enough to make him force a smile to his face.

"I didn't know you hadn't heard," she said quietly. "Yes. Charlie and I got engaged last month."

Will nodded, but he couldn't be sure it didn't seem a little spastic. "When's the big day?"

"We're still trying to figure things out. We don't want to step on Gemma and Stephen's toes, so we might wait a little while."

Will blinked at her.

"Oh wow, yeah, you've been gone a while. Um, Gemma and Stephen got engaged at Christmas. They're planning a winter wedding."

"Weddings all over the place. I'll have to drop into the bakery and tell Gemma congratulations."

"She'd like that." Liv smiled at him, but there was an undercurrent of pity this time that made him want to escape. "It's really good to see you, Will. I'm glad you're back. Drop by the shop sometime before you go. I think you'll be impressed with what we've done with the place."

"I'm sure you did a beautiful job. You always do." He smiled and gave a little wave that immediately made him cringe at his own awkwardness.

Liv smiled, though, and Thomas escorted her over to the table, where he set down two menus, one in front of her and one opposite. Will pulled out his wallet and threw a couple of bucks on the counter for the coffee, then drained the last of the dark liquid from the mug just as the owner returned to the counter.

"That was my cue," Will murmured to Thomas. "I'll catch you later."

"I'm sorry you got blindsided with that one. I really thought you knew."

Will just flashed a smile that he knew wasn't terribly convincing and headed for the door. Just as the man he was trying to avoid appeared on the other side of it.

He stifled a groan. Now he really was going to have to play nice. This morning just kept getting better. He reached for the door and held it open for the other man.

Charlie Castro, Liv's fiancé, was dressed for his day as a contractor in a pair of jeans, work boots, and a button-down flannel, pretty much the polar opposite of how Will dressed for work. But it was the caution in the other man's eyes that took Will by surprise.

"Hey, man," Charlie said with a slight smile. "Didn't know you were back in town." He held out a hand, and Will had no choice but to shake it.

"Just got in last night. Congratulations on your engagement, by the way."

Surprise crossed Charlie's face, but he got it under control and accepted the words with a nod. "Thanks, I appreciate that. I'm not sure what your plans are up at the house, but let me know if you need me. I'll have some time over the next couple of weeks."

"Sure, I'll do that," Will said easily as he stepped toward the door. "See you around."

Not a chance in the world. Bad enough that he'd inadvertently set up this relationship by asking Charlie to help Liv back to her house with some books she was going to sell for him, but he certainly wasn't going to have him spending all his time up at Larkspur House, where he could face his regrets on a daily basis.

Funny how he'd been sure that he was completely fine with being back, with the fact that Liv had moved on with someone else, until he was confronted by it.

This was turning into the best trip ever.

Will was in an admittedly foul mood when he returned to his vehicle and turned it back toward the Larkspur House. He hadn't managed to get breakfast, and now he didn't want to stop by the Broken Hearts Bakery, knowing that Gemma would probably want to talk about both her own and her best friend's engagement.

His stomach still rumbled, and now it slightly soured because the only thing in it was a cup of strong coffee.

Perfect.

At this rate, he should just go back to bed and start the day over.

Except the minute he pulled into the driveway of the Larkspur House, he knew that wasn't in the cards.

A petite redhead was currently struggling to load bags into the back of her Volvo.

Will put his SUV into park, then jumped out. "What are you doing?"

Rose started and drew away from him, making him instantly regret his sharp tone. "I . . . I'm getting ready to go. It's clear that Erin overstepped, and I'm not going to get in the middle of whatever family . . . thing . . . is going on here."

It was exactly what he'd wanted, but no doubt Erin would hold him responsible for it. "Is that what Erin told you?"

"She's not awake yet, but I figured this would just be easier."

Will pinched the bridge of his nose. "You would think so, wouldn't you?" He stepped past Rose, hauled her suitcase out of the cargo space, and slammed the trunk lid closed.

"But . . ." she protested.

"Two weeks," he said, dragging the suitcase up to the front door. He pushed it open with his elbow and hauled the suitcase inside. What did she have in this thing? Rocks? Cannonballs? It must weigh a hundred pounds. How Rose had gotten it into the car in the first place was a mystery, given that she probably stood all of five-foot-three.

"I'm sorry?"

"You can stay for two weeks. I'll pay you whatever Erin promised you, plus room and board as discussed. But after that . . ."

Rose was staring at him, wide-eyed, which made him feel like an ogre, but he didn't have the mental or emotional energy to smooth over her feelings right now. Instead, he started for the staircase and hauled the suitcase up, one flight at a time, aware of Rose trailing silently behind him. He deposited it outside the door of the bedroom she'd occupied last night.

"I don't want to take your bedroom."

"It's fine."

"No, really. I was already an unwelcome surprise." She lifted her chin, and while he didn't know her, he could already tell that this was a well-worn gesture of habitual stubbornness.

"This is my house, so I get to choose where everyone stays. And you're staying here." He lifted an eyebrow at her, as if daring her to argue with that point.

She swallowed hard, but she nodded anyway. "Thank you."

"No problem. And feel free to wake Erin up any time. She'll sleep until noon if you let her."

With those words, he turned on his heel and headed down the hallway to the tiny bedroom he'd claimed for himself, feeling unaccountably irritated by the exchange.

Two weeks. It was only two weeks. And then he could go back to Chicago, back to his normal life, back to the person he was there. Because for good or for ill, there was something about Haven Ridge that brought out the worst in him.

When he was here, he didn't like who he'd become.

CHAPTER SIX

Rose watched Will Parker's departing back as he strode down the hallway, every line of his body speaking of irritation. Her stomach twisted in apprehension. She should be glad that she'd gotten a two-week stay of execution, some time to figure out what she was going to do next, but instead she felt like she'd been dropped into a pressure cooker, while the heat cranked up with each passing minute.

Clearly, there was a history of familial drama here that she didn't understand. There was no doubt from the way that Will looked at his sister that he loved her, but he also handled her like she was made of glass. It didn't take much imagination to figure out that probably had something to do with the scar on Erin's wrist. But it didn't really explain why he seemed so put out at Rose's presence. Was it because he resented having to bow to his sister's whims, because he was scared of what she might do if he didn't?

Or was it just that he didn't like Rose herself?

He doesn't know you, she reminded herself, but it seemed equally likely that he wasn't interested in getting to know her. She was an interloper, a witness to whatever family dysfunction was going on here, and it was clear that if he had his way, he'd stick her straight into her car and send her back to Milwaukee.

Well, that wasn't an option for her. She simply had to make these next two weeks count. She'd been hired as a house assistant—which she figured meant a combination of cleaner, organizer, and now cataloger— so that was what she was going to do.

Rose dragged her suitcase across the room into the walk-in closet and began unpacking the clothes she'd just stuffed into it an hour before. Her books—of which there were a considerable number—went onto the ledge of the window behind the settee, so she could read in the evenings after she was done with her work. The suitcase itself, she slid under the bed, concealed by a heavy, old-fashioned dust ruffle.

Her things put away, she stripped off the blouse she'd put on earlier and exchanged it for a graphic tee that proclaimed *I like books better than I like most people*, slid her feet into sturdy running shoes, and tied her hair back in a high ponytail. Then she climbed down three sets of stairs and started searching for the cleaning supplies.

She finally found them in a broom closet off the kitchen, complete with a floor polisher and an old-fashioned canister vacuum. She grabbed a brand-new package of disposable dusters, a scrub brush, and some rags, and then filled a bucket full of cleaners and polishes. She had no idea what she was going to need yet, but if she was going to start somewhere, she might as well start with her own bathroom.

Rose marched back up the stairs, huffing by the time she reached the top—the altitude really did kill her stamina—and went back to her room. It wasn't as if the place was dirty exactly. There was no grime or mold, and it was clear it had been thoroughly cleaned at some point in the past. But cobwebs hung in the corners, and there was a layer of dust on everything she hadn't yet touched—the top of the mirror, the light fixtures, the corners of the tile floor. She retrieved her headphones from her purse, selected some music on her phone, and got to work.

Surprisingly, the time sped by while she cleaned. She wasn't afraid of hard work. In fact, it had annoyed her that Jordan had insisted on hiring a cleaner for their huge Wilshire home, claiming that no one in the neighborhood actually did their own work, and besides, she was better off spending her energy where it could do some good—with the charity.

Now she knew that he hadn't wanted her poking around their home, where she would have found evidence that his expenditures were even more extravagant than their privileged lifestyle hinted at. He'd always said that they had the six-thousand-square-foot house in the nicest suburb of Milwaukee because of family money, so she'd never questioned how he could live there on $150,000 a year. It hadn't been until the police arrived with a search warrant that she learned of the Jackson Pollock in the guest room closet or the tens of thousands of dollars of jewelry in the downstairs safe ordered from online jewelers—none of which she'd known about even though Jordan had stacks of receipts for them in her name.

When she'd seen that, she'd finally realized that this was no accident, that her husband had purposely set her up. Fortunately, he wasn't nearly as good a liar as he thought, and Rose's shock and dismay had played as genuine to the police.

Rose scrubbed the tile in the shower even harder at

the recollection, gritting her teeth against the memories, against the pain that surfaced with them. That had been over six months ago. The day after the police had called her in to answer Jordan's outrageous claims against her—claims that were backed up by his parents and brother, all of whom were directors on the charity's board—she'd found a divorce lawyer and filed the papers.

He hadn't contested it. The final hearing had been three weeks ago. And that's when she'd really understood that because the house was his parents' and he'd bought everything over the course of their three-year marriage with stolen funds, she was walking away with nothing but the clothes she'd brought to the union and a handful of savings bonds she'd received as childhood gifts.

Enough to buy a three-thousand-dollar Volvo and enough gas to get to Colorado.

A rivulet of sweat ran down Rose's cheek, even though it was still cold in the house, and she rubbed it away with the back of her wrist before she realized that it wasn't sweat but tears. No. She wasn't going to cry over Jordan or the lie that was her three-year marriage or the fact that she'd abandoned her family legacy for a man who most definitely didn't deserve the sacrifice. She wasn't even going to cry over the fact that what was supposed to be her reprieve from the mess her life had become was even more temporary than she'd initially thought.

She was going to do her job, earn her keep for the next two weeks.

No, that wasn't good enough. She was going to help Erin preserve *her* family legacy.

She was going to help prove the surly Will Parker wrong.

Rose glanced at her watch, saw that it was now past

nine o'clock. Good enough. She pulled off her rubber gloves, wiped her sweaty palms on her jeans, and marched next door to Erin's room. She rapped sharply on the door until it was yanked open from the other side and Erin stared at her, bleary-eyed and confused. "What's wrong?"

"We only have two weeks," Rose said. "Get up and get dressed. We have a house to save."

* * *

To Erin's credit, she was dressed and in Rose's room within ten minutes. While Rose finished scrubbing, she took one of the dusters and removed the layer of fine silt off every conceivable surface. But once the bathroom was clean, she stripped off her gloves and gave Rose a significant look.

"As much as I love your enthusiasm, this place has forty-three rooms. We could spend the next two weeks simply dusting and not get anywhere."

Rose sat back on her heels and pushed a strand of hair from her face. "You're right. I just couldn't stand for my place not to be clean. Somehow it seemed like the most basic duty of the job, you know?"

Erin perched on the edge of the bathtub. "I know. I just think we need a plan. If we're really trying to find something of value in the house that could be sold, we should focus on the places where those would most likely be."

"Well, art is probably the most obvious possibility. Paintings, sculptures, that sort of thing. Followed by antique furniture and rugs, rare books . . ." From the determined look that formed on Erin's face, Rose had a feeling that she would sell off every last item in this place to keep the house, even if they had to refurnish it in IKEA ready-to-assemble.

"Let's start in the library then. The books are gone, but I know there's old art in there. I just don't know if it's particularly valuable."

Rose didn't have any better ideas, so she nodded and started packing the cleaning supplies into the bucket. When Erin looked at her questioningly, she said, "You hired me as a caretaker. I might as well dust while I'm in there, right?"

Erin winked at her. "I hired you as a partner in crime. Just don't tell my brother."

Rose forced a smile, but the mention of Will Parker dulled her mood. She followed Erin out of the room and down the hallway. "What's with your brother, anyway? Is he always that uptight?"

"Well, to be fair, he didn't expect you to climb into bed with him."

Rose flushed at the recollection. "I don't mean that. I mean this morning. He seemed mad at me. He roared into the driveway and practically yanked my suitcase out of my hand. How do you think I knew he gave me two weeks?"

Erin paused. She obviously hadn't thought it through. "I don't know. He's just not a fan of Haven Ridge in general, spends as little time as possible here."

"Why?"

"Too many bad memories." Erin led the way down the stairs and then turned toward the room where Rose had found her playing the day before. "He was really close to our grandfather. He passed away last year. And then his best friend died a few years back. . . I think being here just reminds him of what he lost."

That gave Rose pause. It did seem like a lot of loss for one person, especially one who was relatively young. She guessed she couldn't blame him for that. But it didn't explain the way he glowered at her as if this whole thing had somehow been her idea. She'd just answered an ad, for goodness' sake!

But Erin was still talking. "Honestly, he has always had this overdeveloped sense of responsibility. He used to stay home with me on Friday and Saturday nights instead of going out with his friends, because he didn't want me to be alone. He wanted to go to UCLA, but when I got into Boston College for music, he decided to go to BU instead." Erin shot Rose a look. "It's suffocating sometimes, but he means well. I just don't think he knows how to actually relax."

Rose couldn't help but think about those scars again. She had no idea when that had happened, but maybe she could understand why Will wouldn't let his twin out of his sight, even now. After all, she was "on leave" from the symphony. What had happened to cause that?

"Is he. . . married? Or involved with someone?" It seemed hard to believe a guy his age was only living to look out for his sister. Then again, the lack of a relationship didn't exactly mean he was lonely and celibate. "A lot of someones?"

Erin slanted her a searching glance. "Why? Are you interested?"

"Oh, no. He's not my type."

"Yeah, there seems to be a lot of that going around lately." Will's deep voice rang out in the hallway, and instantly, heat rushed to Rose's face. Seriously. This house had to be over thirty-thousand square feet. And he just managed to be right behind her when she said *that*? She cringed so hard she thought she might have pulled a muscle. Slowly, she turned.

"Sorry, I didn't mean—"

He lifted an eyebrow, clearly not about to let her off the hook.

"I'm just here to do a job," she said lamely. "I'm not looking for anything else."

"Good." His voice was terse. "When you're done with Erin's projects today, come find me. I could use your help outside." And then, without another word, he turned on his heel and strode off.

Rose stared after him, then turned to Erin. "I screwed up, didn't I?"

She expected Erin to shrug it off and tell her not to worry about it, but the other woman's brow furrowed as she watched him walk away. "I don't think so. That wasn't his mad face. Though I have no idea what he could want your help with. I guess you'll find out."

And while Erin seemed so nonchalant she figured she had nothing to worry about, the possibility of having to spend time with the grumpy, enigmatic Will Parker did nothing to quell the butterflies in her stomach.

CHAPTER SEVEN

THE LIBRARY WAS A BUST. Despite the fact that it was beautifully decorated with old-fashioned furnishings, it seemed that the majority of them were handmade. To Rose, that wasn't a drawback—everything in the place was beautiful—but it offered no magical solution to their problems.

Likewise, the selection of oil paintings might have been impressive, but no amount of visual searching on their phones could decipher the signatures on the paintings to know if they were valuable. Given the fact that many of them seemed to be landscapes of Colorado, Rose suspected they might have been by local artists.

Again, that would be a selling point had this been a hotel or guest house, but not so much when they were looking for a big score to allow them to make the necessary repairs.

By the time they finished the room, dusting and vacuuming as they went, Rose felt fully demoralized. Why, she couldn't say. Erin, by contrast, still seemed optimistic that they would find something amazing.

And Rose literally had no skin in this game. Success or failure, she was still out of here in two weeks. She was just labor, and as Erin hinted, companionship.

"I still need to go to the grocery," Erin said as they closed up behind them. "Do you want to come?"

"I'm supposed to find Will and help him with. . . whatever it was he needed help with," Rose replied. "You can go on without me."

"Are you sure? I can wait."

Rose glanced at her watch. "It's already three o'clock. If we want to eat dinner any time tonight, I guess you should probably go now. Just grab some basics. Chicken and vegetables maybe. I'll throw something together later."

"Okay. Maybe we can head back to town after, grab some goodies from the bakery."

"I could be convinced." Rose smiled as Erin went back to the staircase, ostensibly to return to her room. Rose, on the other hand, wandered to the third floor, looking for Will. She didn't find him anywhere on the third floor, and the second floor likewise turned up no sign of the man. Until she heard the low hum of a male voice.

Frowning, Rose followed the sound to a half-closed door and pushed it open gingerly. It was the study she'd seen earlier, complete with a wall of bookshelves and a large, sturdy desk. Will was standing with his back to the door, his cell phone pressed to his ear.

". . . send over everything when it's complete. I don't want to draw any conclusions until I see the full packet." He paused, listening to someone on the other end. "Assign that to Brandy then. She's quick at data entry—"

Will turned and froze, stumbling over his words when he saw Rose. Feeling as if she'd been caught

eavesdropping rather than doing exactly what he'd
asked her to do, she mouthed, "Are you ready?"

Will held up a finger, which she took to mean *one
minute* but he didn't attempt to close the door on her
like she would have expected.

"Okay, thanks, just text me when it's all together and
I'll get started. I should be back in Chicago in two
weeks, tops."

He said his goodbyes, then punched off the call and
shoved the phone in his pocket. "Done already?"

"Just the library. Erin's going for groceries now."

"And you didn't want to go with her?"

"You said you needed help. That's what I'm here for.
To help."

Will's dark eyes appraised her as if he wasn't quite
sure whether to take her at face value. What was with
this guy? He must have some major trust issues. But he
finally nodded. "Follow me."

He brushed past her through the doorway, not
looking back to make sure she was following. She wasn't
sure whether to be more distracted by his arrogance or
by the smell of his cologne, masculine and expensive,
that lingered in the hallway behind him. Reluctantly, she
followed at a distance, down the remaining stairway,
through the kitchen, and out toward the side of the
house.

But rather than going to the double doors of the
carriage house, he circled around back to a single,
regular-sized door. He fished a key ring out of his
pocket and unlocked the padlock on an iron hinge that
held the door shut. It squeaked as he opened it, and he
gestured for her to go inside first.

The smell of machine oil and sawdust tickled her
nose, but she could see precious little in the beams of
light that seeped through the seams of the carriage

house. Her stomach leaped again, thanks to a too-active imagination. When was going alone into the dark with a strange man ever a good idea?

And then Will reached past her and flipped a switch. Old fluorescent lights flickered on with a hum, illuminating the garage space in glaring white light.

No, not a garage. A workshop.

Everywhere she turned, she saw equipment. Not just the regular table saws she'd expect, but lathes and planers and machines that, despite her one-time HGTV obsession, she couldn't even name.

"This was my grandfather's workshop," Will said quietly. "He made a lot of the furniture in the house."

"Wow." That explained the well-made but unbranded furniture they'd found in the library. "I think I saw some of his work inside. He was really talented."

"He was. When I was little, I used to sit out here with him while he worked. Sometimes he'd let me turn a leg on the lathe or he'd have me glue and clamp joints. By the time I was in high school, I was completing whole pieces under his supervision."

Rose stole a look at Will. His voice was completely level, dispassionate even, so if she were only listening, she would think that it was a straightforward recitation of facts. The look on his face as he looked around, though—she couldn't tell if it was nostalgia or pain or regret, maybe even a mix of all three. But whatever it was, it was not dispassionate.

"Were you close?" she asked softly. "You and your grandfather?"

The expression vanished and he turned to her. "Close enough. I was hoping you might be able to help me do a little research. All this equipment is extremely expensive, at least it was once. I'd like you to help me figure out what it's worth and if there's a market for it."

"Okay," Rose said slowly. "I'd be happy to, but I don't understand the secrecy. Why didn't you just say that earlier?"

Will turned to her, that hard expression back. "I know Erin has grand hopes of finding, I don't know, a Renoir or a Rodin somewhere in this house, but I know this place backward and forward. There's nothing of real value here. I mean, a thousand dollars here and there, but nothing of the scope that could actually save this place. Except this."

"Are you sure you want to sell it?" Rose asked quietly. "It seems like you have a lot of good memories out here."

"It doesn't do me much good if we have to sell the house. It's not like I can set them up in my condo in Chicago."

That was an artful dodge of a question if she'd ever heard one. "Level with me here, Will. Do you want to keep this place?"

He averted his eyes. "Of course I do."

Now it was time for Rose to give him the lifted eyebrow. "Do you really? Because from where I stand, it looks like you've given Erin just enough hope for it to all come crashing down in two weeks."

"You've been here all of twenty-four hours and you think you've got us figured out?"

Rose sighed. "I'm not saying that. And I know it's not my place. But there's no way we're getting through forty-three rooms and a garage in two weeks. We could tear this place apart and it would still take all month to look up every last piece to see if it's worth something. I don't know a lot about woodworking, but I do know small towns, and I know that you'll be lucky to be able to get a fraction of what this is worth up here."

"So, what . . . I don't try? Just tell my sister, too bad, it didn't work out?"

"You and I both know that this is no silver bullet." Rose tried to soften her tone, but there was no nice way to say it. "If you really want to help Erin, if you really want to save this place, selling off some equipment isn't going to do it."

Will's jaw tightened at the proclamation. "At least I'm doing something. And you're right—it's not your place. So how about you stick with helping Erin with her project and let me know if you find anything? I'll do the research myself." He held out a hand toward the door, a clear order for her to leave him to it.

Rose bit her lip, the regret already rushing in. She should have kept her mouth shut. She was just an outsider here, a hired hand, and one who probably wouldn't be able to do very much to help. But she also knew something else, to the very depths of her soul.

Half-measures and wishful thinking would not save this place. Unless one of the twins was willing to do something drastic—and Rose couldn't even begin to think of what that might be—they had absolutely no hope of success.

CHAPTER EIGHT

WILL INSTANTLY REGRETTED HIS HARSH WORDS the second they left his mouth. Rose looked like she'd been physically struck, and if he wasn't mistaken, he'd seen the glimmer of tears in her eyes before she'd turned on her heel and left the workshop.

He was behaving like an absolute tool.

He rubbed his eyes wearily. He didn't know what was wrong with him. No, scratch that. He knew exactly what was wrong with him. Haven Ridge. He'd been unsettled from the moment he crossed the town limits and it got worse the longer he was here. It was bad enough that he had to break his sister's heart, but now it looked like she'd roped Rose in with her.

If she'd just confine herself to the job she was hired to do and stay out of our family business, it would be fine. The grumpy thought rose up within him, even though he knew it wasn't completely fair.

Because she was at least partially right.

This was a pathetic offering, a Band-Aid on a gushing wound. He'd known full well that this equipment would at most fetch ten thousand dollars.

And that was only if he were lucky enough to find someone who appreciated the value of the equipment, how well-built the vintage machines were compared to their less-sturdy modern counterparts. If he thought it would do any good, he'd even humble himself enough to call Charlie and see if the contractor could use them. But he'd heard enough talk to know that the other man was just getting his contracting business up and running again, and he was doing far more structural work on the town's facilities than woodworking.

Will sighed and went to the shelves to get a brush and rags. Slowly, painstakingly, he began cleaning the left-over sawdust from the machines with the brush, wiping down dusty surfaces, oiling the parts that had started to get gummed up from age. He knew these particular machines just as well as his grandfather had; some of the furniture in the house had been of his own making, in fact. Selling the equipment felt like a betrayal.

More of a betrayal than selling the house itself? came the unwanted voice in return, one that sounded suspiciously like his grandmother's.

Maybe, he thought, *but you were the one who told me I had to take care of family at any cost. And Erin is way more important than any house.*

She wouldn't ever consent to moving in with him, but if she didn't go back to her orchestra job, Will knew for a fact she would lose her condo. For that matter, he wasn't entirely sure how she was making the payments while she was on leave. So that meant she would need someplace to live. . .and while Will made a pretty healthy salary at his job, it didn't stretch to supporting two households in an expensive city like Chicago.

But if they were to sell Larkspur House and take the proceeds to "invest" in something smaller and more manageable that could eventually turn a profit, then he would be doing what was best for the trust and Erin would be participating in the family legacy.

He only felt slightly guilty over the mental gymnastics and manipulation involved in that whole thought process.

When he finished cleaning all the woodworking equipment, he pulled out his phone and began taking down all the salient information: manufacturer, model number, and serial number of each piece. It might not be able to save this place—Rose had been right about that—but he also hadn't been lying about not having the space to take it all home. What was he going to do, fill his one-car garage with equipment he'd never use and park his car out in the snow? It was better to pass it on to someone who would appreciate it and use it to make beautiful, functional things. Even if it hurt to let it go.

He finished up by taking photos of all the equipment from multiple angles so he could list it for sale online, then shoved his phone in his pocket. It was getting late, and as much as he'd prefer to hide out here in the carriage house workshop all day, Erin would eventually come looking for him. Probably with frozen pizza or lasagna or whatever else she'd picked up from the prepared foods section at the big box store—he'd assumed that was the destination when he'd heard the rumble of the old pick-up on the other side of the dividing wall.

So he was shocked by the delicious aroma of home-cooked food when he walked through the kitchen door. He was even more shocked when he saw it was Rose standing in front of the large stove.

"What's all this?" he managed, looking between the new hire and his sister who was somewhat ineptly chopping vegetables at the butcher block island.

"Rose is making dinner," Erin said brightly, grinning

at him. "You might actually get some real meals while she's here."

"I get real meals," he shot back, "when I cook them myself."

Rose threw a cautious look over her shoulder. "Well, don't get your hopes up too high. I neglected to give Erin a list and what she brought back was more like a *Chopped* mystery basket than anything resembling a recipe."

Erin grinned, completely unperturbed by the statement. "That is very true. But she wasn't answering her phone, so I couldn't ask her for specifics."

Rose's eyes flickered over him briefly before she went back to her cooking. He understood the implication. She had missed the call because at that moment Will had been busy chewing her out over her interference.

Ugh. He really was a jerk.

"Well, it smells good," he said, hoping to save the moment. "Do you need any help?"

"No—" Erin began, but Rose cut her off.

"As a matter of fact, I could. You see that loaf of bread there? Can you slice it for me? Forty-five degrees on the diagonal, maybe three-quarters of an inch wide."

Rose grabbed a pot holder, took the pan off the burner, and shoved it into the oven compartment. She didn't even look back at him, fully expecting him to comply. Despite himself, a smile lifted the edges of his lips. He went to the knife block and pulled out a long, serrated bread knife, then plopped the French loaf onto the countertop.

Carefully, he began slicing the bread to Rose's exact specifications, until he caught Erin's grin directed his way. "What?"

"Look at you. Actually doing something in the kitchen."

"I can cook!" he protested.

"Heating up Hamburger Helper does not count."

"Hey, I can do more than that. Remember, I made a rack of lamb one time."

"And how long ago was that?" Erin countered.

He grimaced. "I don't know. Eight years ago?"

"Yeah, when you were trying to impress that chef you were trying to date."

"She owned a catering company, and I was not trying to impress her . . ." He broke off and gave his sister a wry smile. "Okay, fine, I was trying to impress her."

Rose came over to the counter with a bowl of what looked like dressing ingredients. "Was she impressed?"

Will hesitated. "She would have been had I not gotten a business call and burned it."

Erin burst out laughing, and even Rose cracked a smile.

"Okay, fine, I'm not a very good cook. But you don't have any room to talk, Erin."

"Oh, I know I don't. But I'm not the one who's trying to make myself out as competent in the kitchen."

Erin had a point. He wouldn't even argue the point if Rose weren't here. "To be fair, I work really long hours so I'm never home to cook. But I do make amazing pancakes."

"You do," Erin conceded with a doting smile. "He used to make them for me when we were kids. He'd put in chocolate chips in the shape of a smiley face."

Rose glanced up at him as if surprised, but he couldn't tell if she was shocked he'd do a nice thing for his sister or that he could even make pancakes. "It's true. I do make a killer pancake. Our grandmother taught me." He gave Erin a look. "And usually, it was blueberries. You just always begged me for chocolate chips."

Erin grinned. "True. And you usually gave in."

When it came to her, he always gave in. He barely repressed a sigh as he went back to cutting the French bread.

"That looks good," Rose said finally, whisking her salad dressing, but he didn't know if it was directed toward him or Erin. Then an alarm went off on her watch and she swiveled away to pull the pan from the oven.

Will craned his neck to see what was in the pan. "What are we having?"

Rose wagged a finger at him. "It's a surprise. Let me just say that Erin didn't leave me much to work with, bringing home cabbage, chicken breasts, and Havarti cheese."

Will stared at his sister. "What on earth?"

She grimaced. "I was intending to make a chicken salad. I grabbed the cabbage by mistake. And I did get crackers to go with the cheese. But chicken breasts work with about everything, don't they?"

"They do," Rose confirmed. "Fortunately."

She worked with her back facing him at the counter next to the stove, so he couldn't see what she was doing until she returned with three plates, holding beautifully grilled sandwiches. "Voila," she pronounced, setting a plate in front of each of them on the island. She took the bowl of cabbage that Erin had shredded and carefully tossed it with the dressing, then spooned some out on the plate next to each sandwich.

"This looks delicious," Will said honestly. "What is it?"

"Chicken and Havarti grilled cheese with raspberry jam and a side of cole slaw. Well, kind of cole slaw," she amended.

Will took a bite and couldn't hold back a murmur of

appreciation. It really was delicious, the chicken thinly sliced, the cheese melting around it. The raspberry jam was a surprisingly welcome counterpoint to the salty and savory flavors from the meat, cheese, and buttered grilled bread.

"You're right. You can cook."

He didn't miss Rose's look of surprised pleasure before she hid it behind her sandwich as she took her first bite. "This is not half bad. But maybe next time I'll send a list."

Erin grinned. "But you do so well when you have to improvise."

Rose laughed and for a second, the mood in the kitchen was so friendly that he could almost imagine they were all there by choice and not because various life circumstances had derailed them.

"What do you think about heading into town and grabbing some dessert from the bakery?" Erin asked Will, and just like that the illusion was shattered.

"I need to look over my work emails," he said, "Make sure I'm not missing anything important. But grab me an eclair if Gemma has any?" He rose and took his plate to the sink, where he rinsed it before putting it in the dishwasher.

"Sure thing," Erin said, but it was clear she thought his behavior was strange. He never begged off an outing based on work. He normally got up early and worked before Erin ever got out of bed, so they had time to do whatever random activities she had planned while he was in town. Rose said nothing, just followed him with an appraising gaze.

He escaped quickly, going straight up to the second-floor study to plug in his laptop. As soon as it booted up, he hooked it to his portable WiFi, since Larkspur House didn't have its own internet connection.

But his only new email messages were the automated notifications that new files had been added to his company's server. He deleted the notifications and shut his laptop again. Those could wait. All the documents— financial statements, bank statements, police reports— would be trickling in over the next couple of weeks, while the ones that weren't electronic were entered into spreadsheets by their data-entry-clerk-slash-office-assistant. Once they had all the files in house, then he could start examining them, looking for a trail of transactions that indicated wrongdoing.

Everyone might tease him about accounting being boring, but first and foremost, he considered himself an investigator. He just dealt with numbers rather than fingerprints and surveillance video. As far as accounting jobs went, it was about as exciting as one could get. And yet the thrill of anticipation that usually came with starting a new case eluded him.

Because while he could unravel any kind of financial mystery that came across his desk, he still couldn't figure out a way to save Larkspur House for his sister.

CHAPTER NINE

OVER THE NEXT COUPLE OF DAYS, Rose and Erin fell into a comfortable routine. They got up around eight a.m.—early for Erin, late for Rose—and then Rose made a simple breakfast downstairs in the kitchen while they decided on which new section of the house to tackle. Each morning she held her breath, wondering if Will would make an appearance, and every day they ate alone, even though she saw signs of him being up and about even earlier than they were. Why it mattered to her, she didn't know. Maybe she thought that if they could just have a conversation, if he could see how much this house meant to his sister, maybe he'd give in, give them more time. Their days were ticking down toward the two-week mark with relentless regularity.

Except she always came back to his words in the workshop. *It's not your place.* He'd meant the situation between Erin and him, but she couldn't help taking it more literally. Even as she fell in love with the graceful proportions and beautiful antique furnishings of the Larkspur House, she felt deeply that she was a stranger here. An interloper. Someone who was here by the whim of chance and not by design. Not like Erin and Will who could trace their lineage directly to the original builder of the house more than a hundred years earlier.

And yet, she felt the pressure to find something useful even more strongly than the twins. Because this might be their home, but she was failing at her only purpose in being here. At the rate they were going, Will could decide that she wasn't worth the expense and let her go.

That didn't mean they didn't find fascinating items as they cleaned, packed, and discarded. In one of the third-floor bedrooms, they found an antique wind-up jewelry box in perfect condition, the lid glimmering with jewels. For one bright second, Rose was excited, wondering if they'd found something of real value. They had, but only of sentimental value—it was etched with the name Marie, who was the daughter of Andrew Bixby, but the jewels were paste. It was an artifact of local historical interest, but to the rest of the world, it was worth about $100, at least according to eBay. Still, they tucked it away in one of the boxes they'd designated as "keep"—the things the twins would take away before they sold the place.

In another room, they found what appeared to be a scrap of a blueprint—one that turned out not to be original, but of one of the many remodels the house had undergone since its building. A quick search of the local planning office told them the plan was from the 1970s. Interesting, but hardly historical.

"I don't want to be negative or anything," Rose said at the end of one particularly frustrating day, clearing out the room that had once been the grandfather's study. The man kept check registers from 1982 but nothing of actual value. "But it feels like we're getting nowhere fast."

Doubt flickered across Erin's face, but it quickly disappeared into a cheery smile. "We'll find something. I can feel it."

What Rose could feel was her reprieve slipping away with each passing day.

Because she really did love it here. When they weren't working on cleaning out one of the forty-three rooms in the mansion, she was reading a book in the conservatory or wandering the house looking at every careful detail of its architecture. It was clear to her that this wasn't simply a house that the owner had left up to his builders to design. Someone had taken the time and effort to specify every single detail, down to the ornate moldings in the hallways. Every floor had a similar motif, but each was unique in some way. The first floor used carved larkspur as cornices where the wall met. The second floor featured columbines. The third were poppies. But the fourth used roses, which were most definitely not native to Colorado. That meant that a member of the Parker family had loved them and had them built into the architecture as a personal, private pleasure.

Rose found herself taking pictures of all these things and detailing them in a journal, knowing full well that she might be helping to write the real estate listing that would take it out of Parker hands.

Oddly enough—or maybe not so oddly, considering he was acting as the timekeeper—Will stayed out of their way. Rose thought he was working in the background, just separately. One day she saw a truck roar up the lane and park in front of the carriage house. It left an hour later, loaded with a large, shiny piece of metal equipment that glinted in the light.

Somehow, it made her inexplicably sad. She almost wanted to say something to him, to offer her condolences, even though she knew they wouldn't be welcome, but he was either absent or had his head bent over his computer in the second-floor study.

"What exactly does your brother do?" Rose asked one day while they were digging through boxes in the closet of one of the unused fourth-floor bedrooms.

"He's an accountant," Erin said, absorbed in the textiles she pulled out of the box—pretty, but probably not immensely valuable.

"Yeah, I know, but what kind of accountant? Like, taxes? Or bookkeeping or what?"

Erin caught the interest in her voice and finally looked at her, a smile playing over her lips. "Why do you want to know?"

Something in Erin's tone brought a flush to Rose's cheeks. "I was just curious. He seems so serious when I pass by the office, like the fate of the world is resting on his concentration or something."

"That's just Will. He's always had an overinflated sense of self-importance." Erin grinned to soften the dig. "Seriously, though, he does work hard. He's a forensic accountant."

"Like . . . with law enforcement?"

"Not quite, though sometimes he does work with the police or FBI. Mostly companies hire his firm when they think that an employee is stealing but they can't quite prove it. He combs through every last bit of their financial information until he figures out exactly who did what and when."

"In Chicago."

"Yeah, why? Do you know his firm or something?"

"No, of course not."

But the blood had already drained from her face, settling someplace near her heels. Will Parker was a *forensic accountant.* She hadn't actually needed elaboration on what that meant. She remembered all too well what the police had said when they'd released her after questioning: *We may have more to ask you after the forensic accountants get done with the files.*

Because it didn't take too much imagination to think that Will would have heard about her case.

Milwaukee and Chicago were only an hour and a half away from each other by car. They might have their own economies and their own cultures, but it wasn't unusual for a company to have offices in both cities. It certainly wasn't unusual for someone to call in a consult from Chicago when Milwaukee didn't have the local resources.

And it wouldn't be unusual for a forensic accounting firm to know about the biggest fraud case to hit Milwaukee when it involved one of the most well-known families in Chicago.

Rose pressed a hand to her forehead, not sure why the realization had hit struck with such a blow. It wasn't like she was going to be here longer than another week anyway. The likelihood of him actually knowing the details of her case were slim; the chances he'd make the connection to her nearly non-existent. She'd gone to her maiden name of Cameron as soon as the divorce was final, to distance herself from Jordan and the rest of the Kelly family as quickly as possible. But even if Will were to find out, it wouldn't matter. The worst that could happen was that he cut her loose a few days early and she'd hardly be worse off than before.

So why did the idea of being found out bother her so much?

"You know, I think I need to get some air," Rose said, pushing to her feet. "Or maybe even run into town for a few minutes. Should I pick up some cookies?"

She'd been stacking the deck with the cookies

remark, knowing how much Erin loved the Broken
Hearts Bakery. "Oh yeah, if they have some pecan
sandies today, bring me some of those. Literally the
best thing I've ever tasted."

"Done." Rose didn't wait another second, just
hightailed it out of the room and upstairs to change out
of her dusty T-shirt into something a little cuter. Five
minutes later, she was headed out to her car, tossing the
key nervously in her hand. Twenty minutes after that,
she was pulling into downtown Haven Ridge with her
windows open, a breeze in the air, and a much lighter
heart.

She parked at the very end of Beacon Street where
the commercial and residential sections met and locked
the car behind her before setting off on foot. The sun
beat down with a sting that was out of proportion to
the moderate temperature of the day, and she wished
she'd remembered to put on some sunblock. Her fair
Irish skin went from pale to sunburned in approx-
imately thirty seconds. Maybe she'd find a Haven Ridge
hat in that gift shop that Erin had mentioned the other
day.

But even the threat of impending sunburn couldn't
ruin the rapid lift in her mood. This was why she'd had
to get out. She'd instinctively known that a sunny stroll
through the charming town would be an antidote to the
worried, close atmosphere of the historic house. She
took her time, peering into windows of empty and
occupied shops alike, noting the date placards built into
the tops of the brick buildings. When she finally got to
the bookstore, she pushed right through, took a deep
breath . . .

. . . and found herself right at home.

The bookshop had a pleasantly cluttered, winding
interior, wooden bookcases set at odd angles, every

nook and cranny filled with volumes. That scent of paper—old and new—was better than any pill for her blood pressure. There was only a single older lady browsing at this time of day and there was no one behind the counter, so Rose took her time perusing the shelves.

"Let me know if I can help you with anything," a pleasant female voice came from somewhere in the shop.

Rose twisted to see a pretty blonde amble into the front of the store, a small cardboard box in her hands.

Impulsively, Rose moved toward the counter. "Do you happen to have any Edith Wharton?"

The surprise on the woman's face said she got more requests for modern thrillers and romances than classics. "I do, as a matter of fact, right over here." She set her box on the counter and then led Rose a little deeper into the historic building, stopping before a modest section with a hand-lettered sign. She browsed the shelf for a long moment, then tipped off a clothbound book. "*The Age of Innocence*. First edition." She handed it carefully to Rose. "It actually came from a local collection. Are you familiar with Larkspur House?"

Rose let out a little laugh. "Considering I'm staying there right now?"

The woman's face melted into understanding, and she laughed. "I wondered if that was you. I'm Liv Quinn."

Rose shifted the book into her left hand and held out her right. "I'm Rose Cameron."

"I know. Welcome to Haven Ridge. How are you finding it so far?"

"I've only been here a week, and I haven't spent much time in town, but so far it's charming. So is this bookstore. Is it yours?"

Liv smiled. "It is. We opened last year. But you probably know that."

Rose blinked. "Why would I know that?"

Liv's friendly smile faltered. "Oh. I just assumed since you were staying up at the house. . . the Bixby Trust owns this whole block of buildings. I lease this space from them."

"No, I had no idea. But Will Parker is not particularly forthcoming on the topic. On any topic, really."

Liv grimaced. "Yeah. I'm sorry about that."

"Why would you be sorry?"

Now Liv looked like she really regretted bringing it up, and she vacillated, clearly torn over whether to continue. "I suppose you could just as easily ask anyone in town and they'd tell you. Will and I have. . . history. And I'm afraid he was a bit blindsided by my engagement when he came back this time."

Rose opened her mouth, then closed it firmly. Sunday morning, when she'd been trying to leave, he'd roared back to the house, in a foul mood. "So that's where he was on Sunday. No wonder he was in such a bad mood."

Liv looked genuinely surprised, before her expression shifted to pain. "Will is a great guy. He was here for me after my husband—who happened to be his best friend—died. But I think he just read more into the relationship than was there. I take full responsibility for that. I didn't realize. . . " She shook her head. "Just go easy on him. It's been a rough few years."

"Apparently so," Rose murmured. She looked back at the book in her hands, carefully flipping through it even though she didn't take in more than the most cursory observations. So Will had been in love with a woman who was now engaged. She could see why he would hate being back, why he'd been so surly. That couldn't be easy for anyone.

But more importantly. . . stiff, grumpy Will Parker actually had real, genuine feelings?

"I'll leave you to browse," Liv said, and that was how Rose realized she'd been silent for too long. She tucked the book under her arm and looked through the rest of the classics section, noting how many old volumes were tucked here on the shelves. Were these all from Larkspur House?

Resisting the impractical—and impossible—urge to buy up all the old books to refill the house's library, she took her time exploring the rest of the bottom floor before she brought *The Age of Innocence* to the counter. "Just this one, please."

Liv smiled. "Good choice." She carefully wrapped the book in brown paper and tied it with a piece of string—an old-fashioned affection that immediately made Rose love the place even more—before ringing up the book on the register. Rose tried not to gape at the price on the tablet in front of her and held back her cringe when she tapped her debit card to its screen. It wasn't as if she had money to spend on frivolities like this, but she also knew she couldn't leave the book forlorn and unappreciated on the shelf.

Call it a souvenir of her short time in Haven Ridge.

And then Liv tucked a paper bookmark beneath the strings of the package. "These are about our book clubs. We have two different ones that each meet once a month. The first is a classics club—we're currently reading *Jude the Obscure*—and the second is pop-fic. We just finished *Project Hail Mary* and next month we're starting the new Emily Henry book."

For a second, Rose imagined herself sitting in a circle in this welcoming space with other readers, but just as quickly, the bubble burst. "Unfortunately, I don't think I'm going to be here that long. This is only a temporary job, and it would be a nonexistent job if Will had his way."

Liv cocked her head and studied her, but what she was reading from her face, Rose couldn't guess. "Give him some time. He takes a while to warm up to new people. But when he does, you have a friend for life."

"Well, I think I'm probably running out of time," Rose said with a sad smile. "But thanks again for the book. I'll be in again before I leave."

She took a deep breath as she crossed the threshold beneath the jingle of bells, her euphoria of moments before fading to sadness. How strange that less than an hour before, she'd panicked over the idea of people finding out who she was, but Liv's instant recognition when she'd introduced herself had made her feel right at home. She supposed it was the difference between famous and infamous—one was positive, the other negative.

Or maybe it was just that for a split second, she'd had that strange feeling of *home* that she'd felt when she was in Larkspur's conservatory.

Without realizing it, she'd proceeded down Beacon Street, seeing but not really registering the various businesses there—an art studio, a music shop—and found herself in front of a cheery store signed as *Haven Ridge Gift Shop*. A blue bicycle sat out front, its basket filled with a real pot of geraniums and a sandwich board in old-fashioned writing that advertised *Gifts—Apparel—Local Art*.

Granny Pearl.

Rose pushed the door open and stepped inside, immediately enveloped by the scent of lilacs and roses and vanilla—no doubt from the wide selection of candles by the front door. Carved wood signs lined one side of the shop; beautiful watercolors and oil paintings lined the other. Rose found herself standing in front of a stunning painting of a pack of coyotes done in sunset colors and a pointillistic style, wondering how someone could have the talent to render mere dots of paint with such emotion. She could practically feel the wildness and the freedom in the swirls and groupings of colors.

"That's one of my favorites, too."

Rose twisted her head to find Granny Pearl had come up behind her, soundless in another colorful pair of Jordans, this time wearing a simple T-shirt and jeans. "It's lovely. Local artist?"

"You know him," she said with a smile. "My grandson, Thomas."

"Wait, *Thomas* Thomas? Like, cafe owner,/town mayor Thomas? He's a painter too?"

"Used to be an art professor, as a matter of fact. But yes, that's him."

"He's . . . amazingly talented." Rose turned to the old lady. "Is there something in the water here? Because it seems you have a lot of talent for a small town. Erin is . . ."

"Remarkable," Pearl finished with a smile. "We knew it from her first recital at the school. Picked up a bow and it was like she'd been playing the cello her whole life."

"I know. I could listen to her forever. Makes me wish that I'd been born with just a little of that talent."

"We all have our gifts," the old lady said. "Sometimes it just takes the right time and place to find them. Now what can I help you with today?"

"Oh." Rose had forgotten about her mission . . . she'd wandered into the shop like she'd been drawn there. "I was hoping you might have some hats. I've only been out there for twenty minutes and I think my nose is already starting to burn."

"Of course." Pearl guided her toward the rear of the store, where a metal grid on the wall held a wide variety of embroidered hats. Some had a simple *Haven Ridge* in various fonts; others had a reproduction of the *Welcome to Haven Ridge* sign, which Rose herself had not yet seen. She browsed several designs before she picked a white one with a simple orange and pink logo and brought it to the counter.

"That will be $17.99," Pearl said without ringing it up. Once more, Rose cringed at how fast her bank account was dwindling, but she was saving herself the pain of a sunburn later, so she handed over her card. A minute later, Pearl handed her the receipt with her hat. "Thank you, dear. Enjoy your afternoon. We're glad you're here."

Rose didn't think much about the comment until she was out on the street again, walking down the sidewalk to the end of the block, where she turned west. *We're glad you're here.* Why would that be? Was it just a nice thing she said to all tourists to make them feel welcome?

And yet there was something about the serious way Granny Pearl had delivered the words that made Rose think it was more than just a polite farewell.

Geez. Now she was doing it. She'd scoffed a little at the idea of town magic. It was magical, all right, but it was the magic of history and familiarity, a combination that was fading fast. While the world around them favored progress and development, Haven Ridge was sticking to its roots. Rose had always spent so much time living in the past, given how disastrous her present had become, it was no wonder that would be appealing to her.

And yet . . .

Hadn't Erin said something about how Granny Pearl was a bit of the town's guardian as descendant of the original founder, Elizabeth Strong? Wouldn't that mean that if anyone would have an idea of how to help Larkspur House—or at least information they could use to help Larkspur House—it would be her?

Almost without having made a conscious decision, Rose turned on her heel and walked back up the street to the Haven Ridge Gift Shop. When she pushed back through the door, the old lady was bustling around her shop with an old-fashioned feather duster. But the way Pearl turned to her with a smile made her think that her return was no surprise.

"What do you know about the Larkspur House?" Rose asked slowly.

Granny Pearl smiled and lowered her duster. "I thought you'd never ask. Meet me at the Brick House Cafe in two hours."

CHAPTER TEN

I<small>T WAS FAR LESS DIFFICULT</small> to kill two hours in Haven Ridge than Rose thought. She started by texting Erin as soon as she left the gift shop.

Got hung up in town. Do you mind if I take the rest of the afternoon off? I'll be home in time to make dinner. She'd already pressed send before she realized she'd used the word *home* instead of the word *back*, wondered if it was a significant slip or just habit. Either way, it didn't take long for Erin's reply to come through in return.

No problem. Haven Ridge has the tendency to do that. Have fun!

Rose smiled. Erin really was completely unlike her brother. She expected had she texted Will with the same thing, he might have reminded her of her responsibility to her job. But considering she'd been working ten hours a day, combing through boxes and sweeping floors and dusting every conceivable surface, she figured he didn't have much room for complaint.

If he even noticed her absence in the first place.

Permission to play hooky granted, Rose shoved the phone in her pocket, pulled the hat down a little lower to shield her face, and started on her leisurely walking tour of Haven Ridge. Back down Beacon Street she went, across Alaska Avenue, and up Columbine. This street seemed like it was a little slower to find its revival, unlike the two that flanked it, but even here there were signs of renewal. She smiled at the tiny children's consignment store, which had cheery dresses and adorable overalls in the front window, but she didn't go inside, even though she did offer a prayer of thanks for the fact that she and Jordan had never had kids. This whole situation had been bad enough with just the two of them.

Up the street, several buildings in a row seemed to be undergoing facelifts, with scaffolding reinforcing their brick faces. Directly across from them in a similar building, new vinyl lettering adorned fresh plate glass proclaiming *Columbine Apothecary,* with a handwritten sheet of paper in the window announcing *Join our grand opening on August 1st!* followed by a Sharpie happy face. Rose paused and pressed her nose up to the glass, peering through the opening left by the peeling kraft paper. The interior was dark, but she could already see shelving half-filled with bottles and antique tables stacked with boxes. She smiled as she pulled back, making a note of the opening date before she realized that she would be long gone by then.

The rest of the businesses on Columbine were strictly functional—a hardware shop that looked like it hadn't changed a bit since 1950, a stationery store that looked like it mostly carried business supplies, and a combination chiropractor/acupuncturist's office. She stopped at the quaintly named Koffee Kabin, where she ordered a mocha, then wandered back up Dogwood. Which eventually landed her in front of the Broken Hearts Bakery.

The heavenly scents of sugar and vanilla enveloped

her as she stepped inside and took in the clean, quiet, pretty interior. Behind the counter, a tall, dark-haired woman transferred a tray of pastries to the glass case. She looked up when Rose entered and closed the case's sliding door. "Welcome! How can I help you today?"

"Do you have pecan sandies?"

"I sure do. You must be Rose."

Rose blinked at her.

"I'm pretty sure the only person who comes here specifically for pecan sandies is Erin Parker," the woman said, "so I only make them when I hear she's back in town." The woman held out her hand. "I'm Gemma Van Buren."

"Nice to meet you, Gemma. I am indeed Rose." She shook Gemma's hand with a little laugh. "You were one of the first people Erin mentioned."

"I would say the same, but truthfully, Granny Pearl beat her to it." Gemma laughed and moved over to the bakery case, where she used tongs to transfer a dozen of the small crunchy cookies into a glassine bag.

"I'm almost afraid to ask what she said."

"Don't be. In her usual Granny Pearl way, she was complimentary. Something like, 'finally someone to bring some order to the chaos out there.'"

Rose wasn't sure how to take that. She supposed it could be seen as complimentary, but how on earth could Pearl have surmised that from a single ten-second meeting? Besides, with Will involved, it seemed hard to believe anything about the Larkspur House could be considered chaotic. He was one of the most orderly, rigid people that she'd ever met.

Fortunately, her attention was diverted by the selection of baked goods in the case. Her gaze snagged on a tray of sugar cookie hearts iced in pastel colors with snarky sayings. "Can I get a couple of these?"

"Sure, which ones?"

Rose bit her lip. "How about *Good Riddance* and *2 Good 4 U Anyway*?"

"Excellent choices," Gemma said with a wink, adding those to a second bag. Fortunately, she didn't ask exactly *why* those two spoke to Rose. "Anything else?"

"No, that's it. No, wait, on second thought . . ." She perused the case. "Could I get one of the chocolate eclairs, too?"

Now Gemma's expression turned knowing as she retrieved the pastry. "Let me guess. Peace offering?"

Rose grimaced. "How could you know?"

"Small town. And . . . Liv is my best friend."

"Ah." Rose understood the subtext there easily. In a town this small, everyone would know when Will was in a bad mood, and almost everyone would know exactly why. For a moment, she actually felt sorry for him. It was bad enough to have your heart broken in the big city with no one to care. Even worse when every single person you passed looked at you sympathetically. It almost made her rethink her assessment of the charm of the small town.

Except the attention didn't seem malicious or even petty. What would it be like to live in a town where everyone actually *cared* about each other? Rose had thought she'd had friends in Milwaukee until the divorce, but she'd quickly learned that they were either hangers-on interested in the prestige that came along with the Kelly name or petty people who seemed to take a perverse delight in seeing how far she'd fallen. In fact, other than her parents—whose pity came laced with a heavy dose of *we tried to tell you*—there wasn't anyone in her life to care about what the scandal and subsequent divorce might be doing to *her*. She had a distinct feeling that wouldn't happen in Haven Ridge.

Gemma rang her up at the register and then handed over a paper bag containing the individually packed treats—she knew exactly to whom each of those items would go. But just as she turned to go, Gemma called out, "Hey, I know you're probably busy up at the house, but we're having a cupcake party here on Thursday. You're more than welcome to come."

Rose paused, her interest piqued. "Cupcake party?"

"Yeah, kind of a 'decorate your own cupcake' thing. It's $20 per person. I supply the cupcakes and the supplies to decorate them, you take them home." Gemma flashed a wry smile. "Fair warning, it will be mostly teenage girls, but they're a good crowd. And Liv and Mallory usually come."

Right now, being surrounded by giggly teenage girls seemed preferable to her scowly host, so she nodded. "That sounds like fun. I'll see if I can make it. Thanks."

"You're welcome," Gemma said. "Welcome to Haven Ridge."

And for that moment, even knowing that her time was ticking down and she would be out of here in days and not weeks or months, she did feel welcome.

She spent the rest of her two hours wandering Haven Ridge, looking into windows and nibbling slowly on her sugar cookies, washed down with the mocha. It seemed pretty clear that food was the heart of this town, though the hot springs seemed like a close second. She washed her hands in the hot spring fountain in the park, taking a quick sip of the mineral-heavy water, and then wandered a few blocks over to an old-fashioned, low-slung brick building under construction. The sound of power tools drifted from inside, though the only signs of actual people were the dusty work trucks parked at the curb. A chain link fence surrounded the dirt lot, the signs wired to the fencing proclaiming *Castro Construction* and *Alvarez Plumbing*. And on the opposite side, a vinyl banner that said: *Haven Ridge Spring House Recreation Center, Coming Soon.*

Interesting. Was this an old-fashioned bath house that they were opening to the public? She laced her fingers into the chain link, peering in to get a better look, but the dark interior told her nothing. She pushed away the thought that she was never going to get to see it finished, surprised by how sad it made her.

She was being ridiculous. This was not her town. This was just a momentary stop on her journey to wherever, and the fact she had *no* idea where she was going next didn't mean this should be her final destination.

Why not? that tiny internal voice challenged. *Just because they don't need you up at Larkspur House doesn't mean you're getting kicked out of town.*

Except from the looks of it, Haven Ridge didn't exactly seem to be an employment mecca. Unless she was going to go get a job at a big box store as a checker or a stocker—which wasn't exactly the small-town dream—she would be surprised if there was actually anything to do here. She was a failed literature PhD who had most recently worked as a fundraiser and marketer for a literacy nonprofit. Somehow it seemed like those sorts of jobs would be in short supply.

She was so lost in thought that when she glanced at her watch, she realized she only had five minutes left to get to the Brick House Cafe. She tossed her empty paper cup in a trash can on the corner and then hustled her way back to the cafe.

She'd expected Mallory and Pearl to be waiting for her, but she did not expect the vast variety of materials spread across the counter, arranged into orderly stacks. Pearl twisted around at the jingle of harness bells, a

smile spreading across her wrinkled face. She waved
Rose over and patted the stool next to her.

"Wow," Rose said, hopping onto the vinyl seat. "I
don't think I fully understood what I was asking."

Mallory laughed. "Beware anyone who wants to
know anything about the town. Granny Pearl and I are
probably the foremost Haven Ridge experts in, well,
anywhere."

"I believe that," Rose said, wide-eyed. There was a
bound manuscript that had to be at least four hundred
pages—the name Mallory Rivas on the cover said this
must be her finished dissertation.

"That's just a copy," Mallory said when she saw Rose
looking at it. "You can take it home and thumb through
it if you want. I don't think everything will be relevant
to your interests, but the history of the town does tie in
with what you were asking about the Larkspur House.
You might find it useful for your purposes."

"Which are. . .?" Rose had just wanted to know a
little bit about the house's history, hoping it might give
her some direction in their search.

"To save it, of course," Pearl said. "We all know that
William Parker does not want to sell the Larkspur
House, most definitely not to an investor who's going
to come in and turn it into some posh event center. It's
not good for the Bixby Trust and it's not good for
Haven Ridge."

"From what I can tell, Will doesn't much care for
Haven Ridge in general."

Mallory's expression softened, and her tone was
tentative. "I'm just a newcomer, but even I know that
Will has had somewhat of a difficult life. You can't
blame him for having bad associations with the town."

Rose cocked her head curiously. "How so? I mean, I
know about his friend, Jason, and I picked up that he's

still a little stung by Liv, but that's just. . . regular life stuff."

Mallory and Pearl exchanged a look, and the cafe owner shook her head. "You're going to have to ask him that. It's really not our story to tell."

Well, if she was relying on Will Parker to bare his soul to her, she'd never find out what they were talking about. She shook off that thought. It didn't matter. She wasn't doing this for Will anyway. She was doing this for Erin and for the fact that she was falling in love with the historic house with every room they sifted through.

And maybe, if she were completely honest with herself, she hoped that she might find some small way to make a place for herself there. After all, if there was a reason to keep the house, might there be a reason to have a house assistant too?

"As much as I love all the thought you've put into this, I really just need to know the basics on the Larkspur House. I'm already playing hooky from my duties there this afternoon."

Pearl fixed her with a reproving look. "I would think that you of all people would already know at least part of it. After all, the house was built by Andrew Bixby."

Rose gaped. "No. The novelist Andrew Bixby? *Dawn Over the Mountaintops*? *The Miner's Folly*?" She hadn't even made the association. After all, he was a minor novelist from the early twentieth century, and his work didn't fit neatly into either of the major movements of the era. His work was too nostalgic to be consider realist, and yet too unflinching to be classified as romantic. As a result, she'd excluded him from consideration of study, simply because she didn't want to spend her entire dissertation trying to prove why he should belong in one camp or the other.

Mallory moved farther down the counter to a

banker's box, lifted the lid, and pulled out three Penguin Classics paperbacks. She set them next to each other in front of Rose. "In case you want to read up. The manor house in *The Miner's Folly* is thought to be referencing the Larkspur House by a different name."

Rose picked up one of the books and leafed through it, skimming the prose. It was formal, but somehow it wasn't old-fashioned. The little she'd read of Bixby's work had impressed her with its modern sensibility. She found herself getting drawn into the beauty of a passage's clean prose and then snapped it shut. She knew what she was going to be reading tonight.

"Thanks," Rose said finally. "That's helpful. What else should I know? Short version?"

Granny Pearl reached for a stack of photo albums, opening and putting aside each one until she found the one she was looking for. "Short version: Andrew Bixby was the heir to a mining fortune in West Virginia, but he had a strong case of wanderlust. His wife, Amelia, was a Philadelphia socialite—her parents were new money and so of course they were scorned by the old-money set in New York and Boston. Bixby knew her father, actually approached him for a business deal, and from the few letters we have, it seems to have been love at first sight between the two. Being a bit more free-thinking than the Knickerbocker set, Amelia's parents actually approved of the union. They were less than thrilled when Andrew wanted to go west, however."

Mallory stepped in when Pearl paused. "Andrew Bixby knew he had to impress them and assure them that they were not sending their daughter off to a mining camp. So he traveled for almost two years, looking for the perfect place to build their home and start his business. He invested in several of the mines in the area, which had switched from gold and silver to lead and nickel, and when he found the site for Larkspur House, he knew that's where he was going to build a manor that would impress not only the locals but his in-laws in Philadelphia."

Pearl flipped open the photo album to a page with three lone photos pasted in with aging yellow corners. She tapped the first photo with her fingernail. "This here is the house when it was just being built. And that is Andrew Bixby."

Rose swiveled the book toward herself so she could take a better look. Bixby was somewhat unremarkable-looking in a dark suit and a bowler hat, appearing like every other man from the era. The half-finished house, on the other hand, was incredible, the shell of stone walls already starting to rise from the landscape.

The photo beneath it was of the finished house by itself without any of the landscaping that Rose assumed would come later. There were a few details that were different—the trim along the arched windows looked to have been switched or updated in later years—but overall, the house hadn't changed much from its original design.

Finally, the last photo of Bixby was with a pretty woman, dressed in pale clothing in the Gibson Girl silhouette—broad shoulders and a wasp waist, with a cascade of curls falling down from beneath a stylish hat. From the corner of the picture peeked an old-fashioned car, little more than a carriage on four high white-walled wheels. Rose gave a faint smile at the display of wealth: Andrew and Amelia Bixby must have been the most stylish couple in Haven Ridge.

"How long did they live there?" she asked.

Pearl looked to Mallory, who answered. "Andrew Bixby died in 1921. Amelia lived there until the 1930s when their children were completely grown, and then she moved back to Philadelphia. The house fell into disrepair until the 1940s, when an heir came back to restore it and establish a trust to ensure that it didn't happen again. So the Bixby Trust dates back to the late '40s."

"So if the trust is named Bixby, how is it under control of the Parker family?"

"The usual way," Pearl said with a smile. "The last Bixby heir had only daughters. The eldest married a Parker and from then on, it's been the Parker family's responsibility."

Rose nodded slowly. It was a fascinating history, if a bit thin. "Thank you. That's all very interesting. I'm not sure that it really helps us, though. I mean, if Andrew Bixby was as famous as Hemingway, there might be some justification for preserving the house, for giving tours. But as it is now . . . it's been thoroughly modernized. It would take more money to restore it to its 1906 state with all the period furniture than it would be to make the structural repairs. And even that's out of reach."

Mallory looked at her sympathetically, but Pearl seemed unperturbed. "I don't believe that its fate is to get sold off," she said. "That means you have to keep looking. Something will present itself."

"Maybe so," Rose said, but inwardly she was unconvinced. Still, she lifted the dissertation. "Can I take this? And the novels? I'll return them before I go, of course."

"Of course," Mallory said with a smile. "Call me if you have any questions."

Rose said her goodbyes and stacked the manuscript and books in her arms, regretting that she hadn't parked closer to the cafe. The chances of her getting these back to her car without dropping at least one of them were not high.

Surprisingly, though, she made it to her Volvo without losing any of the books, though they managed to slide onto the floor as soon as she dropped them onto the passenger seat. She rolled her eyes as she put the key in the ignition and reached across to retrieve them. It was sweet of Pearl and Mallory to lend her the books, but her hopes were hovering lower than ever. It might be interesting history, but it was devoid of any kind of sizzle that would help them save the property from its inevitable fate. Sure, Bixby was an interesting writer, but while he'd achieved contemporary popularity, his books hadn't endured in the literary landscape. There simply wasn't enough information available or a wide-enough catalog to encourage serious scholarship on the topic.

Which meant that the whole literary angle was a dead end.

Rose mulled over the problem on the way back to the Larkspur House. Maybe they were looking at this the wrong way. So far they'd been focusing on stopgap measures—making enough money to repair the house so they didn't have to sell it. But maybe they should be looking at the ways they could make the house self-supporting. Pearl had made an offhand comment about how they didn't want some developer coming in and turning it into a soulless corporate event center.

But what if they were the ones to do it, minus the soulless, corporate part?

Rose pulled up next to the rental SUV in front of Larkspur House, the vehicle reminding her of the single biggest reason her plan wouldn't work. Will. She had the feeling that, coming from a stranger, the suggestion wouldn't hold the same weight it would from someone he respected. And as much as she hated to say it, his relationship with Erin didn't exactly put them on equal footing when it came to business ideas. He'd just think his sister was rushing into a half-baked scheme to keep the house in the family trust. He wouldn't take it as a serious business proposal. Which meant that she'd need to find someone else entirely to broach the subject.

The bigger problem was, she had no idea who that might be.

She sighed and put the vehicle in park. There was only one way she was going to find that out.

She was going to have to make friends with Will Parker.

CHAPTER ELEVEN

"Erin, are you home?"

Rose's voice echoed through the hallway, drifting through the open doors of the conservatory. Will sighed and lowered his book into his lap. When he'd figured out that both women were gone, he'd thought it was the perfect opportunity to get some reading done in his favorite space. The sun was starting to dip toward the horizon, painting the grounds in glorious hues of gold and orange, yet another one of the spectacular Colorado sunsets that characterized Haven Ridge.

For a second, he thought about remaining quiet and leaving Rose to her own devices, but that wasn't fair. Just because she'd been an unwelcome surprise didn't mean that he wanted her to actually *feel* unwelcome. From what he could tell, Erin had chosen well in her hiring. Rose was a hard worker, smart and polite, and she was an excellent cook. In fact, he hadn't eaten so well in the last several years as the nights that Rose took it upon herself to make dinner for everyone. Even considering that Erin's grocery shopping habits leaned toward the whimsical.

He simply resented what she symbolized. Pointless hope. A last gasp for this house, when they would be better off just making peace with the situation and moving on.

Rose was still calling, though, evidently not having seen the open doors of the carriage house that indicated Erin's absence. He sighed again and raised his voice. "Erin left for a while. She'll be back later!"

The house fell silent, but a moment later, the tap of footsteps approached the doors to the conservatory. Rose's tentative voice called out, "Will?"

"In here."

Rose stepped through the doorway, glancing around until she found him in the corner on the lounger. "Oh, hi. Did I just hear you say that Erin is gone?"

Will gave a faint smile. "She decided that what we really needed tonight was s'mores so she went to get all the supplies."

"Oh, that sounds fun." Rose hovered awkwardly by the door, clutching a stack of paper to her chest. "I won't interrupt you then. Can you just let her know that I'm back when you see her?"

"Sure," Will said. But as she turned to walk away, words spilled out of their own volition. "Don't feel like you need to leave on my account. This place is big enough for the two of us."

She hesitated, then turned. "Are you sure? I don't want to disrupt you."

"You're not. Not really." He held up his book. "It's not that interesting anyway."

The little flash of a smile that she gave him as she crept back in tugged on him in a surprising way. Rose wasn't actually *scared* of him, was she?

"What have you got?" He indicated the papers she was clutching to her chest.

Rose looked down as if she'd forgotten what she was carrying. "Oh. This is Mallory's dissertation on Haven Ridge. And these are all Andrew Bixby's novels." She held up the three slim paperback volumes.

"Not all of them," Will said off-handedly.

"What?"

"Those are just his published volumes. There were more than that."

Now he had her full attention. Rose moved over to his side and took the chair that sat beside his on the other side of a small wicker table. "Oh yeah? How do you know that?"

"Well, for one, it's in the foreword of one of those books. *The Miner's Folly*, I think." He held out his hand, and after a moment of confusion, she handed the book to him. He flipped open the front cover, skimming the foreword quickly until he found what he was looking for. "Here it is. 'In a letter to his publisher dated January 1918, Andrew Bixby makes mention of another novel about the changing fortunes of a widowed woman and her children, living in a falling-down mansion. Some believe that he may have been displaying prescience of his impending death—or perhaps secret knowledge of a danger to his health—because it was not much later that he withdrew from society. However, some scholars believe that it was merely Bixby's way of reassuring his publisher that the much-diminished sales from his previous novel would be improved with another volume, most likely one taking advantage of the new taste for the modern Gothic. Whatever his intention, *The Miner's Folly* was Bixby's last published work, and if there ever was a fourth novel, it seems to be lost to the ravages of time.'"

Will closed the book and handed it back to her, noting the thoughtful look on her face.

"Do you think there actually *was* another novel?" she asked.

"Who knows? I know that generations of Bixbys and Parkers have been over every inch of this mansion and no one has ever turned up any indication of one. Then again, Andrew Bixby didn't keep a journal, nor did his wife keep a diary, so most of what we know has been pieced together from various contemporary accounts."

A slow smile was spreading across Rose's face, and she lifted the dissertation. "You've read this, haven't you?"

Caught. "I have. Thomas asked for my input while Mallory was writing it."

"And?"

He settled back into his chair. "Mallory is a very accomplished historian. She also has a big imagination."

"You don't approve."

"I wouldn't say that. It's just that Mallory is the type who believes that Haven Ridge's best days are still ahead of it. So it colors her conclusions."

"And you think its best days are behind it?"

Will threw her a twist of a smile. "You said it, not me."

Rose braced her arms on her knees and propped her chin on her hands. "Maybe you're right. But does that mean we have to give up on it?"

"We?"

Rose colored, pink rising so easily to her cheeks that it made her skin seem translucent. The warmth of the setting sun lit her red hair, making her look in that moment like a Rosetti painting. It seemed suddenly easy to believe that she'd always been here with the house, her romantic looks reflecting its old-fashioned architecture.

Then again, the glare she was giving him was very, very real.

"I know I'm an outsider, but that doesn't mean I don't like the place. That I can't see what makes Haven Ridge special."

"I think that probably makes you less of an outsider than I am. Because a certain disregard for reality seems to be required for everything that goes on around here."

He cringed at the unintentional bite to his words, but to his surprise, she wasn't offended. She actually laughed. "Not a believer of the magic everyone keeps talking about?"

No point in lying. "Not one bit."

Rose shrugged. "Me neither. I mean, it's a sweet idea. But you and I both know that we're only here because we have to be. Not because the town brought us here for some sort of reason." She fixed him with a look. "Just like you and I both know these two weeks are to placate your sister. There's nothing here that's going to save the place."

Will just stared at her. Of all the things he thought was going to come out of Rose's mouth, this was probably the last. If finding out she was a realist surprised him, the outright cynicism in the words shocked him.

"So why are you here then? If you think it's pointless?"

"It's a job and a place to stay," she said flatly. "I have nowhere else to go. And if it makes Erin happy . . ." She shook her head. "Besides, if you were really serious about keeping this house, we'd be talking about totally different tactics."

"And that is?"

She ticked them off on her fingers as she talked. "You'd get a loan for all the repairs. And then you'd start making money. You'd rent it out for events or weddings. You'd make it into an event center. Heck, you could even run it as a bed-and-breakfast. There isn't even a hotel in this town. You can't tell me you think it couldn't be done."

"Of course it could be done," Will said.

"But?"

"But no matter how capable Erin might seem at this moment, she's not able to manage an endeavor like that on her own. And I have no interest in doing it."

"Because you love your career in Chicago so much?"

"Because of all the places in the world I would want to live, this is very last on the list." He pushed himself to his feet in one swift movement and saluted her with his book. "If you'll excuse me, I have some things to do. I'll let Erin know you're back if I see her."

And before she could say or do anything beyond stare at him with that slightly surprised look on her face, he strode out of the room.

* * *

Well. She'd pushed her luck and now she'd really done it.

She and Will had finally been having a civil conversation, and she'd seen an opening. Thought that perhaps she could show him that she understood his concerns, that she recognized what a long shot it was that this two-week stay of execution would turn up anything more than a dusty bunch of old junk. Thought that, just maybe, she could get him on her side so they could discuss how they could possibly keep Larkspur House in his family.

He'd shut her down in no uncertain terms.

She wasn't even entirely sure why. Sure, he had no intention of staying here in Haven Ridge, but who said the twins had to run the endeavor? She certainly wasn't gutsy enough to put herself forward for the honor, but even if it wasn't her, surely someone had the ability to visualize and execute a project like this.

Besides, she wasn't sure that Will didn't have his sister all wrong. Yes, Rose had only known her for a few days. But she had worked with dozens of different people in her three years with the nonprofit in Milwaukee and she thought she'd become a pretty good judge of character and work ethic in that time. And it wasn't that Erin wasn't capable of doing a good job in a traditional role. It was simply that if she had the choice between doing something the boring way and doing something the creative way, she'd do it the creative way every time.

In Will's strict, narrow, accounting mindset, the serious way was the only option.

She should have just gone with her first instinct, making nice with him, getting him to understand she could be just as reasonable as he could. Instead, she'd let the fact she only had a week left on the clock pressure her without thinking through the consequences of failure.

Though why that should be a surprise, she didn't know. These days it seemed like she was always leaping before she looked, and so far it had brought her nothing but heartache.

She sighed and chewed her lip, then stretched out on the lounge. But her enthusiasm for the dissertation had waned. If Will was determined to sell this house, there was nothing she could do to change his mind. She'd be better off spending her time searching job listings so she knew she had someplace to go in seven days.

But instead of pulling out her phone, she leaned back on the wicker lounge and opened *The Miner's Folly*. Of the three books, this was the only one she hadn't read during the course of her literature studies, mostly because it was considered the poorest of the three.

And yet, as she opened to the first page and began reading, it didn't take long to get swept into the story. She could see why perhaps this wasn't considered Andrew Bixby's best work; whereas his earlier ones possessed a sort of Dickensian tone, this book was more . . . personal, at least in the sense that there was less distance between the narrator and the reader. And as she continued turning pages long after the sun went down and she had to strain her eyes in the dim overhead lights of the conservatory, she could definitively say that she thought the critics were wrong.

The Miner's Folly was a masterpiece.

It simply wasn't the book that everyone had expected after the first two volumes. It was neither Romantic nor Realist. The tone felt surprisingly modern, with more in common with, say, *The Great Gatsby,* which wouldn't be published for another eight years.

Andrew Bixby was a trailblazer.

Rose was perhaps halfway through the short novel before she realized that full dark had fallen outside and Erin should be back by now. She fished in her purse for a scrap of paper to use as a bookmark, then piled her books and manuscript in her arms again before she wandered back out into the hallway. Her hand was on the first-floor stair railing before she caught the drift of voices from the kitchen.

Slowly, she followed the sound and pushed through the door. Will was standing at the stove, Erin plopped atop the island behind him.

"Something smells good," Rose said tentatively.

Will whipped his head her direction, clearly startled, and then relaxed. "Pancakes. You're just in time to tell me which you prefer, chocolate chip or blueberry."

Erin grinned at her. "Not much of a choice, is it?"

Rose laughed. She had been about to say chocolate chip, but now on a whim, she said, "I'll take the blueberry."

"Good choice," Will said easily, reaching for the bowl next to him and plopping a couple berries into the batter already cooking on the cast-iron griddle.

Rose just blinked, glancing between the two. Had she imagined that whole exchange with him in the conservatory earlier? Or worse yet, had she imagined *every* interaction between them in the last several days? Because from where she was standing, he seemed like an entirely different person.

An entirely different person who had stepped up to cook breakfast-for-dinner rather than disturb her reading.

It wasn't as if cooking was part of your job description, she reminded herself. But that's what it had become. Everyone scavenged for their own breakfast and lunch, and then gathered together in the kitchen while Rose prepared dinner.

Will flipped the pancakes expertly, then pulled three plates from the cabinet beside him. When he put her plate in front of her at the island, she made a point of looking him straight in the eye. "Thank you, Will."

A flicker of something—surprise? disquiet?—passed over his face and he looked away. "You're welcome."

He moved away to find the butter and a container of syrup, but Rose dug in without waiting. "Oh, these are good."

A small smile curved up the corners of his mouth. "Oh yeah?"

"Yeah. It almost doesn't matter if this is the only thing you can cook. I'd eat this every day."

He laughed, a genuine, full laugh and it surprised a smile onto her face. "Thank you. I'll take that as a compliment."

"You should, because I am a pancake connoisseur."

Erin was looking between them now, an appraising look on her face. As soon as Will noticed it, though, his smile slipped and he turned away. "It's not much, but we won't starve because someone was too into her book."

Rose froze with her fork halfway to her mouth. Just when she started to think he was a decent human being, he had to go and say something like that. It wasn't as if cooking was her actual job responsibility; she was doing it so they didn't have to survive on peanut-butter-and-jelly sandwiches. And then he criticized her for putting her research on *his* house first?

"On second thought, I don't think I'm that hungry." Rose pushed her stool away from the island, took her plate to the trash where she scraped off the remaining pancake, and then set her plate in the sink. She grabbed her stack of books on the way out, not looking either of the twins in the face as she went.

The door was just closing behind her when she heard Erin's quiet reproach. "Why did you have to go and say that?"

Because he's a jerk.

Because he's determined not to like me.

Because there's just something about me that makes him act horrible.

And while the first or second answer was the most likely to be true, the third one was the one that stuck with her.

She blinked away the little prickles in her eyes that surely had to be strain from reading in poor light and not tears. Because no way was she ever going to *cry* over an insensitive, uptight idiot like Will Parker.

Only when she got back to her room and dumped everything on her settee did she remember the package from the Broken Hearts Bakery in her purse. She opened the bag and took out Erin's pecan sandies first. She'd go and drop them in the other woman's room later. She set aside the remaining conversation heart cookie for later. And then she removed the chocolate eclair she had bought for Will.

She looked at it for a long moment and then took a huge bite.

CHAPTER TWELVE

That night, Rose dreamed of water.

Not of a tsunami or driving into water—the usual subjects of her stress dreams—but the slow, insistent drip of moisture. *Drip, drip, drip.* Over and over, like the insistent ticking of the clock. Or water torture, soaking her by increments.

Rose jolted awake, disoriented and already frowning at the oddity of the dream. Of all the things to dream about, why that? She had plenty of real anxieties in her life to work out without inventing pretend ones.

She shivered in the cold air. And only then did she realize that the water was not in her dreams.

She and her blankets were wet.

Rose leaped out of bed and turned on the bedside lamp, the warm glow illuminating the sodden coverlet. Slowly, her gaze lifted upwards and she gasped. Where there had been smooth plaster only hours before when she fell asleep, now there was a bubble the size of a trash can lid, a stream of droplets falling from its center at regular intervals.

Hastily, she threw a sweatshirt on over her skimpy

tank top and darted out of her room to Erin's, where she knocked as loudly as she dared. She pressed her mouth to the crack in the door. "Erin? I think we have a problem."

A rustle inside indicated Erin had heard her. A moment later, the door opened and the woman's mussed head poked out. "What is it? What's wrong?"

"There's a leak in my ceiling. It's dripping water all over my bed." Rose shivered, reminding her that it wasn't just her bed that had been getting soaked for who knew how long.

Erin swore under her breath and shut the door in Rose's face. When she came back out, she was wearing jeans and a T-shirt, her feet bare. "Okay, show me."

Rose led her back to the room and pointed wordlessly at the ceiling.

"Well, that's . . . not good."

"What do we do?"

Erin made a face. "We call my brother."

That's what Rose was afraid she was going to say. She still didn't have any interest in talking to him, though if they had to be up in the middle of the night, it was only fair that *he* had to get up with them. A smile crept onto her lips. "Let me do it."

Erin frowned at her, clearly confused, but she didn't argue, instead creeping a little closer to the bubble. "It looks like it's seeping through the plaster and just the paint is holding it in."

Rose was already halfway out the door and down the hallway. Unlike how she roused Erin from bed, now she didn't even bother trying to be gentle. She raised her fist and pounded on the door. "Will! Wake up!"

Almost immediately, the door was yanked open. This time, Will was wearing a shirt, though his hair stood on end, smashed over to one side. "What? What's wrong? Is someone hurt?"

"Not yet, but my ceiling isn't looking so good. I've got water pouring out of it and it looks like it's going to collapse." Okay, so that last part might have been an exaggeration, but she was enjoying the little tinge of panic on his face.

"Great." He stepped into the hall and pulled the door shut behind him. "Just what we needed." He strode down the hall like a man on a mission, leaving her to trail behind him. Somehow, in his pajamas and bare feet, marching toward a plumbing catastrophe, he looked more relaxed than he did on a daily basis around her. As if she already didn't feel bad enough.

He stepped into Rose's room and stared at the ceiling for a long moment. "Yeah, that's not good."

"What do we do?" Erin asked.

He rubbed his hand over his face. Rose had seen him do this enough times to know it was his exasperated gesture. "I have to go into the attic, I guess."

"Shouldn't we turn the water off first?"

"If I turn the water off, I won't be able to see the leak. How much worse is it going to get in the next ten minutes?"

On cue, the paint bubble gave way and the entire contents came splashing down onto Rose's bed, bringing chunks of plaster with it.

She looked at him and he grimaced.

"Right. *Now* how much worse is it going to get?"

Rose cast a doubtful look at the ceiling, but the sodden lath stayed intact.

"Be right back."

As soon as Will left the room, Rose looked at Erin. "He seems to be taking this well."

Erin let out a helpless laugh. "Honestly, I think he's more surprised when something goes *right* than when something goes wrong. This is something like the fourth leak we've had. But it's not raining, so that means it's the pipes and not the roof."

"I'm not sure if that's good or bad."

"At this point, I don't think it's going to be good news."

Rose sighed. As much as she'd enjoyed being responsible for Will's rude awakening, this was the last thing she wanted for the house. Just one more reason to call it quits, one more expense they couldn't pay for.

Outside, she heard a scraping sound and moved to the door. Will, now wearing sturdy shoes with his pajamas, was pulling down a ladder from a trap door in the ceiling.

"It doesn't have a proper staircase into the attic?"

Erin shook her head. "It used to, but sometime in the '60s or '70s they reconfigured this level to put in the extra bathrooms and bedrooms. The staircase took up too much space, so they did a pull-down ladder instead. The attic really isn't a real room; it's more of an access space for the utilities. Like the boiler."

That explained the water leak, at least. Rose would be willing to bet the fixture was directly over her bed.

It only took a couple of minutes for Will to reappear with a grim look on his face. "The pipe to the boiler is leaking. We'll have to turn off the water for tonight until I can look at it more thoroughly tomorrow." He glanced at Rose and grimaced. "You'll have to move into one of the other bedrooms after all. Sorry."

"Better than sleeping in a swimming pool, I suppose. I'll move all my stuff tomorrow."

"Come on," Erin said. "I'll show you the other two bedrooms and you can choose which you want."

Rose followed Erin down the hall, but when she cast a look back at Will, he was watching them with a look that she couldn't quite interpret. Why was the man so hard to read? She didn't have the faintest clue whether that expression was irritation or regret.

And at the rate they were going, she'd never have time to find out. "Why do I feel like the house is trying to tell us something?" she murmured to herself under her breath.

Erin caught the words and sent her a sad look. "As much as I want to disagree with you, I'm afraid you might be right."

CHAPTER THIRTEEN

WILL WOKE UP AFTER ONLY A FEW HOURS with a pit of dread in his gut. The late-night awakening was bad enough—as was the fact that they had no water in the house until he could figure out a fix for the leaking pipe—but the absolute resignation on Erin's face had been worse. He'd been trying to convince her that Larkspur House was a lost cause, that simply too much had been lost to disrepair and time, but he hadn't wanted it to be such a rude awakening.

Though to be fair, it had been Rose who had gotten the rude awakening. After she'd been settled in Erin's old room, he'd gone and inspected the damage in the one she'd been occupying and found the mattress and bed coverings absolutely soaked with cold water. She must be a deep sleeper if she'd managed to sleep through a flood. Of course, the sudden collapse of the bubble hadn't helped matters either.

He scrubbed his hands over his face, an automatic reaction to stress that he'd found himself doing more and more since he arrived back in Haven Ridge. No matter what he might think about the future of the house, the problems had to be fixed. He couldn't sell it with a leak in the attic, crumbling plaster in the guest room, and no ability to use running water. So he pushed himself out of bed and dressed in an old pair of jeans and a threadbare T-shirt he'd left in his closet for just this sort of occasion. He'd climb up in the attic with a proper light and see what was actually going on. Maybe it wouldn't be as bad as he thought.

But first, coffee. Nothing was getting done without coffee. Assuming that there was bottled water in the fridge to actually make it.

To his surprise, when he walked into the kitchen, the smell of freshly ground beans already scented the air. He glanced around blearily and found Rose sitting in pajama pants and a T-shirt at the island. "You're up early. I thought you'd want to sleep in after last night's adventure."

"Hard to sleep when you're worried about what comes next," she murmured before taking another sip of her coffee.

"Yeah, tell me about it." He took a deep breath and studied her face. She didn't seem angry with him anymore, which meant she might actually listen to him. He poured himself a cup of coffee and then crossed the kitchen to sit across from her. "I'm really sorry for hurting your feelings last night."

"You didn't hurt my feelings."

His eyebrows lifted. "Oh. Your reaction to what I said—"

"Oh no. You were a total jerk. But you didn't hurt my feelings. I learned a long time ago not to care about the opinions of people who don't respect me."

He drew back, shocked. "You think I don't respect you?"

Her own lifted eyebrows were her only answer.

"That is not at all the truth. I just don't know you. Erin obviously thinks you're great, but—"

"—but you don't respect her either, so her opinion doesn't hold any weight."

Will swallowed hard. Wow. Rose really wasn't holding back her thoughts this morning. "It's not that simple."

"Then tell me, why isn't it that simple? No, start with why you seem to hate being here so much. Because that I really don't understand. Haven Ridge is amazing. And this is coming from someone who has lived all over the country."

It was too early to be having this kind of conversation, especially when Rose was looking at him with a clear challenge in her eyes. Yet he sensed that if he didn't answer her questions, this would be the last conversation she'd willingly have with him. Why that bothered him so much, he didn't know.

It bothers you because it makes you feel like a jerk. And you are being a jerk. The only thing you can do now is tell her why you're being a jerk.

He took a big sip of his coffee while he considered how to start. "In some ways, our childhood in Haven Ridge was great. In others, it was quite difficult. Particularly for Erin. She's always been sensitive..."

The skepticism surfaced on Rose's face and he hastened to explain. "That's not an insult. It's just a fact. She...feels things more deeply than other people, bad and good. It's part of what makes her a good musician. No, it's what makes her a *great* musician. But it's also what holds her back from being one of the best of her generation. And believe me when I say that she's a prodigy. She could be the twenty-first century's Yo-Yo Ma."

"But..."

"But any time she veers too close to greatness, she falls apart. It's as if she's afraid of success. Or maybe she just feels the pressure more acutely than everyone else. When she was fifteen, she was offered a full scholarship to Julliard. I thought she should take it. Our grandparents were less convinced, but I *knew* she had to pursue her dreams. Maybe I put too much pressure on her, or maybe she just felt the weight of all the sacrifices our grandparents had made for her. But she fell apart."

"She tried to kill herself."

He blinked, shocked that Erin had already told this stranger her deepest secret. But Rose shook her head. "I saw the scars."

"Oh. Right. Well . . . I was the one who found her and called the ambulance. Held towels to her wrists to stop the bleeding while we waited. It was not a cry for help. It was a genuine attempt, and had I been a few minutes later, she would have succeeded."

He let his head fall forward and gripped the back of his neck, trying to stave off the guilt he felt every time the memory surfaced. "Had I stayed home that night . . ."

To his shock, a cool hand closed over his free one on the table. "She just would have waited until you were at school. Or asleep. It wasn't your fault."

His eyes drifted to Rose's manicured hand, curled around his, then lifted to her earnest hazel eyes. "I knew she was struggling. And I was tired of dealing with it. I wanted my own life. And that was the price for it."

An empathetic smile lifted the corners of her lips, but her eyes remained sad. "I'm sorry. That's a lot to carry. Haven Ridge has a lot of bad memories for you."

He took a deep breath and slowly pulled his hand away from hers. "It's more than that. We've been happy in Chicago. We've made lives for ourselves. Erin is playing better than ever, or she was until she was promoted. And now, she's back . . ."

"And you're afraid of history repeating itself."

Put that simply, he couldn't deny it. He gave a single nod.

Rose sighed heavily. "I don't know what to tell you, Will. It's a lot of responsibility to carry for another person. At what point do you have to let someone make her own decisions?"

"I don't know. At what point does letting them make their own decisions constitute giving up on them?" The ache in his chest seemed to answer that question for him, but it didn't give him any guidance on what to do. He was smothering Erin, he knew. But every time he'd backed off, every time he thought she was ready to take on her own life without his help, she'd fallen apart. It wasn't just that they were siblings; they were twins. There was a bond that came from that, a sense of responsibility for each other, that no one could understand unless they'd lived it.

Rose remained silent—it seemed she couldn't answer that question any better than he could. To his shock, the words kept coming. "I really wanted to save this place for her," he murmured. "But not if it's going to end up killing her again."

The silence stretched, but unlike his other encounters with Rose, this time the silence felt close, companionable, sympathetic. She seemed to be wrestling with something. She clearly had opinions on the situation. Was she suddenly afraid to voice them? Did she realize she'd overstepped?

But when she finally spoke, he realized he had it all wrong. "I just got a divorce. My parents never trusted my husband from the beginning. They said something was off about him, they had a bad feeling about it. I thought they just objected to the fact I was quitting graduate school to move to Milwaukee with him, to work for his family's business." She lifted her eyes to his face, her mouth in a wry twist. "Ironically, I was supposed to work in *my* family business after I graduated, so do with that as you will."

Will barely breathed, sensing that she was telling him things that she hadn't shared with anyone. After his demonstrated ability to constantly put his foot in his mouth when it came to her, he didn't trust himself to say a single word.

"Anyway, it all went bad. Very, very bad. I lost my house and my job, pretty much walked away with what I brought to the marriage and could fit in the back of my car. My parents, of course, would take me back, but the thought of hearing them say 'I told you so'... I just can't do it." She threw him a wry look. "Even if they didn't *say* it, I'd know they'd be thinking it. And who wants to move back into their childhood room at the age of twenty-eight?"

Will just lifted an eyebrow at her, and she huffed out a laugh.

"Sorry. Right. Anyway, so that's why I'm here. Because if I went back, it would be admitting that I couldn't make it on my own. That my plans failed. That they were right. I'd take the position at my dad's publishing company or I'd finish my PhD and get a professor position at a local college, and then I'd be locked in. They'd be so happy that I was finally living up to expectations that I'd never break free."

Will didn't know what to say. Rose had just laid herself bare... maybe not her deepest secrets, not the dirty details... but the whys of how she came here. And it felt like she was trying to send him a message. But he had to tread more sensitively with her than he'd done so far.

"I'm sorry it all went wrong."

"I'm sorry, too."

He chose his words carefully. "Do you think all expectations are bad then? Are you . . . are you trying to tell me that you think I drove Erin to this because I wanted her to be successful?"

She blinked. "No. That's not what I'm saying at all."

"Then I don't understand."

Rose's expression softened. "I'm saying that maybe the reason you're so unhappy is because you have unreasonable expectations of yourself. And instead of living the life you want to live, maybe you're living the one that you think everyone expects you to live."

The words hit him with the physical force of a blow, but before he could fully process them, Rose was hopping off her stool and heading for the door. "Where are you going?" he managed.

"To change," she said. "One way or another, there are things to be done in this house. And I guess it's time that you have some help."

* * *

So maybe her exit was a little dramatic. Rose would rather Will think that she'd made an exit for emphasis than guess the truth . . . that over the course of a few minutes, she'd gone from being irritated over his existence to feeling empathy with him.

Or maybe you should try being real with yourself and admit that seeing a little bit of what's going on inside that handsome head of his made you actually . . . like him.

Fine. It still didn't make up for the fact that he seemed to insult her every time he talked to her, but now she thought she understood why. It wasn't meanness. It was just carelessness. Distraction. She'd thought that Will was an uptight person who had to have everything go his way, and now she suspected he

walked around with the weight of the world on his
shoulders all day, every day.

The man actually thought it was his fault he wasn't
able to stop Erin's suicide attempt. And lived in fear
that if he made one wrong move, it would happen again.

How could she not understand how that might twist
a person into knots?

Besides, now that she understood what was behind
his rigidity, she wanted to see him break free of it.
Which brought them back to addressing the number one
problem—the house and all its ill-timed breakdowns.

"You are not going to be his Manic Pixie Dream
Girl," Rose told herself sternly as she made the long
climb back to her new room. But that didn't mean Will
didn't need a giant kick in the behind for his life, and
she didn't mind being the person doing the kicking.

Rose went back to her second room before she
realized that all her clothes were still in the first one and
changed direction mid-course. In the walk-in closet, she
swapped her pajama pants for a pair of jeans, but didn't
bother changing the T-shirt. She was just going to get it
dusty anyway, so what was the point in making more
laundry for herself? Now that she thought about it, she
was sure there had to be a laundry room somewhere in
this huge house, but she hadn't yet seen it.

When she walked back into the hall, Will was already
waiting with a steel travel mug in his hand. He held it
out for her with the awkwardness of a child offering a
girl a handful of dandelions.

"What's this?"

"You left half your coffee in the kitchen. I thought
you might want some fresh coffee to go."

"Thank you." She accepted the mug, took a sip, and
realized that he'd somehow figured out how she took it
as well. That was . . . unexpectedly observant.

"You know, you don't have to help."

"Yeah, but I'd really like a hot shower sometime today, so if I can be of use . . ."

Will just shrugged like he'd finally decided not to argue with her and pulled down the folding ladder from the attic trapdoor. He slid his arm through the handle of a plastic bucket and then started climbing the steep ladder. "Stay here until I get the lights set up, okay?"

Rose waited, sipping her coffee, until Will called down for her again. She set aside the mug in the hallway and carefully climbed into the attic.

It was just as Erin had warned, more of an unfinished, crawl space than an actual attic. She peered around in the light of two clamp-on shop lights that Will had hooked up, plugged into some outlet she couldn't see. He was crouched on beams that looked like the size of railroad ties, examining something. "Be careful where you step," he warned. "It's not as fragile as drywall but the lath still probably won't hold your weight. Don't want you falling through the ceiling."

"No, we definitely don't want that." Rose hoisted herself the rest of the way in and gingerly picked her way over to his side, walking on the beams and bracing herself with a hand overhead on the rafters. She stopped where Will was examining a surprisingly small copper pipe. "Is that it?"

"Looks like a nail was resting against the pipe and it corroded. I have some putty tape that should seal it temporarily." He rose from his crouch and picked his way over to Rose's side. "The bigger problem is there. You can see the water ran all the way across the joists to drip into your room. And some of this is stained, so it looks like it was leaking for a long time. We're going to have to take out that section of plaster, dry out the wood, and then replaster it."

Rose frowned as she examined the space. It was hard to visualize where the rooms were located beneath them, considering it was just one large open space crisscrossed with joists, but. . . "I don't think that's my room."

"What do you mean?"

Rose reached up again for balance as she stepped from one joist to the next. "Well, I figure that one right there is the wall of Erin's room, right? Which means that this one here should be the wall of my room."

Will frowned. "No, your room is bigger than that."

"No, it isn't. And I know for a fact that I had to walk more steps to the attic opening than that. That has to be the other bedroom."

"Nope, it definitely isn't, because you can see where the HVAC goes to those rooms. See?"

They looked at each other. "That doesn't make any sense," Rose said slowly.

Will frowned again, thinking. "Wait here. Or come down if you like. I just have to go get a measuring tape."

While she didn't love the idea of being left up here, she also didn't feel like picking her way back across the attic and climbing down. So instead, she walked out of the way where she could view the space from a distance, sneezing at the dust she kicked up.

The attic was huge, and from what she could tell, didn't even encompass the entire floor, just the backside of the house. Even then, it was a vast space that showed her exactly how big this historic house actually was. Down below, she heard a metallic scrape and vibration. She understood what it had been when Will reappeared, a tape measure clipped to his jeans pocket.

"Okay, let's figure out exactly what we're looking at." He picked his way across the joists with surprising agility, then extended the tape to the far wall. "That's

thirty feet right there. So this should be Erin's room."
He indicated the space beneath his feet. "Yours should
start here . . ." He extended the tape in the other
direction and then paused. "You're right. Your room
doesn't extend that far. So that would have to be Erin's
old room, the one you're staying in now."

"Except I know for sure there's no leak in there. Not
any sign of water at all."

Will clearly didn't believe her, so he crept past her
and measured from the other exterior wall, marking off
his old room, Erin's old room, and the guest room. The
tape stopped a full four feet from where he had already
indicated the wall of Rose's first room should be. "That
doesn't make any sense."

"Was it the old staircase to the attic?" Rose
wondered. "Erin told me they reconfigured this space
up here because the staircase took up too much room
and they wanted to steal the space for the bathrooms."

"Possibly?" Will stared down at the lath surface
between them. "I'm just concerned about where all that
water is going. If it's inside the walls . . ." He shook his
head. "The last thing we need is any internal water
damage."

"So, what do we do?"

Will's distant, thoughtful look cleared and he moved
over to where he'd left the bucket. When he
straightened up, he was holding a large power tool with
a saw blade. "We're going to have to repair the plaster
anyway. So we might as well find out what we're dealing
with."

Rose was glad he made that decision, not her,
because she cringed as he plugged in the tool and began
to cut a neat square from the hundred-and-twenty-year-
old ceiling between the joists. Just before he finished
the cut, he levered up the piece and pulled it into the

attic, leaving a neat dark hole below. He pulled a skinny flashlight from his other pocket and shined it down beneath them.

"I don't believe it. Here, Rose, take a look."

Will held out his hand, and after a moment of hesitation, she took the support as she made her way to his side. He shined the light below into the cavity again.

Rose crouched down for a closer look and then gasped. It wasn't just a hole into one of the bedrooms as she'd expected.

There was an entire, windowless room below.

CHAPTER FOURTEEN

"So you're seeing this too." Will looked down into the room and then back at Rose. "I'm not imagining it."

Rose shook her head slowly, almost unable to believe what they were seeing. "No, you're not imagining it. It's like that lady who found an entire apartment behind her bathroom mirror."

"But less creepy."

"No, I'd say this is pretty creepy."

He cocked his head at her, a quizzical look on his handsome face. "Why? It's just a room."

"A boarded-up room in a hundred-year-old mansion?" she said disbelievingly. "This is *literally* the definition of 'skeleton in the closet.'"

Will peered down into the space again. "I'm going down there."

"Are you crazy?"

"Not last I checked. Seriously, what's going to happen?"

This was not the Will Parker she had come to know so far, Mr. Mitigate-All-Risks-For-All-Reasons. Give him a secret room and all of a sudden he turned into

Indiana Jones. "You could get stuck down there! And if you do, there's no way I could pull you up again."

"I'm not going to get stuck. There's furniture down there. I'm just going to drop down to that desk and take a look around. And then you can lower down the Sawzall. If worse come to worst, I'll cut myself a doorway."

"Yeah, because that's what we need. Another doorway in a strange place that you need to patch." Why was she being so contrary? Why did she care if they put another hole in the wall? It wasn't her house.

Because, she realized, she wasn't quite sure what to do when she and Will were on the same side of anything.

Will stared at her as if he were thinking the same thing. "Have we switched places or something? Because I would have been willing to bet that of the two of us, you'd be the one champing at the bit to explore a secret room."

"Yeah, you'd think, wouldn't you? Though Erin would probably have us both beat in that department." Rose wrapped her arms around herself, the quiver of nervousness—or maybe it was anticipation—worming back into her stomach. "Fine, go down there. But don't say I didn't warn you if you get sucked into another dimension or something."

"You have my full permission to say *I told you so* if I get sucked into another dimension."

Rose couldn't hold back her laugh, and Will gave her a surprised smile in return before he lowered his legs through the hole and prepared to drop down. He handed the flashlight to her. "Shine that down there for me, if you would. And wish me luck."

"Don't die or open a portal to the underworld."

"Close enough." He braced his arms between the

beams that framed out the hole, his fingers gripping the wood, and lowered himself down like an American Gladiator on some sort of weird Iron Cross apparatus, reminding her of the glimpse of bare skin and toned muscle she'd gotten the first night they'd met. As soon as his foot touched the edge of the desk, he gave himself a little swing and dropped his full weight onto its dusty surface. The furniture creaked ominously.

"Uh, what was that?" Rose called down, cutting the beam of the flashlight around the space for better visibility.

"Just the desk, I'm fine." She heard a thud—jumping off the desk, it seemed like—and then he sneezed. "Can you drop the flashlight down here?"

Rose scooted to the edge and leaned over as far as she dared, even though it made her stomach seize with anxiety. Didn't matter that it was only perhaps an eight-foot drop into the room. It might as well have been a hundred for the sense of vertigo it summoned.

But he was standing in the dark and looking up at her expectantly in the glow of the flashlight. "Okay, on three. One, two . . . " She dropped the flashlight through the hole and he snatched it out of the air, then turned it on his surroundings. The beam illuminated dust motes swirling in the air, disturbed by his presence.

"I'm going to see if I can find a light switch." Both Will and the beam disappeared, leaving only a faint yellow glow through the opening.

Moments stretched, and unreasonable as it was, Rose's stomach jittered. "Will, what's going on down there?"

"I'm not finding a light switch. Or a light fixture for that matter. I'm not really sure why this is here, actually."

"To hide the bodies. It's to hide the bodies, isn't it?"

He laughed, and the husky sound hit her unexpectedly hard in her chest. "No bodies. Not even a
closet. Just an old armchair, and a writing desk, and a
steamer trunk."

"A steamer trunk? What's in it?"

"It's locked. Hold on a minute."

More sounds—what seemed like a drawer opening,
faint rustling and rummaging. "Will? What's happening?"

"I'm looking for a key." A faint zipper sound reached
her, and then he made a huff of satisfaction. "This
might be it. Hold on."

There was a metallic scraping and then more sounds
that she couldn't place. Then a creak. "Oh wow," he
said. "You should see this."

"What? What is it?"

Will stepped back beneath the hole, shining the
beam toward himself to illuminate his face. He was
grinning. "Nope. You either come down and see it
yourself or you'll never know."

"That's not fair."

"Never said it was."

Rose gritted her teeth while she considered. They
were going to get stuck in there and die, she just knew
it. "How small is the room?"

"Kind of like a large walk-in closet." Then his voice
changed. "Wait. Are you claustrophobic?"

She grimaced. "Just a little?"

"Well, I promise you, this is not a tiny room. It's
bigger than the walk-in in your guest room. If you can
handle that, you can handle this."

Rose bit her lip, torn between the desire to see what
he'd found and the fear of lowering herself into a
drywall coffin. "Okay. Fine. But I'm sending the saw
down first."

"Fair. Lower it by the power cord."

Rose carefully picked her way back to the outlet so she could unplug the power tool, then wobbled back to the hole. "Okay. Coming down now."

She lowered the saw by the cord until the pressure lifted off the cord.

"Got it," he called, and the cord slithered in after it.

Rose took a deep breath. "Okay. I'm coming down. How do I do this?"

"Just lower your legs through and I'll get you. I promise, it's not as far as it looks." The sound of furniture scraped and then Will's face was close to the opening, illuminated by the flashlight that was now stuck in his shirt pocket.

Slowly, Rose inched herself over to the space, pushing her legs through, even while her stomach rebelled at the very idea. But it was one thing to pepper him with humorous, ridiculous objections and another to actually let him think that she was a coward.

"Okay, I'm coming down."

"I've got you. Don't worry."

Rose took a breath, braced her arms, and started to lower herself into the hole.

Just when her muscles began to tremble and she was about to freak out about her legs dangling in space, strong arms wrapped around her thighs.

She had *not* thought this through.

"Let go," he said. "I've got you."

She had no choice but to trust him, so she let go. He loosened his grip so that she slipped through his arms, sliding down his body until they were face-to-face, his arms wrapped around her waist.

"That wasn't so bad, was it?"

Even through the gloom—the flashlight now dimmed, trapped between their bodies—she thought she caught a glint in his eyes. Amusement? Something else?

"No," she said, breathless, and this time she was sure she saw the flash of a smile. Abruptly, he let go and jumped off the desk, then held out both hands.

She had no choice but to take them, even though it felt like an electric shock the minute they touched again. He supported her weight as she hopped off the desk and then immediately let her go, turning away and plucking the flashlight from his pocket.

The relief she felt was quite out of proportion to the situation.

And then she was distracted from the unexpected sensations coursing through her body, because her attention was fully focused on the steamer trunk in the corner, illuminated by the beam of the flashlight. "Wow."

He turned and grinned at her. "I told you. Wasn't it worth it?"

"We'll see. Is that a—wedding dress?"

"Looks like." Will stepped back out of the way and trained the light on the trunk while she delved into it.

It certainly *looked* like a wedding dress, white or ivory satin—silk, she thought—trimmed with yards of lace. She wiped her hands on her jeans, hoping they weren't too dirty before she carefully moved it aside. Beneath it were several cardboard boxes, their careful construction speaking to age.

"This looks like a hatbox," she said, pulling the top one from the trunk.

"What's in it?"

Rose lifted the lid from it and laughed. "Unsurprisingly, a hat. It's white, so I think it probably went with the wedding dress."

"Reasonable guess. What else?"

Rose put aside the hat, careful not to set it on the wet floor, then looked in the next box. "Baby clothes. A christening gown, I think? At least, it's all lacy and stuff."

"It probably is then. Is that it?"

"I don't think so . . ." Down at the bottom was a flat brown pasteboard box, about twice the width of a normal ream of paper, roughly the size of the stationery sets she'd loved as a child. She lifted it out and moved over to the desk, choosing a dry spot to set the box down. Will immediately moved to her shoulder to train the light on her find. She lifted the lid to find a stack of paper on top. "Oh wow."

"Is that . . . a manuscript?"

Rose scanned the typewritten page, noting the old-fashioned font. "I think it is. It looks like a . . . book."

Will went completely still. "You don't think . . ."

"I don't know. I might." It was one heck of a coincidence that they'd just been discussing the possible existence of Andrew Bixby's fourth novel and now they'd found what looked to be a novel. Then again, there was no guarantee this wasn't an amateur attempt by one of the children or even one of the various guests of Larkspur House. "I'd have to look at it more closely to know for sure."

They looked at each other in the dim glow of the flashlight. Rose's own excitement was unmistakably reflected in Will's face.

"How are we going to get out? Are we going to have to cut our way out?"

"I might not have thought this through," he admitted. "I should have had you lower down the saw while still attached to the extension cord."

Rose closed her eyes at her own foolishness. Of course there wouldn't be an outlet down here. She really was stupid.

"But let me mark the studs before we go back up." He found the saw and moved to a section of the wall between two studs. Rose trained the light on the area, noticing what she hadn't noticed before. One wall was finished lath and plaster, but the other ones were fairly modern two-by-fours, covered with drywall. Will raised the saw blade and punched it through the drywall right inside the stud on both sides, marking the opening. "There. We'll cut into it later so we can get the rest of the stuff out."

"But we're taking the manuscript?"

"Of course we're taking the manuscript." Will grinned at her and climbed back on top of the desk, holding out his hands. This time she barely had enough time to stretch her leg onto the desktop before he hauled her up. "Well, come on then."

Rose looked at him doubtfully. "How exactly am I going to get back up there?"

Will interlaced his fingers and held out his hands to form a step. "Like this."

"I'm going to kill you!"

"I'm not sure whether to be insulted over your impression of my strength or amused at how much you overestimate your weight."

Rose rolled her eyes. "You're plenty strong, I'm sure. What you're overestimating is my athleticism."

Will just stood there and stared at her.

"Fine." She waited until he bent over again and then placed her foot in his hands, holding onto his shoulders for balance. He straightened, raising her head into the hole. She reached out and grabbed onto the beams on the sides of the openings and with one easy push, he lifted her up far enough to get her arms under her and haul her backside onto a safe perch.

"Ye of little faith," he said from below, still grinning.

"Still haven't figured out how you're going to get up here . . ."

"Saw and box first."

Getting those out proved to be slightly harder, because she had to lay on her stomach to take the items from him one at a time. Then she got out of the way and hoped that she wasn't going to have to be the one to cut the wall apart to get him out.

She shouldn't have worried. Will stretched up to grip the beam, squatted to give himself a little jump, and hauled himself up into the attic with the ease of a gymnast. She just stared at him. She'd known that Will Parker, CPA, or whatever he called himself, wasn't a weakling, but that was . . . "Impressive."

"Hardly," he groaned, stretching his arm across his chest and giving her a look at taut muscle. "I'm out of shape. I haven't been to the gym since I got here."

"Doesn't look that way to me," she muttered. Immediately, she gave herself a mental shake. *Brain, keep those kinds of thoughts to yourself. The last thing you need is for him to think . . .*

Will raised an eyebrow. "Was that a compliment?"

Too late. Blood rushed to her cheeks. "I was just saying, if it were me, I'd be stuck down there permanently."

"Mmm." He didn't seem confused, and curse the man, he actually seemed like he was hiding a smile.

No, curse herself, because when he looked at her that way, the suspicion gone from his expression and his handsome face relaxed into amusement, she found herself wondering what other expressions she might be able to elicit from him given the right motivation.

She cleared her throat. "Let's get out of here. I've had enough of dark dusty spaces for one day."

"After you," Will said, hauling himself to his feet before he grabbed the manuscript.

Rose picked her way back to the attic stairs, bracing herself with a hand overhead, then climbed down, her stomach twisting in anticipation the entire time. She told herself the feeling was strictly due to what might be in the box that Will carried.

But even as she thought it, she knew it was not entirely the truth.

CHAPTER FIFTEEN

WILL HEADED STRAIGHT FOR THE STAIRCASE leading down two floors to the study he used as an office, feeling the need to find neutral ground. And he suspected he wasn't the only one—now Rose wouldn't look him directly in the eye.

He didn't know what had happened. One minute, they could barely speak without being at each other's throats and the next, there was this . . . tension between them.

No, it wasn't as if he didn't know why. The minute that he'd had his arms around her, her soft body sliding down the length of his, it was as if a switch had flipped. And now it was his responsibility to flip it back.

Rose was his employee. A temporary employee. One who didn't even like him, no matter how her eyes sparkled when she teased him. The errant thoughts that zipped through his mind in unguarded moments weren't just unwanted, but wildly inappropriate.

As soon as they entered the study, Will set the box on the desk and then moved back a few steps to make room for Rose. She flicked him a little glance, then fixed her eyes on the box as she slowly drew off the top and began to unpack the contents.

The first thing out was a stack of paper—the manuscript. Even from a few paces away, he could see that it was a pale cream, not the aged yellow he would have expected from an antique. "What does it say?"

"*From the Western Woods.* Does that ring a bell?"

Will shook his head. "No, I've never heard of that before. It doesn't have an author name or anything?"

Rose shook her head. "No." Carefully, she shuffled through the pages before aligning the edges and straightening the pile. "I'd have to read it before I could tell you if it was a Bixby, and even then I might not be able to say with any certainty. We might be able to consult a Bixby expert, but he was a minor literary figure of the time, so there's just not a lot of scholarship on him."

"Understood." Will edged closer, but stopped when Rose flicked him a cautious look. "What else is in there?"

She moved aside and looked into the box. "An old newspaper, dated 1921 . . ." This paper was exactly as he'd expect antique paper to look, fragile and yellowed, almost too delicate to touch. She treated it with the care with which one would treat a priceless artifact, opening it flat on the table beside her. "*Haven Ridge Register.* The front-page story is the death of Andrew Bixby."

Will's eyebrows flew up. That was interesting, and potentially historically significant. He hadn't even realized that the *Register* existed that far back, though he shouldn't be surprised. Just because it was a dwindling town—admittedly one on the cusp of revival—didn't mean it hadn't been a thriving community in the past. "A family member probably collected that. It's an encouraging sign that this trunk probably belonged to a Bixby."

"I thought the same thing." Rose delved back into the box and this time came out with a small leather-bound book. "Ohh."

This time, Will couldn't hold himself back, curiosity overcoming the need to put some physical space between them. "Is that a journal?"

"I think so." Rose carefully opened the old cover, revealing fragile yellow pages covered with beautifully old-fashioned script. After a moment, she began to read. *"April 15, 1921. Andrew has fallen ill again. He insists that it is just the change in the weather, but I know the truth that he has been hiding from me. I've insisted on calling for Dr. Maxwell, but I'm afraid of what he will surely tell me."*

Will and Rose exchanged a look. Slowly, he asked, "Is this Amelia Bixby's journal?"

Rose blinked and turned several pages. *"We laid him to rest in the town cemetery today. Andrew would have been proud of William and Leslie, but Marie is too young to understand. It breaks my heart every time she asks for Papa. I don't have the heart to tell her that Papa isn't coming back, so I have simply told her that he is on a long trip. I don't know how I will make her understand."*

Rose's eyelashes fluttered, and he could tell that she was trying to blink away tears. Instead, he went for straight facts. "I don't remember the younger children's names, but I do know that Andrew's son was named William."

She flicked startled eyes to his. "And his daughter was Marie. This really is Amelia Bixby's journal."

"It would seem so."

"What do we do now? We should go wake Erin. She's going to want to see this—"

Will's hand shot out to grasp her arm before she could move too far from the desk, but when her startled gaze landed on his grip, he let go immediately. "I don't want to get her hopes up until we know if we really have something here."

Rose started to protest, but she apparently followed his train of thought, everything he'd revealed about his sister, and then nodded. "I don't like it, but I do understand. How are we going to authenticate it?"

"Well, fortunately, we have the two foremost experts on Haven Ridge living here *in* Haven Ridge. I think this calls for a trip to town."

* * *

Thirty minutes later, Rose and Will were walking through the bell-adorned door of the Brick House Cafe. To say that the drive from Larkspur House into town in Will's rented SUV was tense would be understating things, but Rose couldn't tell if it was the anticipation of thinking they might have found Andrew Bixby's lost novel or the sudden awareness that crackled between them every time they were within two feet of each other.

It was annoying.

Least of all because now, she didn't even have her dislike to fall back on. Engaged and interested Will Parker was a totally different person than stuffy bean counter, Will Parker; his eyes sparkled with excitement, and when he looked at her, he didn't seem to see her as an unwanted guest, but a co-conspirator. When he was in this mood, he was . . . undeniably appealing.

Too soon and too stupid, Rose told herself. She'd been separated for six months and divorced for a few weeks. There wasn't a better definition of a rebound than the interest she was feeling right now. Having feelings for the first guy who was actually nice to her after the end of a bad marriage was the reddest of all red flags.

Except she realized that she had not thought about

CARLA LAUREANO   149

Jordan a single time since she'd arrived at the Larkspur House. It was as if her marriage and the scandal had belonged to a different life in a different universe. And that alone should bother her, because it meant she was ignoring the undeniable trauma from the situation instead of dealing with it. At some point, it would rush in and crush her.

Right now, though, she was trying not to let any of those thoughts show on her face.

"Let me guess," Mallory said, the minute she saw them standing at the counter. "You're not here for pie."

"I could go for pie," Rose said. "It's not that far off from a donut, and we have those for breakfast all the time."

Mallory winked. "A woman after my own heart. Pie and coffee, then? Anything for you, Will?"

"Just coffee, thanks. You have a minute to look at something we found?"

"Of course." Mallory's tone perked up, her interest piqued. "Why don't you head to the office in the back? I'm assuming you don't want half the town to know your business before you do."

Only then did Rose realize that the restaurant was partially filled and at least half the heads in the space were turned in their direction. "Good plan," she said, looking to Will. "Lead the way."

Will lifted the box from the counter and led her through the cafe, down the back hallway toward the bathrooms, and through an unmarked door into a small, sparsely decorated office. He set the box on the desk and then gestured to one of the leather sling chairs in front of the desk. Less than five minutes later, Mallory breezed in with two mugs of coffee and a plate of pie on a plastic tray. She set their food down in front of them before she slipped behind the desk.

"I take it you found something interesting up at the house?"

"A manuscript," Will said.

"And a diary," Rose added quickly.

Mallory's eyes lit up and she gestured to the box. "Really? May I?"

"Be our guest."

Our. Rose didn't miss that unconscious usage.

Carefully, Mallory unpacked the items in the box and laid them out on the desk. "Well, I don't think I need to tell you that the manuscript is somewhat modern."

Rose had thought as much, but her heart fell anyway. "How old do you think it is?"

"The paper itself? Fifty or sixty years old. I'm pretty sure this was typed on an IBM Selectric."

Rose's hopes plummeted. "How can you be so sure?"

"Because I own one. And this looks exactly like the Courier font I currently have loaded."

Rose let out a long, disappointed breath and threw a look at Will. "I'm sorry. I knew it was a long shot, but I was still hoping. . ."

"Well, just because this copy is new doesn't say anything about the person who wrote it."

Both Rose and Will jerked their attention to Mallory. She continued, "I don't want to get your hopes up, but just because it was typed sometime after 1960—and I think it was probably much later than that—doesn't meant that it wasn't originally written by Andrew Bixby. It just means someone typed it. An original manuscript would have probably been handwritten. Typewriters were definitely available in the early 1900s, they just weren't all that common outside of certain professions."

She did have a point. Edith Wharton, writing slightly later in Paris, handwrote all her manuscripts in black ink on blue paper and physically cut and pasted her changes together. The typed manuscripts that she sent to her New York publisher were done by a typing service in Paris.

When Rose said as much, Mallory nodded enthu- siastically. "We know that Bixby wrote his first novel longhand and then sent it back to Boston to be typed. What we don't know here is who typed it and why or where the original is. It could have been discarded by someone who didn't know any better."

"I can understand if a descendant was concerned about preserving his legacy and made a copy once the original manuscript started to deteriorate. But if that was the case, why wouldn't they have tried to publish it?"

Mallory shrugged. "It wasn't like he was Harper Lee. Finding an old manuscript wouldn't be a guaranteed financial success for a publisher, particularly in the 1970s. My instinct is that perhaps they typed this in an attempt to get someone to buy it and no one would."

It was actually a pretty reasonable explanation for what they'd found. Mallory continued, "So we'd just need some way to link it back to Andrew Bixby."

"Well, we do have a journal. But it looks to be written by Amelia Bixby."

Mallory perked up. "Oh, is it in here?"

Will and Rose both nodded simultaneously, and Mallory dove back in with enthusiasm. This time, when she drew out the book, she handled it with a care that bordered on reverence, and Rose was reminded of the dissertation she was publishing as a book. This was another potentially interesting chapter.

"Amelia should be easy to authenticate, since we have plenty of examples of her writing," Mallory said. "After Andrew died, she handled all the accounts for Larkspur

House, so we have correspondence and ledgers and the like with her initials and her handwriting. I would have to compare the two, and obviously I'm not a handwriting expert, but . . ."

"Please," Will said, "keep it and let us know what you think. If you want to transcribe it for your book and give us a copy, I wouldn't object either."

It sounded like a sneaky play to get out of hard work, but Mallory lit up like it was Christmas. "I'd appreciate that. It won't take me all that long to get through it, I don't think. I can email you a copy as soon as I'm done."

"That sounds wonderful," Will said, and he sent Rose a little conspiratorial wink.

The answering leap of her heart was somewhat less wonderful. She put that feeling in an imaginary box and slammed it shut. She was not going to start to think of herself and Will Parker on the same side, particularly because Erin had hired her and she wasn't entirely sure that Will and *Erin* were on the same side right now. It felt like a betrayal.

Almost as if she needed something to punctuate that decision, Will said slowly, "Would you do me a favor and not mention this to anyone, including Erin? I don't want to get her hopes up. Chances are good that all this is interesting, but isn't going to help us save the house."

Mallory nodded slowly, but Rose could tell the secrecy didn't sit right with her either. But Will and Thomas were friends, from what Rose understood, so she'd go along with it.

Rose didn't know how she felt about that. Erin didn't strike her as so unstable that she couldn't handle the disappointment. On the other hand, she'd hadn't fished her out of a bloody bathtub and held her until the paramedics arrived, so she wasn't sure she got a vote.

It was a reminder that as charming and kind as her hosts could be, they had as much baggage as she did.

Mallory stood and placed the manuscript back in the box, but she kept the journal. "Let me know what you find out about the manuscript. You might also consult Liv. She's not really an expert on this time period, but considering she worked in New York publishing for a lot of years, she may have resources that can help you if you get stuck."

"We will," Will said. "Let us know if you see any mention of a book title in the journal. That would probably be the fastest and easiest way to find out if this is really an original Andrew Bixby."

The meeting hadn't gone long enough for Rose to even touch her pie, so she took a big gulp of her coffee and a couple bites of the pie, so she didn't seem rude. "Can we pay outside?"

Mallory waved her off. "Don't worry about it. You've made my day with this journal. I'll be in touch."

Rose and Will said their goodbyes and carried their plates and cups out with them, the box tucked beneath Will's arm. They dropped their dishes on the counter and then headed out to Will's SUV.

As soon as they were carefully tucked inside, Rose glanced at Will. "I can't decide if that was a success or not."

"If anyone can help us, it would be Mallory."

"What's her story anyway? I mean, I know she and Granny Pearl are the unofficial town historians, but how did that happen exactly?"

Will backed out of the parking spot and started up the street, headed out of town. "Her car broke down here while she was working as a writer for a magazine and she ended up doing a story on Haven Ridge. It was what gave the town the little tourist bump that it needed to start its comeback, and she ended up staying. She was so fascinated by the history, she decided to finish the PhD at UCCS she'd abandoned, focusing on local Colorado history. It was pretty much the perfect place for a historian to land, falling into a town with a significant, but previously unknown, history."

The revelation gave her a pang of regret that felt suspiciously like shame, and she stared out the window while she willed it away.

But Will still seemed to pick up on the shift of mood. "What?"

"The story just hits a little close to home," she said. "I left my own PhD program to get married."

"She's proof that it's not too late," Will said. "If you were so inclined."

"That's the problem, though. I know I should probably do that. But I don't know if I'm so inclined."

Rose caught his frown from the corner of her eye. "So why is that a problem?"

"Why isn't that a problem?"

The edge of his mouth tipped up. "You mean besides the fact that 99% of the population get along without a PhD to their name?"

"Yes, but 99% of the population do not have two brilliant literature scholars as parents."

"Ahh."

Now she whipped her head toward him. "What does that mean?"

"It doesn't mean anything. Just that I understand why maybe you weren't eager to go back, considering the family expectations."

She blinked at him. "You're one to talk about family obligations."

He opened his mouth as if to argue, then closed it firmly for several seconds. "You're right. It's none of my business."

Rose could almost physically feel him withdraw from her. She should be fine with that, right? That's what she'd wanted. A way to shut down the sudden spark of feeling between them, this sense of commiseration, whatever else went along with it. She should keep her mouth shut, let the sharp comment ride, and just finish out her two weeks without having any sort of personal investment in this family and this house.

Except they'd already gone long past that. She was invested in the story of the Larkspur House, and it was inextricably linked to the Parker twins.

"No," she said finally. "It's not that it's none of your business. It's just that I don't like disappointing people any more than you do. You just stuck around and lived up to the expectations while I ran away. You saw how that worked out."

"Did they actually say that?"

"No, of course not. But I heard it all the same. They never liked my husband, hated the fact that I gave up the final bits of my education for him, and now I've just proved them right. I haven't been able to face them yet."

"Which is why you're here, embroiled in our family drama instead of your own." His tone was calm, but she thought she caught the barest hint of self-deprecation in it.

"Something like that." She studied his profile for a long moment. "What would you do with your life if you didn't have to live up to those obligations? Would you have done anything different? Been a soccer player? Moved to Europe?"

He actually looked startled at that. "I am doing what I wanted to do with my life. I love my job."

"Really? Accounting?"

"Investigation," he said firmly. "I deal with mysteries

all day long, but the evidence is in the numbers, not in physical clues. What's there not to like about that?"

"Well, the numbers to start."

He laughed, a full-throated, unrestrained laugh that startled her as much as it warmed her. "Let's just say that I feel about numbers the way that you feel about words. But in my case, numbers don't lie."

"If that was the case, you wouldn't have a job."

"It's people who lie," he said. "You can pretend to be someone you aren't, you can lie to everyone around you, but I can tell exactly who you are and what your life is like from your account information alone. So I stand by my statement. Numbers always tell the truth."

He didn't mean it to be, but it felt like a slap in the face, knowing what she was holding back. True, she was innocent. Her numbers would show no wrongdoing whatsoever. But at some point, he'd come across the news coverage on her husband's case. At some point, he'd realize she'd been hiding far more than just the end of a bad marriage. That part of her shame about crushing her family's expectations was because she'd given it up for someone like the people that Will helped put in jail.

She just hoped that by the time he made the connection, she'd be long gone. At least then she wouldn't have to see that same disappointment in his eyes that she knew she'd see in her parents'.

Because for some strange reason, all of a sudden, what Will Parker thought about her had actually begun to matter.

CHAPTER SIXTEEN

ROSE'S DAY WENT DOWNHILL FROM THERE.

When she and Will got back to the house, Erin was already up and wondering where they'd been. Thankfully, Will had thought of that at the last minute and they'd swung by Haven Ridge's small store to pick up fresh donuts and the flavored coffee creamer that Erin liked, so they had an excuse for their absence. They did not have an excuse for the fact that they'd gone together, as evidenced by the sly way Erin's gaze skipped between the two of them when they arrived together.

In short, Rose felt like a horrible person. Not only was she hiding the truth about her past from her hosts and employers, but now she was holding back a very important detail from Erin, who had been nothing but nice to her. She deserved to know about the manuscript that was now safely in Will's second floor office. She deserved to know that they had something that could potentially help save their house.

And yet seeing the optimistic way Erin attacked yet another room, examining every item as if it might be the one to save them, made Rose understand, at least a little, why Will was holding things back. That optimism and sweetness was so rare, he didn't want to destroy it with the high likelihood that they'd found absolutely nothing.

And not even that was true, at least not entirely. They'd found a lot of interesting things. A beautifully carved set of toy animals set away in the closet of one room, along with a porcelain doll with a slightly tattered dress. Erin and Rose speculated about the time period, and after a few internet searches on their phones, settled on somewhere in the 1950s. They found old books and magazines with ads so politically incorrect they gaped in horror at the same time they rolled with laughter. Rose's personal favorite, however, was a folder full of report cards that turned out to have belonged to the twins.

"Look," Erin said with a grin, pointing to her name at the top. "Third grade at Haven Ridge Elementary School. Cs in everything but music. And every single teacher marked me as *too talkative.*"

Rose grinned. "I can relate to that. I never shut up as a kid, unless I was sneaking a book under my desk. But look at Will's. Straight A's. Are we surprised?"

"Oh no, my brother is brilliant. He was in sixth grade math by third grade."

"Really?"

Erin nodded. "Yeah. He looks at numbers and they just make sense to him. We used to throw out these stupid crazy four-digit multiplication factors and he could just do them in his head. He's a legitimate genius."

"I guess that doesn't surprise me."

"Yeah, he does seem the type, doesn't he?"

"No," Rose said, "I mean it doesn't surprise me that

you're both built that way. He's good at conventional math. And you're good at music. Which is basically just applied math."

Erin stopped and sat back on her heels, staring at Rose. "I never thought of it that way."

Rose studied the other woman, saw the slight lift of her chin. "I mean, I guess it's technically physics, but isn't physics just applied math too?"

"I don't know," Erin said with a grin. "I didn't take physics." But her mood had seemed to lift from that slight dip while she'd compared her grades to her brother's.

It must be difficult to be a twin, Rose thought. *To always be compared to each other, to be thought of as someone else's other half rather than your own person.*

But at least Erin's good mood was back. "Oh look, here's Will at the Mathlympics."

"Let me see that." Rose snatched the faded photo from her and studied it with a gleeful grin. "He was such a nerd!"

Erin giggled. "He really was. You'd never know it by looking at him now."

"Not a bit," Rose said, and she must have put too much emphasis into her tone, because Erin was looking at her knowingly again.

"You know, I think he likes you."

"I think he tolerates me," Rose said, though she immediately flicked back to that unreadable look in his eye while he still held her, the lengths of their bodies pressed together. If she hadn't known better, she might have defined it as *heat*.

Which was not a synonym for Will Parker in any way, shape, or form.

"Will doesn't tolerate anyone," Erin said. "He either likes you or he doesn't. He's a binary thinker. On or off.

Which is why he can be such a gigantic pain in my rear, because he wouldn't recognize a gray area if it bit him on the nose."

Despite herself, Rose laughed out loud. Five hours ago, she would have agreed. But now she wasn't so sure. He certainly was lukewarm towards her; he no longer suspected her or disliked her as she'd thought when she came here. But she wouldn't go so far as to say that he was *on* toward her.

Was he?

She shook off that thought before she could even decide if she really *wanted* that switch to flick on. Because she could clearly see his devotion to his sister, his family, the well-being of his responsibilities.

Rose didn't fit here. She was leaving. She would only disappoint him.

Those thoughts kept her quiet through dinner, which she prepared silently while the twins chatted at the table behind her. Just as simple fettuccine alfredo, which she topped with grilled chicken and served with a glass of white wine from one of the bottles chilling in the fridge.

"Everything okay?" Will asked quietly, halfway through the meal.

"Yeah, I'm fine. Just a little tired. I thought maybe I'd go read a little bit and then go to bed early." She caught Will's eye on the word *read* so he understood what she meant.

"You've been working hard and you've gone way beyond our expectations," he said quietly. "Go. Erin and I will clean up here."

Erin turned to her brother in surprise, but she didn't say anything.

"Thanks," she said. "Good night to both of you."

She scraped the last little bit of food off her plate into the trash and placed the dish into the large sink, then turned and headed up the stairs. But instead of going to her room, she went to Will's study, where she'd stashed the manuscript along with Mallory's dissertation, the three paperback books, and a spiral-bound notebook. She had far more than reading ahead of her—it would be in-depth analysis, comparing sentence structure, word choice, voice, tone. It wasn't that she wasn't prepared for the work, just simply that it was outside the scope of her expertise. Authenticating literature was a lot different than criticizing it.

She had only gotten through about ten pages of the manuscript, though she'd filled several notebook pages full of her flowery script, when a knock sounded at the door. She jerked her head up, then swept the manuscript into her lap before she called, "Come in?"

The door opened slowly to admit Will. She let out a breath of relief and brought the manuscript back to the desk before her. "I thought you were Erin."

"Erin went up to her room. I think she's binge-watching *Downton Abbey*." He smiled and then held up a mug. "I brought you some tea. I thought you might need it."

"Thank you," she said, surprised. "I could use it. This is slow going."

"You find anything interesting yet?" He moved to the desk and perched on the corner, setting the tea down in front of her.

Rose took a sip—again, he'd prepared it exactly how she liked it, with a lot of milk and a teaspoon of sugar—before answering. "I'm not sure. Right now, I'm just making notes of things that seem particularly significant. Like obvious pet sentence structures. Repeated words. Every writer has their favorite things, whether they realize it or not. So I'm looking for this author's 'tells' and then I'll compare them to Bixby's."

"That sounds like a lot of work."

"Weeks," Rose admitted ruefully. "Especially if I have to hide it from Erin."

"You think we should tell her."

"I think you're going to run out of time if you don't. I guess the question is, do you really want to save this place or not?"

Will ruffled his hair with his hand, an unconscious gesture that seemed so out of place for a man who was always so put together. "I do. Not just for Erin's sake, but because I'll feel like I've failed if I sell it. I just haven't failed as much as if I bankrupted the trust after my grandfather put me in charge of it."

"How old were you when you took over?"

He grimaced. "Twenty-eight. About the time Grand-dad went into the nursing home."

For the first time, Rose really understood the pressure that Will was under. Andrew Bixby was probably the best-known figure from Haven Ridge's past, more so than Elizabeth Strong, even if she was more significant. And he'd been tasked with main-taining Bixby's legacy in a town he hated, at an age where he should be living his own life, building his career, getting married. A bit more sympathy crept into her for him. It must feel like an impossible task.

"So let's save it."

He blinked at her. "Isn't that what we're doing?"

"No. We're looking for a reason for you *not* to move forward with the sale. That's not the same thing."

He fell silent for a long moment. "What do you suggest?"

"Let me stay. I can't finish this in the week that you've given me. And it would be a shame to not know the truth. You like to solve your mysteries. Well, I like mine. And this is mine."

"And then what? What if it turns out to be a book written by some random person and not Andrew Bixby?"

"Then we figure out who it *was* written by, just so we have some closure. And then we think of alternatives to you selling the house. But we'll never know if we don't try. Wouldn't you like to be the person who found Bixby's lost manuscript?"

She could tell that she was winning him over, but it was as if the practical side of him rebelled at something so open-ended. "Rose. I don't think you realize how dire the situation is."

"I think I do," she said. "Or you wouldn't be breaking your sister's heart over it."

That seemed to strike home, and he looked away quickly. Then he gave a sharp nod. "Okay. Find out the truth."

"And we tell Erin?"

He took a deep breath. "We'll tell Erin. *But* we make it clear that chances are better than not that it won't help us. I can't get her hopes up."

Impossible, Rose thought. The minute they told her, her hopes would shoot through the roof. But maybe that wasn't such a bad thing. Will needed motivation, and not disappointing his sister was a big one.

Will might know the numbers. But Rose was a fundraiser, a marketer, a connection-maker. And deep in her heart, she knew the Larkspur House could be saved, even if she couldn't quite understand why it meant so much to her.

CHAPTER SEVENTEEN

"WHEN EXACTLY WERE YOU GOING TO TELL ME?"

Will grimaced at his sister's screech. That went about as well as he'd expected. As soon as Erin had come down for breakfast, he'd sat her down at the kitchen island and explained what he and Rose had found: the secret room, the manuscript, everything. And as predicted, her eyes flashed with fury that he'd been holding back from her.

But Will kept his voice measured and reasonable. "I'm telling you now. You know full well that if we'd told you as soon as we found it, you'd be full speed ahead on proving that it's Andrew Bixby's."

"Of course I would! This might be what we need to save the house! Besides"—now some of the anger faded into excitement—"what part of *secret room* did you think wouldn't appeal to me? When can I see it?"

Will couldn't help but laugh. Enthusiasm was never an issue with his sister, which was exactly the point. "I thought we might cut open the wall to the hallway so we can get everything out. I know Granny Pearl and Mallory are going to want to see the old clothes and things that are in the trunk."

Rose pushed through the kitchen door and faltered, looking between him and his sister. "I take it from the smile on her face that you told her?"

"He did." Erin narrowed her eyes. "I'm feeling a little betrayed by the fact *you* didn't tell me though."

Rose blanched, looking suddenly like an animal caught in a snare. "I wanted to, but I didn't—"

Erin jumped from her stool, her own expression alarmed. "I was just joking, Rose. I didn't mean it. Here, sit down and have a cup of coffee. We're figuring out the plan of attack for the room."

Will watched as his sister ushered Rose to the island and then poured coffee into a mug. He would never say it—he knew better than that—but she looked blearier and more ill-rested than he'd seen her since she'd come to Larkspur House. He slid the plate of bacon and toast across the island so she could reach it as she took a seat next to him.

"Did you stay up very late?" he asked, trying to keep his tone casual.

He didn't fool her. Her voice was wry when she asked, "Is it that obvious?"

"No, but I saw the light was still on in the study when I went to bed, and it was already late."

Rose rubbed her eyes. "I got about halfway through my first pass of it. *Pages* of notes. And I still have no idea whether it's Andrew Bixby's or not. The writing style seems similar, but the subject matter is just so much more personal than any of his other books. I can't quite reconcile it."

Erin leaned over her crossed arms. "But is it any good?"

"It is, actually." A smile came to Rose's face now, a sparkle of excitement through her weariness. "Not only is it beautifully written, but it's a poignant study of grief and I'm hoping, redemption, in the end. We'll see, I suppose. I couldn't help but picture Larkspur House as I read. It feels pretty obvious that it's the model for Mesquite Hall in the book."

Will studied the two women as they chatted, feeling a bit of his earlier apprehension dissipate. He'd been so concerned about how Erin might take disappointment that he'd forgotten she loved literature and culture, how much she actually knew about both. Once more, he'd underestimated her, reduced her to just the bullet points of her history.

He couldn't help but think maybe he'd done the same thing with Rose. He'd seen *expense* and *interloper* and *outsider*, but she was also vibrant and intelligent and seemed to truly care about helping them. Why, considering they were strangers, he couldn't imagine, but at this moment, it was hard to doubt her sincerity. And this was the happiest and most animated he could remember seeing Erin in a long time. She'd been settled in Chicago, calmer and less volatile, but he'd never really known whether she was actually happy.

"So what do you think?" Erin was looking at him now, and he realized he'd missed an entire important section of the conversation while staring at Rose.

"I'm sorry, repeat that?" Heat rose up his neck and he tugged at his collar, hoping no one had noticed.

Erin's repressed smile said that was a vain hope. "I was suggesting that we call Mallory out here to see what you found."

He blinked. "Oh. Yeah, that's probably a good idea. She might be able to identify the era of the wedding dress. And maybe she's made progress on Amelia's journal."

"You found a wedding dress *and* a journal?" Erin screeched, her eyes accusing. "I'm never letting you out of my sight again."

After that, there was no beating around the bush. Erin called Mallory and told her what they'd planned for the day, extracting her promise to bring the journal with her so Erin could examine it. Then she and Rose trailed Will upstairs, where he once more climbed into the attic and jumped down into the secret room—this time, being smart enough to attach the extension cord to the Sawzall before he did. It took a couple of pilot holes to make sure he was in the right place, but once he'd determined the locations of the studs in the hallway wall, he carefully cut out a section of the lath where the new doorway would go. He had to pull his T-shirt up over his face against the plaster dust—he hadn't been smart enough to bring a mask, even though he had safety glasses—but at last a section of the wall just smaller than the doorframe they'd build came out in several large pieces. As soon as the dust settled, Erin's dark head poked in, searching the gloom.

"Creepy," she said. "Are we sure there are no bodies in here?"

From somewhere out in the hall, Rose's voice came, "That's exactly what I said!"

Will shook his head with a laugh and stepped out of the way for the two women to enter. "We should probably bring in a light here so we don't have to keep using flashlights." But his suggestion fell on deaf ears, because the two women were already attempting to drag the trunk away from the wall.

"I appreciate your enthusiasm, but that thing probably weighs two hundred pounds empty. You should wait until we have a little help."

"Oh, sorry, I guess we should leave this to a big strong man?" Erin shot back.

A second male voice drifted from the hallway. "Did someone call?"

Erin laughed as Thomas stepped through the doorway, looking around the tiny room with interest. "You're just in time. We wanted to bring the trunk out where we can look at it."

Mallory popped her head in next. "Wow. This is really cool. I wonder why they walled it up. You sure there aren't any bodies in that trunk?"

Will just sighed. He was surrounded by women who thought they were in the middle of a true crime podcast.

"Will thinks we're being ridiculous," Erin said, clearly reading his mind.

"It's a reasonable question!" Mallory said. "It's the twenty-first century. Why else would you give up square footage?"

"To be fair, it's not exactly square footage that's in short supply here," Rose put in. "Thomas, if you can help Will get this out in the hallway and maybe into the next room, we can take a look at what's inside."

Thomas didn't answer, just moved to one side of the trunk and took hold of the iron handles while Will mirrored his position on the other side. Even with the help, his muscles strained as he lifted. Correction: this thing probably weighed three hundred pounds, and it was not easy to lift using only an iron ring and grip strength. Between the two of them, however, they managed to crab walk the steamer trunk out of the room—shaving off the edges of the makeshift doorway as they went—down the hall, and into the spare guest bedroom.

"Hey there! Is anyone home?"

Another voice floated from downstairs, freezing Will in place. He threw an accusing look at his sister. "Erin, why is Liv here?"

"Up on the fourth floor!" Erin called, before turning

back to him. "When I talked to Mallory, I mentioned this all came about because of a water leak, so she suggested calling Charlie and having him take a look. I didn't have Charlie's number, so I called Liv."

This day just kept getting better and better. Mallory and Thomas were one thing—he considered Thomas a friend, and Mallory was his wife, not to mention a Haven Ridge expert. But Liv and Charlie. . .Will swallowed and moved back out into the hallway, suddenly aware of Rose's attention on him.

The couple came up the stairs a few minutes later, Liv looking fresh and ready for a day of work at her shop, Charlie already a little dusty and holding a tool bag in one hand. She must have pulled him away from the job site to come take a look. As much as he didn't want to like the man simply because of his relationship with Liv, he couldn't fault his work ethic. Or his devotion to his fiancée.

Charlie took the lead, offering his hand. "Erin said you had a leak in one of the pipes in the attic? You want me to take a look?"

Will clasped Charlie's hand firmly enough not to seem weak, not so tight that it seemed like he was trying to make a point. "If you don't mind. The attic access is right down the hall."

"Sure thing." Charlie headed down the hall to where the ladder was still extended.

Will turned to Liv, who was trying not to look ill at ease. "How have you been?"

"Experiencing far less excitement than you by the looks of it," she said with a smile.

"That's fair. Have you met Rose?"

Liv cocked her head as if to study him a little closer. "I have actually. She dropped in at my shop a couple days back."

Oh, right. She would have when she explored the town. The Beacon Street Bookshop was one of the few attractions that would draw visitors. "Right. Well, come see what we've found. The ladies are probably already unpacking the trunk."

Will led Liv into the spare bedroom, feeling slightly awkward, like he didn't quite know what to do with his limbs. This time it wasn't because he was struck by the remnants of his old feelings, but because . . . he wasn't.

Did that mean that he was getting over her?

Or did that just mean his brain had finally gotten the message that nothing was ever going to happen between them?

Inside the spare bedroom, Erin and Rose were both bent over the trunk, carefully removing what looked like the wedding dress, yards of ivory satin that just seemed to keep coming as they pulled it out.

"Ooh!" Mallory exclaimed when they laid it out on the bed. "May I?"

"Be our guest," Will said.

"Beautiful," Mallory murmured, examining it carefully. She flipped up the hem to look at the seam, examined the cuffs. "Not hand sewn."

"Is that bad?" Erin asked.

"No, not at all. My guess is that it was made back east and shipped here. The style is much more of what you would have seen in New York or Boston than Colorado. Silk satin, handmade lace."

"What year do you think?" Rose asked.

"1907, 1908, maybe? I'm not really a fashion expert, but this looks to be about where fashions changed to a more streamlined silhouette. I could probably figure it out from photos of the town at that time."

Rose met Will's eyes before she turned back to Mallory. "So this could have been Amelia Bixby's wedding dress?"

"Possibly. I'm almost certain there's a photo of her somewhere in Granny Pearl's albums wearing a dress similar to this." Mallory straightened from her examination. "Women usually wore their wedding dresses to formal events for a while after the wedding. Especially out here where their wardrobes weren't as big or elaborate. Though, I'm sure that probably wasn't an issue for Amelia Bixby. She probably had a wardrobe to rival a Rockefeller. Bixby was known for showing off his money."

Will grimaced. It was a less than flattering portrait of his ancestor, but then again, he'd built an actual castle in the Colorado mountains. The man obviously did not do subtle.

"There's a hat in there too," Rose said.

Erin went back to the trunk and lifted out the flat, cylindrical box, its edges slightly crushed. Mallory opened the box and drew out an elaborate hat covered with ribbons and silk roses.

"Well, that's something," Liv observed dryly. "Dyed a different color, we could probably wear that to the Kentucky Derby."

Mallory laughed. "Probably. I will say, it's remarkably well-preserved for being over a hundred years old. Testament to our dry climate, I guess. Things don't disintegrate quite so badly without the humidity. What else is in there?"

This time Rose did the honors, pulling out the christening gown next—Mallory and Liv oohed and aahed over it—followed by a few last odds-and-ends: a silver baby spoon wrapped in a handkerchief monogrammed with the initials M.B. and a pair of brand-new leather infant shoes. That had the women speculating on why they'd never been used and talking about a depressing quote attributed to Hemingway. And last, there was a first edition of Bixby's debut novel, *Dawn Over the Mountaintops*, with a white rose pressed in the middle of the pages. He had to admit, that one was really cool, especially considering that it looked like it had never been read, just stashed away as a keepsake. Amelia must have kept it in commemoration of her husband's accomplishment, considering that they were all assuming this trunk was hers.

"I'd love to document all this for my book," Mallory said. "I have a copy of pretty much every extant document from the town, so I might be able to find some supporting information for you on these items."

"Will said you had Amelia's journal," Erin said. "Did you bring it? I'd like to see it."

"Oh yeah!" Mallory spun, looking for her bag, then drew out a padded plastic envelope. "Here it is."

"Have you had a chance to look at it?" Rose asked.

Mallory nodded. "I haven't transcribed the whole thing—the handwriting is a bit hard to decipher, so it's slow going—but I'm confident it's Amelia Bixby's. All the events line up with what we know of their lives here, and she repeatedly refers to William, Leslie, and Marie, which we know were Andrew Bixby's children's names. It's quite a find."

"For its historical value only?" Rose prompted gently.

"Probably," Mallory said. "Not to say that you couldn't sell it at auction and probably get a decent price for it, but it has more local significance to Haven Ridge than it does to another collector. Were it Andrew Bixby's journal, that might be another story. There's a reason people referred to him as the Rockefeller of the West."

Will tried to pretend that his hopes didn't deflate with that pronouncement, but at the same time, he felt a little queasy at the idea of selling his great-great-great grandmother's journal, even if it was to save her house. An unpublished novel was one thing. An actual artifact from his family was another.

He was about to ask what their next steps were to preserve these finds, since they'd practically been hermetically sealed for the last hundred years, when Charlie appeared in the doorway.

"What's the verdict?" Will asked.

"Everything else looks fine. That section of pipe should be cut out and a new section soldered in. I could probably do it over the weekend if you like. It won't take long."

"And the patch will hold until then?"

"It should. It's not a high-pressure line. Just bad luck that the nail was resting against the pipes. The plumbing isn't that old, probably redone in the nineties."

Will extended his hand, and Charlie shook it with a look of surprise. "Appreciate it, man. I'm sorry to pull you away from your real work this morning."

"No problem. Plumbing is going in for the hot springs pools this morning, so I'm not really needed at the moment. With any luck, we're going to have a hot springs rec center by the end of the year that will put Salida's to shame."

Rose looked so enamored with the idea that Will couldn't keep the smile from his face. It was just too bad that it wouldn't be finished by the time she left town. But maybe she could come back. After all, they were hoping that the new additions to the town would help make it a tourist attraction. When he looked away, Liv was watching him with a soft smile. He averted his eyes, feeling suddenly, unaccountably guilty.

Everyone started filing out again, Mallory promising to email the transcribed journal as soon as she finished it and Charlie promising to be back first thing on

Saturday morning. Rose followed them out until it was only Erin and Will left in the room with the trunk.

"You know, it's okay to let her go," Erin said softly. "Healthy, even."

Will glanced at his sister, surprised.

"You don't have to take care of her anymore. I know you felt responsible for her after Jason died, and you went above and beyond what your friendship with him required. You're not letting him down. Liv has Charlie to look after her now, not that I think she actually needs looking after."

"I know," Will said, but inwardly, he wondered how much Erin had seen when he thought she wasn't paying attention. Yes, the whole town knew that he'd carried a torch for Liv and she had passed him over for another man. But for Erin to know why it was so hard to let go . . .

Well, they were twins, after all. He'd just been the one doing the looking after for so long, he sometimes forgot that she knew him as well as he knew her.

But Erin wasn't finished. "It's nice to see you looking at another woman like that, though."

That truly did surprise him. "Rose? I like her, but I don't know her. It's not like I . . ."

Erin patted him on the shoulder. "Sure. Keep believing that, brother." And then she left the room, abandoning him to his thoughts.

CHAPTER EIGHTEEN

NOW THAT ROSE DIDN'T HAVE TO HIDE her work, the pattern of her days shifted. Will and Erin were the ones who were digging through the contents of the house, room by room, a growing pile of trash accumulating in the dumpster that Will had delivered partway through the following week. Meanwhile, Rose felt like she was back in school, her mind fully consumed with analyzing the manuscript. She filled one notebook and then another, cross referencing her notes on the new story with Bixby's published novels one by one. And still she had her doubts that she would come to any definite conclusion.

It was early on Thursday evening when Will entered the study and set a mug of tea before her. It had become a ritual. Will and Erin would clean up from the dinner she cooked, and then an hour or two later, he would wander up with a hot drink and sometimes a snack to ask her about her progress. Tonight, he plopped himself in the chair opposite the desk and asked, "So what's the verdict?"

Rose sighed and leaned back in her chair, rubbing

her eyes. "There's enough similarities here to say this was probably written by Andrew Bixby."

His eyes lit up, then narrowed. "Why don't you sound more excited then?"

"Because. . ." She broke off, trying to put her feelings into words. "It doesn't *feel* right. I mean, the sentence structure is there. Some of Bixby's pet phrases, too, particularly when he speaks of female characters. Bixby has always stood out in his treatment of female characters. They're particularly astute. His women have agency and hopes and dreams of their own, even if they're crushed by the machinations of society and familial expectations."

"But . . ." Will prompted.

Rose toyed with her pen, tapping the end on the desk until she realized how annoying that might be and placed it carefully atop her notebook. "There's a tonal shift. This feels more personal than his other works. And it focuses much more on the interior life of the main female character, which is a departure."

"Well, it would make sense if he knew he was dying. He was writing about an imagined future for his family. Perhaps that's why he never published it. Maybe it revealed too much of his own fears for his wife."

"Maybe," Rose said. "And maybe I'm way off base. But I really would like to have more evidence before we try to have this authenticated as an Andrew Bixby or try to sell it as such."

"Take as much time as you need then," Will said. "We need to be sure."

Rose studied him. He'd been different since they'd cut open the room and pulled out the artifacts. More relaxed, more engaged. Almost as if he was finally fully committed to the project. And yet she still caught him looking up information on selling historic real estate, researching agents who specialized in this kind of building. Was it simply that he liked to be prepared for all eventualities, even unpleasant ones? Or was his patience, his commitment to saving the house just a ruse to fool his sister?

She rubbed her eyes and took another sip of her tea. "Maybe I'm just too close to it. Maybe I need to take a break. I'm imagining things that aren't there. Or"—she gave a helpless little laugh—"maybe I'm just out of my league. After all, I never actually was awarded a degree. This isn't my area of expertise, other than the fact Bixby wrote in the same time period as the authors I actually *do* know something about."

"Okay," Will said abruptly, standing. "Now I know you really do need a break. Come on."

Slowly, Rose pushed back from the desk and rose. "Come on where?"

"Do you have a bathing suit?"

"I have every item I own with me right now. Of course I have a bathing suit."

"Then go put it on. And no questions. It will ruin the surprise."

Cautiously, she followed him out of the room and up two floors to where their bedrooms were located. She shot him a curious look as they parted at both their doors, situated across from each other.

"Trust me," he said.

Ten minutes later, Rose emerged from her room wearing her most modest two-piece bathing suit beneath her shorts and T-shirt with canvas slip-ons. Will was already waiting on her, bouncing on the balls of his feet in anticipation, two striped beach towels in his arms.

She stared at him in consternation. Was the new pool open already? Or was there a community space she didn't know about? But she knew better than to ask, because he could be surprisingly tight-lipped when he didn't want to give up his information.

"Come on." He beckoned her to follow him, down through the house, and into the kitchen. On the way to the back door, he stopped at the refrigerator and pulled out a couple of cans of sparkling water, then handed her the lemon-flavored one. She smiled. Her favorite.

Will threw her a smirk. "Don't think I don't notice you swipe half the lemon ones as soon as we bring the box home."

"It's because I hate the grapefruit and berry," Rose shot back. "And if I'm not careful, Erin will drink them all."

Will winked at her. "I know. Why do you think I hide them all in the back?"

A little flutter worked her way into her stomach at that wink, so unlike him. She bit her lip and said nothing, just followed him out the door and across the yard to his SUV. "Don't you need to let Erin know where we are?"

Will shook his head. "No, she went into town. Cupcake decorating."

"Oh no!" Rose exclaimed. "I was supposed to go to that! I totally forgot."

He paused. "Oh. Well, if you'd like to do that instead, I'm happy to drive you. Or you could drive yourself. It's not that I don't think you're capable."

He was acting weird. Nervous. What was going on?

"No," she said slowly. "It's okay. I'll catch the next one if I'm still here. I'm curious what you have in mind."

"You won't be sorry," he said, and then circled to the passenger side of his car to open her door.

Okay, now this was definitely weird. He was acting like this was some sort of date. Was it?

No, surely not. This was *Will*. He was still in love with Liv, and even if he wasn't, she was nothing more than an employee to him. An employee that he was friends with—or at least she'd begun to think of him as a friend since he'd decided not to bite her head off every time she talked to him—but that was it.

He closed the door behind her, ensconcing her in the quiet interior, and then returned to climb into the driver's seat. He started the car and then made a three-point turn in the driveway. Only when they hit the highway did he turn on the radio.

"We're going away from town," she said, peering into the side mirror. "Where are we going exactly?"

"Afraid I'm kidnapping you?" he teased.

Rose laughed. "Not quite. Just curious."

Will threw her a slight smile. "It just dawned on me that you've been here for two weeks and the only part of Haven Ridge you've seen is the house, the town, and the highway. I thought you just needed a break."

"This is a break," she said. "You have no idea how nice it is to just spend hours alone in the quiet, thinking. Without anyone to bother me."

"Should I not have bothered you then?"

"No!" Rose flushed. "I didn't mean that. I just mean . . . my old job was kind of all-consuming, and I got phone calls and visitors constantly. I felt like I never got more than an uninterrupted hour to work at a time. For that matter, I don't feel like I had an uninterrupted hour to myself the entire time I was married."

Will was silent for a long moment. "That doesn't say much about your ex. Was he . . . demanding?"

Rose sighed. The last thing she wanted to do was spoil this evening by talking about Jordan. But Will was actually asking personal questions, wanting to know something true about her, and she didn't want to put him off. . . even if she didn't want to think about *why* she didn't want to put him off.

"I wouldn't say demanding. More like intense. He never stopped. His mind was always working, always looking for an angle. His drive appealed to me at the beginning. I'd thought of myself as that kind of person, and I thought together we could probably accomplish amazing things."

"But?"

Rose looked out the window, studied the painted colors on the edges of the sky as the sun shrank down and the light began to fade into full night. "He only wanted to accomplish *his* amazing things. What I wanted never really entered into it. And by the time I figured that out, I was trapped."

Will went quiet again. "I'm sorry. That must have been difficult. But apparently you weren't so trapped. You got out."

"Only after I discovered some really unpleasant things that I could no longer ignore," Rose said grimly. "If you don't mind, I really don't want to talk about him. I want to put that part of my life behind me. Move on."

"I know what you mean," he said. "But it's not that easy, is it?"

Rose glanced his way, but his expression gave away nothing. "No. It really isn't."

Will put on his signal and made a turn onto a dirt road that seemed to disappear between the crevice of two hills. Slowly, they climbed up, the ruts in the road jostling the SUV's suspension.

"Are we going hiking?" Rose asked. "I'm not sure I wore the right shoes for that."

"Not exactly," Will said. "And don't worry, your shoes are fine."

Finally, he slowed and then flipped a U-turn to park

in a wide turnout on the opposite side of the road, next to a split-rail fence. He shoved the gearshift into park and turned off the car. "Grab your drink. I've got the towels and the flashlight."

A jitter crept into Rose's stomach, but she wasn't entirely sure why. It wasn't like she thought Will was some sort of serial killer, taking her into the hills to murder her. If he was, she highly doubted he'd bother with the towels and the cold drinks. Not that it was even a possibility. And given the way he'd laughed at her insistence that there must be bodies in the secret room, he'd probably think she was insane for even thinking it.

Still, she couldn't help but ask, "Where are we going exactly?"

He stopped. "It's just a little walk. If you're not comfortable, we can go back. I wouldn't blame you. I didn't really think about how isolated it might seem to you."

His eyes were sincere, his brow furrowed in concern, and she let out a shaky laugh at how quickly she'd let her imagination run away with her. "No. Now I'm curious. Lead the way."

Will locked the SUV and flicked on the flashlight, even though the landscape was still lit by the last rays of the sun. Slowly, they started up the narrow path, little more than a goat trail through the long-grasses, Will using the flashlight to mark out hazards in front of them. Occasionally, he offered his hand to help her climb over a boulder or pick her way through a patch of prickly weeds. It wasn't strenuous, but she still felt her heart beating harder than the walk warranted.

And then he stopped. "Here we are."

Rose blinked. "Where are we exactly?"

Will laughed and beckoned her to come closer. "Look."

She gasped. In the middle of the clearing, bordered by native plants and boulders was a pool, the faintest curl of steam coming off the surface. "Hot springs?"

He grinned at her. "You looked so excited about the rec center, I felt bad you might not be there to see the opening. This is kind of the town's secret. Strictly forbidden to outsiders."

Rose shot him a look. "Won't you be in trouble for showing me then?"

"Considering you've already done more than Erin or me to save Larkspur House? That makes you an honorary town member. No one will blame me for making an exception."

Her smile spread as she surveyed the scene. There was something so very charming about sneaking out in the twilight to dip in a hot springs pool that virtually no one else knew about. "And we can go in it?"

"Of course we can." Will held out a hand. "Come on."

Hesitantly, she took it, and the minute he closed his hand over hers, it felt like every nerve ending lit up. She followed him to the edge of the pool where he set their towels and his drink on the boulder and started stripping off clothes.

She tried not to look. She really did. But even in the fading light, it was hard not to notice the lean lines of his body, not bulky but strong and contoured. He glanced back at her and lifted an eyebrow. "You going in your shorts? I mean, that's totally fine . . ."

"No, no," Rose said, blushing again. She stepped out of her shorts and pulled her T-shirt off, glad that she'd picked a vintage-inspired suit that covered up all the important bits. She toed off her shoes and hesitated on the edge of the pool.

Will waded in without hesitation. "It's okay. It's a

little rocky on the edge, but the bottom is sandy. It's not that deep." He held out a hand again.

She took it and carefully stepped into the pool. It was bathwater warm, but not hot, and she relaxed as the water rose only to her waist. Will let go of her hand and dipped down into the pool so his shoulders were below the water, paddling his way to the edge, giving her room.

Rose did the same and sighed as the water covered her back and shoulders. She'd been spending so much time bending over the desk in the study that she hadn't realized how tight her muscles had become. This was heaven. She tipped her head back to dunk her hair in the water and just floated there for a minute, picking her feet up off the ground until she was weightless, relaxed.

When she put them back down and rose again, Will was watching her with a soft look.

"What?"

"It's nice to see you smile."

Rose's mouth dropped open. "I smile!"

"Because you think you have to, not because you're happy."

It was astute, yet another sign he paid far more attention to her than she thought. But it also stung. "You're one to talk."

Will shrugged, his shoulders rising above the water line, a distraction that snagged her attention for a moment before she dragged her eyes to his face again. "I know I'm a grump. But you are not. You're like . . ."

Rose lifted an eyebrow at him. "I'm what exactly?"

He smiled. "Exactly what you seem. A ray of sunshine that brightens everything around you."

"I hardly think that's true."

"I do. Erin is the happiest she's been since you've been here. I think you're her first real friend in a while."

That observation hit with a pang of guilt. Yes, she'd started thinking of Erin as a friend, but the idea that the other woman didn't have any friends except her brother was just sad. "Erin is great."

"She is. But I've only just realized how lonely she probably is."

"What about you?" Rose shot back. "Don't you need friends too?"

His expression, so open a moment ago, shuttered. "I'm not the easiest person to get along with."

Something in his tone put her on guard. "Says who?"

"Says just about everyone, I suppose." He leaned back into the water just like she had done a moment before, and she recognized the words as an evasion. He might pretend like it didn't matter to him, but that pronouncement hurt.

"I don't think that's true," Rose said finally. "I just think that you make it hard for people to get to know you because you don't let anyone close enough to hurt you."

He rose again, paused like he was really thinking about it. "Maybe you're right."

"I know I'm right. What I don't know is why."

He studied her for a moment, his eyes glinting in the dark. "Do you know what it feels like to lose everyone you love, one by one?"

"No." She stilled, not daring to speak louder than a whisper.

"I never knew our parents, but I felt their absence. Particularly when Erin looked to me for things that our dad should have done. Then our grandmother died. My best friend, Jason. Our grandfather. All within a space of a few years." He lifted his face to the sky, letting out a long sigh. "There's only so many times your heart can break before you just don't . . . feel anymore."

Rose's chest ached. He might say that he didn't feel

anymore, but he couldn't hear the undercurrent of grief present in his voice. The stiff way he held himself like he was protecting himself from the next blow. She moved slowly toward him. "How long has it been since you actually touched anyone?"

He blinked at her, and she saw him withdraw a little behind his eyes.

She cocked her head. "I'm just saying that maybe you need a hug."

Now his expression cleared, the pain fading into something like curiosity. "I need a hug?"

Rose laughed softly. "Yeah. Everyone needs hugs." Even though her heart was beating harder now, she waded closer to him until they were face to face. "Do you know that people die from lack of human contact?"

"Even those of us who aren't quite human?" he joked, but he'd gone still.

"Especially those." The mere inches between them filled with the curl of steam in the air from the pool. When he didn't move away, she slid her arms around his midsection.

He froze, stiffening at the contact. After a second, his arms slipped around her and he pulled her close, resting his chin on top of her head. She felt, rather than heard, a sigh squeeze from his chest.

His heart was beating hard under her ear, and a shiver rippled down her back as he combed his fingers through her wet hair. He eased his hold on her so she could slip back, and she lifted her face to his. He was looking down on her, his eyes dark, a slight smile on his lips. She caught her breath.

And then his arms were back at his sides, his gaze darting away. "You're right," he said quietly. "It has been a really long time. I tend to forget I need things like that."

"Good," Rose whispered, but inwardly, she couldn't help the twinge of disappointment. For a second, she'd thought . . .

Mercy, Rose, you're so stupid. You thought this was his way of making a move on you, when really he was just trying to be nice. And then you went and threw yourself at him.

No, she'd just given him a hug. And she stood by the statement that he'd needed one.

It was just that as soon as she'd had his arms around her, his fingers in her hair, she realized it wasn't all she wanted.

CHAPTER NINETEEN

JUST WHEN WILL THOUGHT THE AWKWARDNESS between him and Rose was gone, he went and did something stupid.

He mentally kicked himself all the way home as an uneasy silence filled the SUV. He wasn't always the best on picking up unspoken cues, but the one Rose had given him in the hot springs pool, the message in her eyes when she'd looked up at him, her hands still resting on his bare torso, had been pretty clear.

And he'd been a coward. He'd let go of her, looked away.

Rejected her.

At least that's the way that she seemed to be taking it. Her expression had closed, and she'd lost her enthusiasm for the hot springs soon after. They'd made their way back down the dark path in silence, the whole time Will feeling like he'd been doing something wrong.

When really he'd been trying to do something right.

Because in that moment, he'd wanted to do nothing more than pull her close again and kiss her. He was pretty sure she would have responded. He might be an idiot, but he wasn't *that* much of an idiot.

It was just that all of the reasons why he *shouldn't* had crowded in until he couldn't remember the reasons he *should*. She was an employee. She was only here until they decided what to do with the house and figured out who the manuscript belonged to. If he made a move and he was wrong, she'd leave and his sister would never forgive him. The risks—for someone who was used to weighing risks—seemed to outweigh the potential rewards.

Now, seeing the wedge he'd shoved between them, he knew he'd made the wrong decision. Because this renewed awkwardness threatened her presence anyway, and he couldn't even say he'd had the pleasure of finding out what those beautiful lips felt like.

"So, what do you want to do for the rest of the night?" he asked, trying to return to their earlier light mood.

"I was thinking I would work on the manuscript a little more." Her voice was perfectly normal and level, but if he wasn't mistaken, some of the warmth had leeched out of it. "I want to be completely done before Mallory gets me the transcripts of the journal."

"That's . . . great." Will inwardly rolled his eyes at himself. It was as if he'd forgotten how to speak English. "Let me know if you need any help."

"I will, thanks."

And that was the last thing they said to each other until they arrived at Larkspur House. Will got out of the car, but Rose jumped out before he could open the door and started for the kitchen door. She had to wait for him to unlock it, which created another awkward situation as he brushed by her to put the key in the lock.

"Good night," Rose said with a little wave. "Thanks for the field trip." And then she scurried across the kitchen and out of his presence.

"Wow, what did you do?" The same door swung back open to reveal Erin in her pajamas. She sauntered over to the island and flipped open the small pink pastry box to reveal six exuberantly decorated cupcakes. She plucked one out and took a tiny bite, raising her eyebrows at him. "She couldn't get out of here fast enough."

Will grimaced. "I took her to the hot springs pool."

Erin's mouth formed a surprised *oh*. "You made a move and it didn't go over?"

"No! Of course not! I didn't make a move." He sighed. "And I think she was expecting me to."

Erin covered her mouth. "Oh, that's even worse. You rejected her."

"How is me being a gentleman rejecting her?"

Erin took a deep breath, casting her eyes heavenward, and let out a sigh. "You are the dumbest smart person I've ever met, Will. You take her to what is probably the most romantic spot in Haven Ridge—a place that is obviously the best make out spot of all time—and you *don't* kiss her. She's going to think that you took one look at her in a swimsuit and decided it wasn't worth it."

Will blinked at his sister. That hadn't even occurred to him. Partly because Rose was. . .well, she was breathtaking. It had been all he could do not to let his eyes linger on lush curves and creamy skin; it had been even harder not to explore that skin with his hands when she'd been pressed against him. Had they remained there any longer, she would have had no doubt how attractive he actually found her.

The thought stunned him. He'd known it, but he hadn't really *known* it until he was forced to put words to it, even if only in his own mind.

Wow, he really was an idiot.

"That," he finally managed, remembering that he was supposed to be replying to his sister, "is anything but the truth."

"Yeah, I know." Erin rolled her eyes.

"Wait, what?"

She cocked a hip against the counter. "You guys have been circling each other for days. I was just wondering how long it would take for you to figure out that she was totally into you. And here you had the golden opportunity—you actually did something romantic for once—and you blew it."

Will ran his hand over his face. "I did, didn't I?"

"Yep. You did."

"What do I do now?"

"I don't know. That's your problem." Erin grabbed her popcorn and nudged him as she walked by. "But whatever you do, make it good. Because if you wait too long, she won't be mad anymore . . . but she probably won't care either."

Will stared after his sister, knowing what she said was true even though he hated it.

Numbers were so much easier than people.

* * *

Rose practically raced up the steps of Larkspur House to her room, anxious to get out of her wet swimsuit, but even more anxious to be safely behind a closed door where she wouldn't run into either of the twins.

She was such a fool.

When had Will Parker ever given her the idea that he had any interest in anything but a friendly—and sometimes not even that—relationship with an employee? And then she'd gone and *hugged* him while half-naked. He'd been perfectly nice about it, of course, trying to spare her feelings in the pool, then trying to smooth things over in the car. While the whole time she kicked herself for ruining the best—and only—thing she had going in her life.

At least he would probably just let it go. It would be even more awkward if he talked to Erin and admitted he was uncomfortable with her here. He'd never do that to his sister, knowing that she wanted the help and needed the friend. At some point, the awkwardness would fade and they'd go back to being pleasant over dinner in the kitchen and slightly distant in the hallway. And she would forget that split second moment when she'd thought that maybe, just maybe, there might be something different between them.

You've been divorced for six weeks, her inner voice chided her. *So anxious to get into another relationship?*

Except it had been over seven months since she'd spoken to Jordan without their lawyers present, and if she were being honest, the relationship had been fractured long before that. They might have lived in the same house and slept in the same bed, but she wasn't sure she would ever have called it a partnership.

She'd been lonely since she moved to Wisconsin.

But she had begun to think that maybe she wouldn't be lonely in Haven Ridge. She'd only been here for a few weeks, but already the people in town—Erin and Will's friends—accepted her like she was one of them. That was worth far more than a romance that would probably fizzle out, and then get awkward because all her friends were his friends first.

It was better this way.

Rose pulled off her damp T-shirt and shorts and stripped off her swimsuit with it. She would normally jump in the shower, but she shared a bathroom with Will and no way would she risk running into him again tonight. Instead, she pulled on a pair of sweatpants and a T-shirt, tied her hair up into a messy bun, and plopped onto her bed with her notebook.

The nagging feeling that she was missing something important about the manuscript would not leave her alone.

She sighed and reached for her phone, a reflexive avoidance response, but when she opened her email, there was a message from Mallory Rivas waiting. She sucked in a breath as she read the message: *More or less done with the journal. With Will and Erin's permission, I'd like to get it photocopied so I can review the originals, but I thought you might find it useful in your study.*

Rose tapped the document to open it, but quickly realized that she couldn't possibly read on her phone screen. It was times like these that she really wished that the Parkers would invest in WiFi. She had to dig through one of the boxes she'd brought up before she came up with the proper cable to attach her phone to her laptop and then transfer the file over. Then she settled back against the headboard of the twin bed, her computer balanced on her knees, and began to read.

It was a lovely summer evening, the kind of sunset that leaves you wistful and wanting, and I nearly called Andrew before I remembered that he'd never again watch the sun set over Haven Ridge.

The sadness in the single line gave her pause. It was a beautiful way to phrase feelings Rose hadn't put into words but understood intimately. In fact, if she didn't know better . . .

Rose reached for her notebook and leafed through it, scanning her loopy writing until she found what she was looking for. There it was: *wistful and wanting.*

Interesting. Of course, Amelia and Andrew had been married for over a decade, so it would make sense that they would share some of the same turns of phrase. She put aside the notebook and turned back instead to Amelia's journal. She spoke of the pity with which the Haven Ridge residents regarded her, how she debated whether she wanted to stay in a place that so heavily held her husband's memory. Mentioned how all anyone seemed to focus on was how lucky she was to have the financial resources to care for her children now that Andrew was gone. No one ever understood that he was her "heart's blood, the life that animated my days."

Rose froze. She was absolutely certain she'd read that phrase before. She flipped through the pages until she found it under her notes for *Dawn over the Mountaintops. He was her heart's blood, her body's breath, the life that animated her days.*

A chill ripped over her skin. And just as quickly, the thing that had been eluding her for days, the thing that hadn't settled right in her subconscious, snapped into focus—the foreword to *The Miner's Daughter* that quoted Bixby's letter to his editor about his unpublished book.

It hadn't stood out to her initially, not until she actually *read* the book in question. The broad strokes were the same, but his letter summarized the work like someone who had only heard about it.

Not someone who had written it.

Rose shoved the laptop aside and jumped out of bed, then rushed across the hall to pound on Will's door. Almost immediately, it jerked back, Will's face layered with concern. "What is it, Rose? What's wrong?"

"I've got it," she said breathlessly, a huge smile stretching across her face, her earlier humiliation forgotten. "It all makes sense."

"I'm glad it does to one of us," he said cautiously. "What's going on?"

"The author of the manuscript," Rose said. "This isn't Andrew Bixby's unpublished manuscript. It's Amelia's."

CHAPTER TWENTY

"Okay, repeat for Erin what you told me." Will perched on the edge of the desk in the study, his eyes glimmering and fixed on Rose.

Rose glanced at Erin, who was watching her with such a look of anticipation that she prayed she wasn't reading too much into it. "I've been making notes of all the unusual or unique phrases I've found in Bixby's books and cross referencing it to the manuscript. And there are a lot of similarities. Same pet phrases, same way of structuring sentences for effect in the same types of scenes. The voice is clearly the same. Then Mallory sent over this."

She swiveled around the laptop to show Mallory's transcription. Rose had spent a good twenty minutes using the search function to look for those same phrases, which she'd highlighted in yellow.

Erin stared at her, wide-eyed. "You think that *Amelia* wrote this book. Why? Because they needed the money after Andrew died? Or maybe just to fulfill his legacy?"

"No," Rose said slowly, "I think Amelia wrote *all* the books."

She'd been holding that little tidbit back, and while Erin's jaw dropped, Will didn't look surprised. He'd apparently understood the significance of her discovery from the beginning.

"It makes sense," Rose continued. "Who would be taken more seriously as a novelist, Amelia or her husband?"

"Well, clearly her husband," Erin said, "but that was risky too. He was a well-known industrialist, a mine owner. Why would he risk his reputation over something so frivolous?"

"Because he loved his wife," Will said quietly, looking at Rose as he said it. "He built a castle to prove that he was worthy of her. Do you think he wouldn't publish her books under his own name to get her the widest audience possible, if that's what she wanted?"

"He might also have been protecting her," Rose put in. "Amelia's parents were devoted Methodists. They very well might have thought that fiction was from the devil. There were plenty of odd beliefs about women reading novels, let alone writing them, up until the 1940s. No one was going to contradict someone as rich and well-known as Andrew Bixby. He probably wanted to preserve her relationship with her family."

"So what next?" Erin asked, her eyes glowing with excitement. "Do you have enough to have this authenticated now?"

Rose fell silent, considering. A slow smile spread her lips. "If we had an original manuscript in Amelia's handwriting to compare to the journal, that would be a slam dunk. But. . .absent of that. . .I think there's enough evidence here to make a good argument that this, and all the other books, were written by Amelia Bixby."

Erin squealed and jumped up to throw her arms

around Rose. "We're rich! You've saved Larkspur House!"

Rose chuckled and hugged the woman back. Her eyes drifted to Will over his sister's shoulder. He was smiling at them, but his expression didn't mirror his sister's elation. "What?"

He grimaced. "I don't mean to be the rain cloud here, because this is a remarkable discovery. Truly. But it's possible that this is more of an academic victory. In order for this to mean anything, someone has to want the manuscript."

"Way to spoil the mood." Erin sighed and shot a dirty look at her brother.

"He's right," Rose said. "And anyway, we need an expert to help authenticate it before we can take it to publishers."

"Okay, great. So where do we get one of those?"

"Mallory might know someone at UCCS who could help," Will said. "Or at least her contacts would know who to send her to."

Except Rose knew for certain that there was no one at UCCS that would have the kind of expertise needed to authenticate a manuscript like this. There were perhaps three or four people in the country with the specific knowledge of the time period and enough familiarity with Andrew Bixby's work to make that kind of judgment call. When she came back to the present, Will was studying her.

"You had an idea," he said quietly.

"I know someone." Rose's stomach was already twisting at the thought. "But it's going to require calling in a favor."

* * *

It was too late to make the call tonight, but even if it hadn't been, Rose needed time to prepare herself. They all went their separate ways to their bedrooms, but she lay awake staring at the ceiling into the wee hours. Too much had happened today. First the ill-fated "date" gone wrong, then this incredible discovery. And now . . .

She had to prepare herself for the phone call she had to make first thing tomorrow morning, all the questions that would inevitably arise. All the ones that she'd been trying to avoid for the last seven months.

When she woke the next morning, she felt neither rested nor prepared for what awaited her, but she still rose, showered, and dressed, hoping she was early enough to avoid running into Will. The last thing she needed was to feel more off guard than she already did.

She went downstairs and made herself a cup of coffee, then after a moment of thought, went up to Will's second floor study where it was quiet and private. Then she took a deep breath, pulled up the office number in her phone's contacts list, and pressed call.

The phone rang several times, and then the line picked up. "Hello, this is Dr. Cameron."

Rose's stomach gave a brutal twist. "Hi, Mom."

The silence stretched for one second, then two, and Elizabeth Cameron's surprised exhale whispered over the line. "Rose. What's wrong?"

Rose closed her eyes and shook her head. "I can't just call to say hello?"

"Of course you can. But you don't. I've heard from you once in six months, and that only to say that you were leaving Wisconsin for a temporary job in Utah."

"Colorado, Mom. I'm in Colorado."

"Sorry, Colorado."

The silence stretched again and Rose muffled her sigh. She'd never been particularly close with her mother, but this was awkward even for them. She supposed that's what happened when you avoided going home so you didn't have to hear *I told you so*. To her mom's credit, she'd already been on the line for all of ten seconds now and she hadn't said anything of the sort. That might be a record.

"How's Dad?"

"Good. Busy at work. I'm not sure if you heard, but he managed to lure Alex Kanin away from Random House. Quite a coup."

"Yes, I imagine it is." Rose had no idea who Alex Kanin was—knowing her dad's taste in books, he was probably some painfully literary writer who wrote Very Important Books that Rose strongly disliked. She and her father didn't exactly share reading lists. "I was hoping you could help me with something."

Dr. Cameron huffed out a little laugh. "I should have known this wasn't just a call to catch up."

Yes, because you always make these catch-up calls so pleasant. "Well, I think you'll find this one worth your while. I've been working in a historic house in Colorado, helping identify and authenticate artworks and antiques of value for the owner—"

"Oh. So that's what you're doing now? You're a fine arts authenticator?"

Rose took a breath and let the remark pass without comment, even though her pulse was beginning to beat a watery thrum in her ears, a sure sign that she was close to losing her temper. "—and I discovered a manuscript."

Now a hint of interest lit her mother's voice. "What kind of manuscript?"

"Well, if I'm not mistaken, Andrew Bixby's missing final novel."

"That would be extraordinary if it were true. What makes you think that it belongs to Andrew Bixby?"

"Sentence structure, word choice. And the fact I found it in a hidden room in Bixby Castle along with Amelia Bixby's wedding dress and journal."

There was a long pause, and true excitement colored Dr. Cameron's voice when she spoke again. "That would truly be a find. How can I take a look at it? Is it an original manuscript?"

"No, it's a typewritten copy, unfortunately, which the local historian dated back to the 1960s or 1970s. She thought it was probably prepared on a Selectric. But there's more. I don't actually think it was written by Andrew Bixby."

"But you just said . . ."

"At least not written by Andrew Bixby, the industrialist. I think it was written by the same person who wrote his novels."

"And who would that be?"

"From the wording in the journal? I think they were written by his wife, Amelia."

"Rose." Here came the hint of condescension she'd been waiting for. "I know you think—"

"You know what, Mom? I called you out of professional courtesy. I thought you would like to take credit for being the one to authenticate the missing Bixby novel and maybe even make a significant discovery about their real authorship. But if you're not interested, it's fine. I have other contacts."

Her mother sighed. "Can you send me some scans?"

Just like Rose had thought. Elizabeth Cameron might not like to give her daughter credit for having a brain, but there was no way she would pass up a chance—however slim—to take credit for this kind of discovery. "I'll send them over to you this afternoon. Let me know when you get them."

Rose hung up before she could say what she really

thought and let out an infuriated noise. Leave it to her mother to act like she was doing *her* a favor, when it was really the other way around. Publish or perish, wasn't that what they said in academic circles? Even well-known PhDs like Elizabeth Cameron weren't immune to that rule.

Rose spun away from the bookshelf and then started. Will stood in the doorway, looking somewhat guilty. "How much of that did you hear?"

He moved into the room, his expression sympathetic. "Just the last part. I didn't realize it was your mother you were talking about."

Rose sighed. "Well, I don't talk about her much. The feeling is mutual."

"I'm sorry. Family is never easy, is it?"

"No. It really isn't. But the good news is, she's going to take a look."

"Rose, if this is a problem, we really don't need her—"

"No, we do. She is the foremost authority on western American Romantic literature in the United States. There's almost no one who could come close to her expertise. If she says that this is an authentic Bixby— and written by Amelia, to boot—there's virtually no one in the world who would say otherwise." Which is why she had braved that phone call. Erin and Will were counting on her. They needed this.

"Thank you," he said quietly. "What next?"

"We take the manuscript to town and have it scanned so I can send it along with the journal transcription. At some point she'll probably want to see the original." A wry smile came to Rose's face. "But I'll make her come here to see it."

He chuckled. "That seems fair. Though I suppose we could probably take the journal to Colorado Springs and find someone who can photograph archival materials."

"Possibly. After that, I suggest we get you a literary agent. Because when she proclaims this as an original, there is going to be a lot of interest in publishing it. How much you'll get for it, I don't know, but you'll do far better with someone experienced in your corner."

"Fortunately, I know someone with a lot of contacts in publishing," Will said with a wry twist of his mouth.

"You sure you want to ask a favor of Liv?"

"No. But it looks like we're both doing things we don't want to do for the sake of this book." He chuckled. "What do you say to a trip to town? We can get Mallory to scan the manuscript and grab some breakfast at the same time. I'll buy."

Rose looked at him for a long moment, recognized this as the olive branch that it was. "I'll get my bag."

CHAPTER TWENTY-ONE

ROSE COULDN'T HELP BUT FEEL AWKWARD when she climbed into Will's SUV—this time beating him to the door before he could open it for her. Assuming he *would* open it for her. His rejection at the hot springs still stung, and from the tentative way that he approached her now, he knew it.

Which meant that he knew what she'd expected and how he'd hurt her feelings.

How humiliating.

But she sucked up her discomfort and assumed a pleasant expression as he made a U-turn in the driveway and turned back down the long drive to Larkspur House. An uncomfortable silence fell between them in the car, neither of them really sure what to say now that it was just the two of them enclosed in a small space.

"So how long do you think it will take for your mother to authenticate the manuscript?" he asked finally.

Rose sighed with relief. As much as she didn't want to talk about her mother, it was better than the other things they could discuss. "It's hard to tell. She'll want to do everything that I've already done, comparing this manuscript with all the others and the journal. Then of course, she'll want to find any supporting information that's available on both Andrew and Amelia—letters, journal entries, and the like. She may even contact the heirs to Amelia's family's estate to see if they have any additional primary sources for her to consider."

"So you're saying this isn't going to be quick."

Rose grimaced. "No. Several months, if not longer. Maybe much longer."

He nodded, his expression smooth, unreadable, but she didn't think she imagined the careful breath that he let out. She debated with herself for a long moment, then asked gently, "How bad is it? How long do you have?"

Will threw a glance at her. "Let's put it this way. Utilities on a place that size aren't cheap. If we stay there for even two more months, I won't be able to repair the roof. And if I can't repair the roof, I can't sell it. But there's not the money to keep it either."

Heaviness hit Rose's stomach. "So that's why you aren't thrilled about this."

He looked over again, his eyes wide with surprise. "I'm thrilled. This is an amazing find. It's important to our family's history and Haven Ridge's too, and beyond that it's just . . . cool."

Rose let out a little laugh.

"Don't seem so shocked. Didn't I tell you I liked my job because I got to uncover mysteries all day? This is thrilling, it really is. But . . ."

" . . . but it doesn't solve your problems."

"Not even close. If nothing else, it makes them worse. Because now that there seems like there *could possibly* be some money in the future, that perhaps this house is even more culturally significant than we thought, how do we sell it? How do I tell Erin that we can't keep it? How do I tell her that in seven years, I've mismanaged the trust so badly that for the first time in almost a century, it can't sustain the properties?"

There was real pain in his voice. Rose studied his profile, wondering how she'd thought him so emotionless before. He rarely let that controlled exterior slip, but there could be no mistake a deep well of feeling lay beneath. He felt that this was his fault, and he was never going to forgive himself if it ended this way.

"Somehow," Rose said, "I have a very hard time believing you could mismanage anything."

He just shook his head. "I was overconfident. I put the block of buildings on Beacon Street up for lease last year, thinking surely someone would want to rent them."

"Well, Liv did . . ." Rose trailed off at his quick, wry glance at her. "Didn't she?"

"I leased it to her for five years at the cost of taxes," he said. "That space doesn't bring in a dime over what I put out for it."

"Ohh." Now things were starting to make sense. "And you regret that?"

"Not a bit," he said immediately. "I owed it to Jason to look out for Liv. Maybe I had other motives for a while, but in the end, that was what was important. And it was the last thing that I could do to make sure she was okay." He gave a harsh chuckle. "Let's face it. That rent is just a drop in the bucket compared to what we would need."

Will stared straight out of the windshield as he put on his signal to turn into Haven Ridge proper and Rose studied his profile unabashedly. Darn him. She wanted to stay hurt and mad at him, but every time he did something that made her think that he was a heartless jerk, he showed a little bit more of what was beneath his shell.

This was a man who never stopped beating himself up for his failures, deserved or otherwise.

A little more of her irritation faded. How could she be angry with him when he was probably even more angry with himself? How difficult must it be to go through life like that, always sure that you were letting people down even when you were doing your best?

Yes, Rose, what must *that be like?*

Shut up, she told that internal voice that always seemed to hit too close to the truth. *It's not the same thing.*

But wasn't it?

"Okay, now I'm wondering what you're thinking," Will said with a slight smile, darting glances at her as they started into the residential district of Haven Ridge.

"I'm thinking I'm an idiot," Rose muttered to herself, then darted a quick glance at him. "I'm just thinking. Hoping that some brilliant idea will occur to me."

"Listen, I'm open to all brilliant ideas, particularly ones that will help us sooner than a manuscript that will take a year or more to sell."

So was Rose, but nothing was coming to her at the moment.

Will parked in front of the Brick House Cafe, and once more Rose jumped out before he could open her door, though she was sure by now that he wasn't going to. That one night had been an aberration. Whatever he had been thinking about her, he was no longer. He was probably afraid that she would conflate a gentlemanly gesture into an undying declaration of love and she would try to jump on him the minute they were alone.

Her cheeks burned at the memory.

But he did open the door to the cafe for her, and when they entered, the handful of customers turned their direction curiously, then went back to their meals. In the back, a familiar figure raised a hand to them.

"Is that Gemma?" Rose asked, nudging Will.

He turned and gave a wave. "It is. Do you want to go join her? I can talk to Thomas and see if Mallory is around today." He held up the pasteboard box that contained the manuscript.

"Okay. You're coming to join us?"

"Sure. Give me a minute."

Still feeling slightly self-conscious at the appraising glances that came their way, Rose made her way to the back of the cafe. Gemma smiled at her when she approached. "Hi Rose. Care to join me?"

"I'd love to." Rose slid into the booth across from her. "Will is talking to Thomas. He said he'd join us in a minute."

"Did he?" Gemma said, significance hanging in her tone. Rose frowned, but the other woman didn't elaborate. Instead, she crossed her arms on the table. "So, you've been here in Haven Ridge for, what, two weeks? How are you finding it?"

"I admit, I haven't spent as much time in town as I'd hoped. We've been pretty busy up at the house. But so far I love it."

"It does tend to grow on you, doesn't it?"

There was something in Gemma's tone, though, that piqued Rose's interest. "You sound like you didn't always feel that way."

"Well, let's say that I understand Will a lot better than he probably thinks I do. There was a time in my life when I didn't think I would ever set foot in this town again. In fact, I could think of about a dozen torture methods that sounded more appealing."

"Why's that?"

Gemma looked at her significantly. "Bad memories. This town hasn't always been quite so friendly. Did they tell you about the so-called curse?"

Rose frowned. "There's a curse too? And here I thought it was just a magic town."

Gemma chuckled. "They're one and the same. Let's just say that some very unpleasant things went down here when I was in high school and certain factions were convinced that the town was cursed for it. And that it was determined to make amends."

Rose couldn't help but smile. She didn't believe in magic or curses any more than Will did, and the wry tone in the other woman's voice said she was skeptical about such things too. "And yet you're back? What made the difference?"

"Something—and someone—to stay for." She shrugged, her smile returning. "Let's just say that the Broken Hearts Bakery wasn't named out of hyperbole. It just took me a while to realize it was *my* heart that needed to be mended."

It was such a poetic sentiment to come out of such a straightforward woman that it took Rose aback for a moment. But hadn't she just thought the same thing about Will? Still waters run deep and all that? She took a chance.

"You know the situation. Will is only back here because of Erin and he only wants to save the house for her. If you were me—or them—what would you do?"

Gemma leaned back in her seat, lifting her milkshake and taking a long sip from the bright red straw. "That's a good question, probably one that's best answered by Liv. She's known Will for far, far longer than I have. But I also think I understand him a little bit. The lawyer in me says that he needs an answer to all the risks he sees in keeping the house. But the romantic in me—and trust me, it's there even if it's buried—says that he needs to learn to use his imagination again. To be able to see the *what if?*"

"And what is that *what if?*"

Gemma shrugged, but her expression was sympathetic. "Like I said, I don't know him well enough to say. But in my experience, you can answer all someone's fears and objections and they still won't take a chance until you capture their imagination."

Rose was about to say that she didn't think Will had any imagination, but that wasn't true, was it? She'd seen the excitement on his face when he discovered the hidden room, how he'd transformed from risk-management mode to adventurer mode. The delight when he'd showed her the hot springs because he didn't want her to miss out. The excitement in his voice when he'd talked about why he loved his job—not for justice or money, but for the puzzle. The mystery.

Will Parker had an imagination, and Larkspur House had a story. It was just a matter of getting him to connect the two.

"Speak of the devil," Gemma said with a grin, and Rose looked up to see Will approaching the table.

"Hey Gemma," he said with a smile, before he turned to Rose. "Thomas says that Mallory is upstairs in the apartment and we can go up. She has a scanner there we can use for the manuscript. Do you want to stay with Gemma or do you want to come up?"

Gemma gave her a significant look that she wasn't quite sure how to interpret, but it was clear what she was telling her to do. "I'll go with you. I want to ask Mallory a couple more questions."

"Great." Will stepped back to give Rose room to slide out of the booth, shifting his attention back to Gemma. "How are things? Business going well?"

"Yes, in fact, thank you. Did you enjoy the eclair the other night?"

Will's brow furrowed. "Eclair?"

Rose's face flushed. "I have absolutely no idea what she's talking about. I most certainly *did not* stress eat it when I got home."

Will grinned suddenly, and Gemma stifled a laugh. She nodded at Rose. "Let me know how it all works out. I have a strange feeling that if anyone can figure out this puzzle, it would be you."

Why was it that every time she talked to someone in this town, they seemed like they knew things that she didn't? It was more than a little unsettling. But Rose just said her goodbyes and then followed Will into the back hallway, past the office in which they'd stopped the other day, and then up the stairs at the very back.

"What was that all about?" Will asked curiously, craning his neck to look at Rose as they climbed.

"I honestly have no idea. You ever feel like half of what's said around here is subtext that you just aren't picking up?"

"All the time," he said wryly. "It's irritating."

Rose laughed, but before she could say anything else, they were standing in front of a door marked *1*. Will lifted a hand and knocked. Almost instantly, Mallory opened it with a smile. "That was fast. I didn't know that you were already in the building when Thomas texted me."

"We're not disturbing you, are we?" Will asked.

"No, not at all. Come in, please."

Rose stepped past Mallory and looked around at the apartment with interest. While the cafe downstairs was straight out of the 1950s or 1960s, this place was like going back in time an extra hundred years. Original floors and moldings, beautiful Oriental rugs, some old-fashioned antique furniture pieces. Mallory led them into a wide hallway space out of which she had carved a desk area with an antique roll-top, on which stood a laptop and a portable scanner.

Mallory held her hand out for the manuscript. "This will take a few minutes. I can only feed about twenty sheets at a time."

Will handed over the box. "We can come back if you want."

"No, have a seat in the living room. I'll get this started."

Reluctantly, Rose and Will went back into the living room—or parlor, as it might be more accurately described—and sat on the Chesterfield sofa. She took in the moldings and original fireplace. "This is really beautiful. A little earlier than Larkspur, right?"

"By forty, fifty years maybe?" Will followed her gaze. "This was definitely one of the earliest buildings in town, built way before Andrew Bixby got here. You can tell by the style of moldings and the shape of the windows."

Rose looked at him in surprise. "I didn't realize you knew so much about architecture."

"Only thanks to Mallory's dissertation."

From the hallway, Mallory called, "Don't let him fool you. Will knows a great deal about a number of things."

"Oh?" Rose turned to him with a smile. "What else do you know about?"

"He's quite a talented carpenter, did he tell you that?" Mallory appeared now at the edge of the parlor. "Coffee for either of you?"

"None for me," Will said, just as Rose replied, "I'll take a cup if it's not too much trouble?"

"Sure you won't change your mind, Will?" Mallory asked with a teasing grin, and he sighed.

"Sure, I'll take a cup."

Mallory headed for the adjacent kitchen and Rose called after her, "I did know he was a talented carpenter, in fact. I've seen some of the furniture he helped make for the house."

"Oh, but that's not even the half of it." Mallory threw Will a reproving look. "You didn't tell her about all your work on the upper floors?"

He rolled his eyes and shot a half-hearted glare at her. "Why would I?"

Mallory came back with two mugs, which she handed to them, then disappeared and returned once more with a pink pastry box stamped with the Broken Hearts Bakery logo. "Knowing you, you wouldn't." She grabbed a cookie from the box and seated herself across from them in a wingback chair. "As you probably know by now, the top floors were renovated back in the 1930s to add more bedrooms and bathrooms, back when it was a school."

"Wait," Rose said. "It was a school?"

"Oh yes. A secondary school for girls."

"Like a finishing school?"

"Something like that. Initially, I think it was meant to be a boarding house. Amelia employed out-of-work craftsmen during the Depression to do the renovations. But not long after, World War II broke out. Up until then, most upper-class girls would have gone to France or Switzerland and learned languages, deportment, sports, writing, all the things that it would take to present themselves in polite company or run a large household of their own—or how to direct servants to do so. Now they couldn't travel internationally, so Amelia saw an opportunity to generate income to help keep up the house. She also provided employment for a select few women who were able to escape Switzerland, Austria, and France as the war continued."

Rose listened with fascination, looking to Will. "Did you know this?"

He nodded. "I take it you didn't make it that far in her dissertation."

"It's like four hundred and fifty pages," Rose said defensively, but Mallory just laughed.

"It was a tome, I understand. But you might find it useful if you want to learn more about that era in Haven Ridge."

Rose looked between the two of them. "What does that have to do with Will, though?"

"The work was done well," Will said, "but inconsistently from the rest of the house. It lacked the same ornamentation, I would guess because of the cost. I spent my summers home from college there, reworking all the paneling and molding to match the lower floors."

Rose blinked at him. Hadn't those been the things she'd remarked upon when she'd arrived, the excellent old-school craftsmanship? "Those were yours? All the cornice flowers?"

He actually looked embarrassed. "Yeah. I know it's not—"

"It's amazing," Rose cut in. "I was remarking to myself how beautiful they were, how much care had been taken. The poppies on the third floor and the roses on the fourth, which I noticed for obvious reasons." She just stared at him. "Those weren't simple things you fed through one of the machines."

Will looked away, actually embarrassed. "No. It took me an entire summer to hand carve all the flowers for a single floor."

Rose just gaped as if she were seeing him for the first time. "I'd thought you were very talented when I saw the furniture, but that is . . . art."

Will made a face at Mallory. "You just had to tell her, didn't you?"

Mallory grinned unrepentantly. "Of course I did. You *are* an artist. Even if you yourself don't seem to remember it."

"Well, it was a long time ago," he put in, pink still tingeing his cheeks. "Back when those sorts of things mattered to me."

The whir of the scanner had long stopped, and Mallory pushed to her feet to go feed the next stack of paper through it, leaving them alone.

"You shouldn't downplay your work," Rose said. "It's remarkable."

"Amateur at best," he replied, but if she wasn't mistaken, he might have looked a tiny bit pleased.

At the desk, Mallory gathered all the paper from the scanner and replaced it in the box. "Okay, I think that's done. Do you want me to email it to both of you?"

"Please," they said simultaneously, and then laughed as they looked at each other.

Mallory made a few clicks with her mouse, tapped in the addresses they gave her, and then shut her laptop. "There you go. Should be in your inbox. Let me know what happens, will you please?"

"Of course," Will said, rising. "Thank you, Mallory. We owe you for this one."

Mallory smiled at both of them. "My pleasure. Keep me informed. This deserves a couple of chapters in my book. In fact, I'm going to have to hold off publication while I wait to hear the final determination."

They said their goodbyes, then climbed down the stairs and headed back through the cafe with a wave. They were both quiet on the ride back to Larkspur House, though Rose thought her silence was probably for a much different reason than Will's.

"I'm going to email this off to my mom," Rose said, "and then I'm going to go see if Erin's up."

Will murmured assent, his mind obviously elsewhere. "Let me know if you hear of anything interesting."

Rose wasn't offended that he disappeared the

moment they stepped into the house, because she was far too focused on the crazy thoughts spinning through her head. She raced up the three flights of stairs, directly to Erin's room, and knocked on the door until the woman opened it, sleepy and concerned. "Rose? What's wrong?"

Rose didn't wait to be invited in, just pushed past Erin and shut the door.

"I have an idea."

CHAPTER TWENTY-TWO

IT DIDN'T TAKE LONG FOR ERIN TO GRASP the direction of Rose's thoughts, but the more that she explained, the more the other woman's expression transformed to excitement. "Do you really think it could work?"

"Honestly? Yes. I mean, it doesn't mean that it isn't a lot of work, and it isn't an instant fix . . . but long term? Absolutely."

Erin plopped cross-legged on her bed. "We'll need help with this one. Liv, Thomas, Mallory, Gemma . . ."

"Somehow I have a feeling they might help. Though given the fact that every single person in this town has at least two jobs, I'm not sure when anyone will have time to do half of what we're talking about."

"They'll make time," Erin said, her eyes shining with confidence. "I'm absolutely certain when they see what you're planning that they'll want to be a part of it."

Rose chewed on her lip thoughtfully. "I don't want Will to know until we're ready to present the idea. Gemma told me that the key to getting him on board is to answer all of his questions about risk, and I have to give it all some thought first. I don't want this to be an idea. I want this to be a full plan. A presentation. Something that he can visualize working because we've thought through all the possible issues."

"I agree. Like I said, he's very black and white. If you can demonstrate that this solves all our problems so everyone gets what they want. . .well, I don't see how he can say no."

Rose took a deep breath, jitters in the stomach forming at the scope of what she'd proposed. "You get everyone on board. And I will start putting together a proposal. We just have to do it fast. Now that the manuscript is out of our hands, there's no reason for him to stay here much longer. It could be months before we hear anything about the authentication of that book, and you know that we don't have months before he wants to do something drastic with the house."

Erin reached for Rose's hand and squeezed, but there was a bit of wonder in her face. "Why are you doing this for us, Rose? This isn't what you signed up for."

"This is *exactly* what I signed up for, remember? A partner in crime, a way to save the house. I truly think this might work." Rose took a deep breath. "And I think you're the one who should present it to him."

Erin blinked and something shuttered in her expression. "No. . .I. . . this will come so much better from you. He doesn't think I'm capable of anything of this scale."

"Which is why I think you need to do it," Rose said gently. "It's not that he doesn't think you're capable, he's just afraid. Afraid of what happens if either of you deviate from the plan. Afraid that something bad will happen if he doesn't control every variable. You need to show him what you're capable of."

Erin still didn't look convinced, but she drew a deep breath and then nodded. "Okay. I'll get everyone on board. You put together the plan, and I'll present it. By the end of the weekend?"

It was a massive amount of work, even if they worked all day and all night, but Rose could understand the urgency. Had recommended it. They had only a short window while Will would still be receptive to their ideas before he started making his own plans to turn over the house to someone who could care for it better than him, even if it wasn't what he wanted.

Because now she knew without a doubt he didn't want to let this place go, even if he didn't know it himself. Someone would not spend a cumulative year of his life restoring decorative details that made no practical difference if there weren't some love for this place hard-wired into him. He wouldn't even be here, trying to save it for his sister, if he really believed it was better off out of his family's hands.

They just needed to show him that it made more sense to keep the house, even if they struggled through for a while, than to sell it. That it was part of him and Erin just as much as it was a part of Haven Ridge.

She was going to give him a reason to stay.

* * *

The restlessness that overtook Will on his way back from town didn't go away no matter what he did. He'd gotten another email this morning letting him know that another large chunk of the data entry had been finished on his upcoming case and had been dropped in the document vault, but the minute he opened the files, he knew he wouldn't be able to concentrate.

Because he couldn't stop thinking about Rose. The

way she'd looked at him when she learned about the work he'd done on the house. Like he was an entirely different person.

To be fair, it felt like he *had* been an entirely different person back then. He'd been aimless, floating. Studying accounting because he was good with numbers and he didn't know what else to do with his life. That had been before he knew that they'd land in Chicago, back when he thought that he might actually come back to Haven Ridge, open up a business and put some of that woodworking equipment to good use. He'd argued that his accounting degree with a business minor would never hurt him regardless of which direction he went, even though he was almost certain he wanted to be an entrepreneur.

That, of course, had been before Erin had landed the job with the Chicago Symphony and he'd decided to move to Illinois to do his MBA in case she needed him. Then the contacts he'd made in the MBA program led to a job, which led to another job, which led to a career.

And whatever plans he might have had for Haven Ridge, however painful it might have been to return, had faded.

The person who had thought that fiddling around with wood and stain and lacquer for an entire summer was a better idea than taking on internships in Boston was no more.

And yet now he found himself walking out to the workshop, breathing in the familiar smells of oil and wood and the faintest trace of finishing products, his fingers itching to do something besides punch numbers on a ten-key.

Will let himself in and moved slowly through the space, bypassing the large machinery—the planers and joiners and saws used for the large-scale work that the house actually needed. Instead, he found himself by the bench, rummaging through the bins underneath. There were offcuts of all sorts of wood—maple and oak and beech—but none of those were special enough for what he had in mind.

Finally, in a small plastic bin, he found what he'd been looking for: the small pieces of specialty woods that he'd bought just because he liked them and he could imagine what form they might possibly take, whether they were practical or not. Figured walnut could be a knife handle and olive wood that he'd thought would make a nice spoon. Zebrawood he'd thought to turn into a music box to replace the one of Erin's—the only thing of value their mother had left behind—that had broken during one of their moves. And finally, he set hands on the one he'd remembered, a small block of curly cherry, stunningly expensive in comparison to the cabinet grade he usually used, its wave-like pattern almost luminescent. Everything he'd considered for it had felt too pedestrian and utilitarian for a piece of such cost and beauty. Until now, a decade after setting his tools aside for the last time.

Will smiled to himself as he put on a mask and safety glasses, then plugged in the smaller table saw and flipped the *on* switch. It whirred to life with a familiar hum. He set the guide, grabbed an offcut of Douglas fir to use as a push stick, and slid the cherry through the table saw, cutting off an even square chunk. Then he took that chunk to the lathe.

The wood started to take shape on the lathe under the careful application of a spindle gouge and skew chisel, their sharp blades taking micrometers off at a time. It was a surprisingly delicate process—the wood was just hard enough to take some work, but delicate enough from the figured grain that aggressive treatment would take large chunks out of it. And yet he felt his heart lighten as the general shape of his object gradually began to form under his tools. When he finally turned off the lathe and held the roughly shaped wood in his gloved hand, he felt a surge of satisfaction that he hadn't felt in years.

It was only the first part of the work, the easiest part. The rest would have to be done with hand tools, bit by painstaking bit, feeling his way through what the wood would tolerate. Push too far and he'd ruin it. Don't push far enough and he would be here forever, never making any progress.

It was a surprisingly astute metaphor for more than one area of his life.

By the time Will left the shop, it was afternoon and the truck was gone from the carriage house—a sure sign that one or both of the women had gone. He wasn't even close to finished—this would take him days, at least—but he was tired and thirsty and his face hurt from the mask. In the kitchen, he drained his glass of water and set it in the sink, then made his way up to his bathroom to shower off the fine pink dust that had crept beneath his clothing.

Clean, dressed in fresh clothes, and finally drained of his nervous energy, he intended to head downstairs to the office to get a little work done. Instead, he found himself standing before Rose's door, his hand raised to knock. It took him several seconds to make himself rap on the door.

No answer.

He tried again, and when he still got no answer, he tried the door handle. It opened easily.

"Rose?" he asked quietly through the crack. "Are you in there?"

When he heard nothing, he pushed it open a little

farther and poked his head in. Only to find a neatly made bed and no Rose. Evidently, Erin hadn't gone to town alone.

He closed the door behind him and made his way down to the office, which was what he should have done in the first place, and pretended that what he felt was something other than disappointment.

CHAPTER TWENTY-THREE

IF ROSE HAD THOUGHT THE SCALE of their proposal was enormous, she had still wildly underestimated its scope. She'd been right about one thing, though: every single person in Haven Ridge who heard about their plan was on board. And somehow, every single person also agreed to keep it secret until they were ready to unveil it to Will.

"This might actually work," Erin said on the way back from town. They'd picked up dinner while they were there as an excuse for their absence, even though they probably didn't need one—Will had been nowhere to be found when they left.

"Of course it will work," Rose said with a smile from the passenger seat. "Whether or not we can be convincing enough to get your brother on board is another story."

"Oh, leave that to me. I can be convincing."

Rose laughed, though she had no doubt that it was the truth. Will would do anything for his sister. And even if it took some work, she was confident that she and Erin and half of Haven Ridge would be able to

make him see both the wisdom and the excitement of
what they were proposing for Larkspur House.

She still felt vaguely bad about lying to him, though.
Will liked having everything figured out, liked being in
control. How was he going to feel when he'd learned
they hadn't included him in this process and he was
literally the last person in the entire town to know?

We'll worry about that when we come to it. It wasn't like
they were going behind his back for nefarious reasons.
It was simply hard to present a well thought-out
argument for why Larkspur House should be transformed instead of sold if they didn't have all the pieces
in place.

It turned out she needn't have worried, though.
There was very little opportunity to speak to him at all,
lies or not. He came down briefly to eat dinner with
them—they'd picked up pasta and garlic rolls from the
Italian restaurant in town—and then disappeared outside. Rose didn't question it. The more occupied he was
with other things, whatever those other things might be,
the less he'd be wondering why they weren't making
progress on the clean-out project in the house. . .or
why they were holed up in Erin's room for hours on
end.

And it *was* hours, complicated by the fact they had
to use their cell phones any time they wanted to look
anything up on the internet. "The first thing we're
going to do," Rose muttered, "is to get internet access
and WiFi installed here."

"Agreed," Erin said, scrolling down the tiny screen
of her phone. "We can go into town tomorrow and
work at the cafe."

"Don't you think someone is going to spill to Will if
we're seen in town working too much?"

Erin shook her head. "No. They all know why we're

doing this, and they want the house to stay as it is as much as we do. I don't think anyone would ruin it for us."

Rose had her doubts—it seemed to her like a small town would love gossip and there had to be at least one person who wanted to have the scoop, but Erin knew Haven Ridge better than she did, so she'd give them the benefit of the doubt.

In any case, as quickly as the project was coming together, they wouldn't have to worry about it too much longer. Turned out her time working in proposal and grant writing for the nonprofit came in handy. There wasn't much difference between writing a presentation for someone you wanted to give you money and writing a presentation for someone you wanted to give you permission. It required having a strong vision, a clear sense of the costs and benefits, and passion for the project.

And as the proposal and presentation began to take shape on Rose's laptop, she realized that she had all.

Not that it was solely her work. Erin had experience in the realm they were proposing, and contrary to what Will might think about her artistic nature, she had exacting and clearly articulated desires for the project.

Still, in the rare moments that Rose encountered Will, when they chatted over a cup of coffee in the kitchen or smiled at each other as they passed on the way to their shared bathroom, she couldn't help a sting of guilt that even she couldn't quite explain.

Then, on Sunday evening, she returned to her room to get a fresh notebook and stopped.

There was something on her nightstand.

Slowly, she moved into the room and approached the item, her heart beating unnecessarily quickly. She lifted the object and studied it, her lips stretching into a smile.

It was a beautifully detailed model of a rose in full bloom, carved out of what looked like cherrywood, just the right size to fit comfortably in her palm. Each petal was so delicate and detailed that it seemed impossible that it had been crafted and not simply somehow preserved from a real rose.

It might have been the sweetest gift that she'd ever received. Was this what Will had been working on out in the carriage house while she and Erin were busy with the proposal?

And more importantly, why? What did this mean, exactly?

Clutching the lovely sculpture in her hand, she moved into the hallway again and rapped lightly on his door. "Will? Are you in there?"

No answer.

That probably meant he was down in his study. She made her way down the two flights of stairs to the office. The door was closed, but a sliver of light shone beneath the space at the base of the door. This time when she knocked, Will's voice came, "Come in."

She turned the knob and slowly pushed the door open wide enough to peek through. "Am I interrupting?"

Will rose from his chair behind the desk, removing a pair of dark-framed glasses. "Rose." His eyes landed on the sculpture in her hand, and she could swear that she saw him stiffen. Was he actually nervous?

"I take it this is from you?" she asked softly, holding up the rose.

Even from here, she could see color rise to his cheeks. Gruff, abrupt Will Parker was actually blushing. He cleared his throat, but all he managed was a nod.

Rose stepped closer. "It's beautiful. Thank you." She held it up and looked at it again, unable to keep the smile from her face. "I will treasure it. I've always hated

my name because it's boring, but if it inspired something this beautiful . . ."

"Rose is a beautiful name," Will said immediately. "It
suits you."

Wait. Was that . . . a compliment? Had he just called
her beautiful? No. Surely she had misunderstood. There
was no way that he thought she was anything but aver-
age. She'd given him more than one opening, more than
one signal that she was interested, and he hadn't taken
a single one.

"What I don't understand is why. You didn't need to
give me anything."

Slowly, he circled the desk and leaned against it,
obviously ill at ease from the way he didn't quite meet
her gaze. "I felt bad about what happened at the hot
springs. I didn't mean to give you the impression—"

Rose flushed. "No. I'm sorry. I shouldn't have done
what I did. I didn't want to make you feel like . . ." Her
voice trailed off when she saw he was now staring at her
with amusement, eyebrows raised.

"I didn't mean to give you the impression that I
wasn't interested."

The pronouncement jolted her, sent a bolt of
electricity down through her toes. Surely she was
misunderstanding. But he was just staring at her with
that half-smile on his face. It wasn't until he began to
speak again that she realized that the amusement wasn't
entirely directed at her. "I can get in my head sometimes. Talk myself out of what I want."

"And what is it that you want?"

He held her gaze. "Right now, I want to kiss you."

Rose went still, her mind going blank with shock.
When she didn't respond, a flicker of doubt passed over
his face and she sensed him withdraw a little. "Unless I
misread you."

"No . . ." Her voice came out a little breathy. "You didn't misread me."

A smile tipped up the corner of his mouth and he unfolded himself from the desk. Gently, he took the carved rose from her hand and set it behind him. She caught her breath when he raised his hand to brush her cheek, felt herself melt as he slid it behind her neck and lowered his lips to hers.

His kiss was soft but assured, his lips brushing hers like he had all the time in the world, like he wanted to savor every touch. Warmth spread through her like warm honey, and she sighed against his lips as she brought her hand up to rest on his chest, her fingers curling into the fabric of his shirt.

But it was over all too soon. When he lifted his head, a wash of loss overtook her—she wanted to stay in that lovely moment for just a little longer. She opened her eyes to find him wearing that faint smile, looking down on her with such affection that it made her catch her breath again.

Her brain stuttered. After the sweetest kiss she'd ever experienced, all she could think to say was, "I take it that's your apology?"

He grinned suddenly, and the expression—the first true, unrestrained smile she'd ever seen on his face—hit her in the gut, twisted her inside-out. "I suppose you could say that."

"I'm afraid I can't accept it." Her own smile threatened to break free at any moment, but she kept her tone serious. "I just didn't quite feel the true depth of your regret."

He backed up to perch on the edge of the desk again. "That's probably because I regret absolutely nothing. In fact, I'm trying to decide what else I should do to require another apology."

Rose laughed, inwardly delighted by this suddenly playful side of him. She schooled her expression, and then, all wide-eyed sincerity, said, "I'm actually quite upset about your lack of concern. I demand that you apologize at once."

"You demand, do you?" Will hooked a finger in the loop of her jeans and slowly pulled her forward so she came to rest between his legs. With his tall frame folded onto the desk, she could look him directly in the eye, where unaccustomed mischief sparkled. "In that case, I have no choice but to comply, do I?"

If she'd been impressed by his restraint the first time, now she was struck by his lack of it. He kissed her like a starving man too long deprived of nourishment, devouring her mouth, strong hands holding her in place against him. Rose could do nothing but hold on, fisting her hands in his shirt, her head spinning. The warm glow of their first kiss burned down in the fire of the second until there was nothing but the two of them— no thoughts, no regrets, only sensation and desire.

"Rose, are you in—oh!"

Erin's voice broke through her delicious haze, and she and Will broke the kiss at the same time.

"You have terrible timing, sister," Will practically growled, glaring at Erin over Rose's shoulder.

Rose twisted to see Erin backing out the door, grinning. "My apologies. I'm just going to . . . "

Erin shut the door behind her, but it was too late. The moment had been shattered, and to her surprise, Will looked a little abashed. "Rose, I . . . "

No. She wasn't going to let him overthink this. She smiled at him. "Apology accepted."

He blinked at her, then laughed, even though he still looked slightly embarrassed. "I feel like I owe you a real one now."

Rose leaned forward and whispered in his ear, "Save it for later."

And then before either of them could ruin what might be the single best kiss of her life, she turned and left the room.

* * *

Rose went upstairs, but she didn't go straight back to Erin's room. Instead, she locked herself in the bathroom, staring at her reflection in the mirror. Her flushed cheeks and kiss-swollen lips told anyone who cared to look exactly what she'd been doing.

She didn't regret it for a moment. She had a feeling the passionate side of Will Parker was seldom seen; she flushed with pride to have been the one to bring it out of him.

She just couldn't go around with it written all over her face.

Rose pulled her hair back into a ponytail and then bent over the basin to splash cold water on her face. She needed to cool down before she could return to Erin's room and get back to work.

Who was she kidding? Her concentration was ruined for the night. The minute she sat down to write her Larkspur House proposal, all she'd be doing was replaying the feel of Will's lips against hers, the way his fingers dug into her hips, that surprising, knee-weakening grin.

How any woman could resist that smile, she didn't know. Liv was obviously blind or stupid.

The thought of Liv gave her pause for just a second, before she pushed it away. For one thing, a couple of kisses wasn't a promise for the future. She had no right to be jealous of anyone that came before her. And for another, she hadn't seen a single sign that he was still hung up on the other woman. The only thing she'd picked up was a vague embarrassment that his former feelings had been so well-known.

When she'd dried her face and convinced herself that she no longer looked like she'd been making out with her employer in his office, she returned to Erin's room. Only to be confronted by the woman's knowing smile.

Her bravery fled instantly. "Please tell me I'm not a rebound. Or a temporary replacement."

"You're not a rebound or a temporary replacement," Erin said immediately.

Rose looked at her in surprise.

"Will doesn't do rebound. Binary, remember? On or off. And if he's on with you, he's off with Liv. Guaranteed."

Rose let out a surreptitious breath, not wanting to admit how much she'd been hoping for that answer. "Good. That could get really awkward."

"More awkward than me walking in on you?" Erin said with a smirk. "I think he wanted to murder me."

"Let's not talk about that." At least for all the passion in the kiss, everyone's hands had been in appropriate places. She wasn't going to wish that sight on anyone's sister.

But Erin just laughed. "Nah, he deserves it. He blocked every single one of my dates growing up. It's about time I return the favor. What was the big gesture, by the way? For making up for being an idiot at the hot springs?"

Now Rose's cheeks flushed. "He told you about that?"

"Yeah, he knew he messed up. He just didn't know how. If there's one thing you need to learn about Will, it's to be very direct. No ambiguity."

No ambiguity. That was a tough order considering their situation. Her very presence here at the moment was ambiguous. And then she honed in on the first part of Erin's statement, the big gesture. "Oh no! I forgot to take the flower!"

Erin frowned. "Excuse me?"

"He carved me a rose. Out of cherrywood, I think. I had gone down to thank him."

Her eyebrows flew up. "He hasn't touched a chisel in a decade."

"I gathered that. Mallory spilled the beans about his work on the house when we were there on Friday and I told him how impressed I was with the flowers."

"So he carved you your namesake." Erin smiled. "Despite his claim that he's done with all that. Hmm."

Rose settled into the armchair with her laptop again, even though the implications made her stomach go jittery. She'd known he'd put in a lot of effort—the craftsmanship and hours of work that had gone into something so detailed was clear—but she hadn't realized he'd broken some unspoken ban for her. That had to mean something, didn't it?

Did she want it to mean something?

Ugh. She had been right about her concentration being shattered. But this changed nothing. She didn't think just because she and Will had shared a couple of kisses—even really good kisses—that he would suddenly change from his normal, practical self. They still had to convince him not to cut this major tie with Haven Ridge.

Besides, the more they worked on this proposal, the surer she felt that it was something that Haven Ridge needed. And not just the town, but Will and Erin too. Something to honor their family legacy and the contribution the Bixbys had made.

And if it had the side effect of keeping both her and Will here so they could explore the attraction between them?

She would be completely fine with that.

CHAPTER TWENTY-FOUR

WILL WATCHED ROSE LEAVE THE ROOM, frozen in place on the edge of the desk. He waited for the regret, the recriminations to wash in. After all, Rose was technically his employee. And he had just kissed her like he hadn't kissed anyone in . . . well, ever. And yet despite all the reasons why it shouldn't have happened, why he should have talked himself out of it, all he felt was . . .

Happiness.

The realization made him pause. When was the last time he'd felt anything approaching real, uncomplicated happiness? The surge of excitement at the prospect of romance, the pleasure in a simple kiss? He hadn't even felt that with Liv—their friendship, his feelings were all too mixed up with the grief of losing Jason. By now, he should be kicking himself for loosening that tight control he had over his feelings and actions, but he felt zero recrimination.

Only anticipation for the next time she would allow him to "apologize."

He rose from the desk, and only then did he realize that she'd forgotten the flower that he'd carved for her.

He smiled to himself as he lifted it and brushed his fingers over the smooth oiled surface. That was another thing he had forgotten: the pleasure in making something just because it was beautiful, just because he could. Even the detail on the moldings for the house hadn't been purely aesthetic; he'd been thinking of historical accuracy and resale value. But even if it weren't for the clear appreciation from Rose, he had to admit he'd enjoyed the work, every painstaking detail. He'd take it to her later.

He circled around to the desk chair, but his concentration was ruined for the night. It wasn't as if he were doing anything important, just answering questions for other associates and doing some last-minute wrap-up for the case he'd just finished. He'd avoided looking at the documents on the server for his upcoming case. He knew from experience that once he dove into the spreadsheets and financial records for his client, he wouldn't come up for air for weeks. There was still too much to do here.

Like figure out how on earth they were going to manage to pay for the repairs that Larkspur House needed while keeping the lights and the water on while they waited to see if the manuscript could be authenticated. This was the windfall that they'd been looking for—he'd always known it was going to take more than the sale of a few antiques to be able to keep the place. He just needed to hold on for a bit longer.

He pulled up his banking app on the phone and reviewed his personal accounts. He had a sizable nest egg from spending far less than he earned and living well below his means for the last decade, even with the high cost of living in Chicago. He supposed if push actually came to shove, he could probably transfer a few thousand dollars to the trust. As a donation or perhaps as a loan. Just to pay the bills until they found out if anyone wanted to buy the book. It was a short-term solution, and honestly, he had no idea how much the manuscript would even fetch if someone wanted it. Like everything else, it was just a Band-Aid on a gaping wound.

The fact was, the Larkspur House wasn't much good to anyone just sitting here empty the entire year.

Will tunneled his fingers through his hair. They'd discussed more than once the possibility of opening it as a museum, but even with the increased tourism, the history of Haven Ridge and Andrew Bixby wasn't much of a draw. To the school children in nearby towns, perhaps, but that was what? Six or eight schools that visited once a year, perhaps a class or two at a time? Even charging admission, that barely covered the cost of keeping the lights on.

They needed a long-term solution. He just didn't know what that was, and he certainly wasn't going to figure it out tonight when every time he tried to do something useful, his mind just wandered back to how it felt to have Rose in his arms, the way she had met every ounce of his demand with equal fervor.

She was something else. Beautiful, upbeat, determined. She'd obviously been through a painful divorce—or perhaps it had been the marriage that had been painful—but she'd still managed to come out of it believing in the good in people. The fact he didn't know the details about her former relationship made him realize that they'd spent precious little time talking about personal things. Theirs was something like an office romance, born from proximity, not any deep understanding of each other.

And was this even a romance at all? Or had it just been a couple of stolen kisses between two people who found each other attractive?

He wasn't sure, but he knew he wanted to find out. He owed it to himself and to her. It was time to ask her out on a proper date.

He shut the lid of his laptop and tucked it under his arm, then grabbed the carving and left the room, filtering through all the possibilities. Haven Ridge had plenty of things to do for the outdoor enthusiast, but it was remarkably short on traditional date activities, unless the woman in question happened to be an avid hiker or mountain biker. And while he shouldn't discount anything, he didn't think that fit Rose. There were several nice restaurants in the surrounding towns of Salida and Buena Vista, but he instinctively knew that she would be drawn to something that was exclusive to Haven Ridge.

And then just as he was falling asleep, he had it.

Which might have been why when he ran into Rose the next morning in the kitchen—looking mussed and pretty in her pajamas with a cup of coffee in hand—he blurted without preamble, "How do you feel about horseback riding?"

A smile curved her lips, eyes lighting with amusement, and she perched on the edge of the stool behind the island. He was momentarily distracted by her shapely legs below the hem of her shorts. When he raised his eyes to her face, her widening smile said that she'd noticed too.

"How do I feel about horseback riding in general? As a mode of transportation? As an Olympic sport?"

Will chuckled, though he felt heat rise to his cheeks. He hadn't exactly gone about this directly, had he? "How do you feel about horseback riding with me at some point in the near future as a date?"

"I think," she said slowly, her eyes glinting with mischief, "that sounds delightful. There's a riding stable around here somewhere?"

"Not quite," Will said with a smile. "But I do know someone who has horses and he'll be very happy to have someone come exercise them for him."

Now her expression turned a little worried. "These aren't working horses or show horses or something, are they? Because I can ride, but not well. I just used to do some trail riding back in North Carolina."

How had he not known she was from the South? Maybe it was because there was only the faintest trace of an accent in her speech, and that could have just as easily been a faded Midwestern twang. There was far too much that he didn't know about her still.

But he hadn't answered her question. "Not even close to show horses. More like fat, lazy ponies that get treated like pets and need some movement in their lives."

Rose chuckled. "I can relate to that. When?"

Erin entered the kitchen on the tail end of the sentence. "Oh good! You told him!"

"Told me what?" Will frowned at her.

"Sorry," Rose said quickly. "I got distracted. Your brother just asked me out on a date. To go horseback riding."

"Ooh," Erin said, winking at Will. "Good one, bro."

"I thought so. Tell me what?"

"We have something we want to show you."

Will looked between Rose and Erin, who both looked like they were holding back excitement. That alone should make him suspicious. "Is that what you two have been doing this weekend? Don't think I didn't notice you weren't cleaning out any of the rooms."

"And here I thought he was too busy carving you presents to notice," Erin said to Rose teasingly.

"Oh, I notice everything," Will shot back. "But it's not like you don't deserve a weekend off once in a while, especially after what we found."

"This is a proper presentation," Erin said. "So when could we make an appointment for a little of your valuable time?"

"How about now?"

"How about when I'm wearing something other than pajamas?" Rose shot back with a grin. She hopped off the stool, and he followed the movement again, got a smirk from his sister which he ignored. "I'll go change now. Meet in the office in twenty minutes?"

"Sounds good. Though now you've got me curious." Were it just Erin alone, he'd be worried, but whatever it was, Rose seemed to be involved. Hadn't she said that she worked at a nonprofit organization back in Milwaukee before she got divorced?

"Twenty minutes," she repeated with a smile that he felt in his gut, and then she slipped out of the room, coffee mug still in hand.

Erin watched him watch her go. "Oh, you're done for."

Will snapped his attention back to his sister. "We barely know each other."

"And yet you can't take your eyes off her. Or your lips, from what I saw last night."

Will rolled his eyes. "Yes, I forgot to thank you for that. You have impeccable timing as always."

"I would say that I had very good timing. From what I saw, another couple of minutes, you would have been sweeping the contents of the desk to the floor."

"That's where you're wrong," he shot back. "I have far too much respect for her to do something like that."

"Who says it would have been your idea?" Erin looked at him significantly. "Just be careful. I know you're not on the rebound, but she might be. She really doesn't talk about her ex at all. I don't think the marriage was happy, but she's only been single for about six months."

"You're afraid I'm going to hurt her?"

"No. I'm afraid she's going to hurt you. And I hate seeing you hurt." Erin gave him a sad smile and squeezed his arm as she passed by. "Twenty minutes in the office. Be ready."

Will watched his sister go and then went to the coffee pot to pour his own cup. Somehow, he'd never thought Erin was paying that much attention to his life. She'd been so busy and she was so relentlessly upbeat— until she wasn't—that it was easy to think that she passed through life oblivious to other people. Obviously that wasn't the truth.

He probably should give Erin a little more credit.

But now, he was more than curious to know what the two had up their sleeves. Had they done more research on the manuscript and found something that was best shown in visual form? And why would that require an actual presentation in the office?

He didn't have long to wait, because Erin and Rose marched into the office exactly twenty minutes later. Rose was wearing jeans and a pretty blouse, but Erin had thrown on a knit blazer and pointy-toed flats with her usual sundress.

"Must be serious if you had to pull out the blazer," he quipped.

"This is serious. Now behave and listen until the end, because Rose and I have been working hard on this."

Erin placed a laptop on the edge of the desk so they could all see the screen and brought up a presentation, professional-looking in color blocks of green and gray. "We would like to present our proposal for the Amelia Bixby Arts Center and Conservatory."

Will sat back in his chair, his eyes widening. But a quick warning look from Erin had him keeping his mouth shut while she clicked over to the next slide.

"In 1941, the Larkspur House opened as a finishing school for young girls who would have traditionally gone to Europe to complete their education." Erin clicked through to a black and white photo of a young woman bent over a desk in what appeared to be one of the downstairs parlors. "However, its headmistress Amelia Bixby somewhat unconventionally emphasized the arts over other domestic skills: writing, painting, music." She clicked through a few other photos, no doubt dug up with the help of Mallory. Despite the fact that Will had been there when Mallory had told them about this part of the history—and the evidence that this had been Rose's idea—he watched the slides with interest.

"With the recent discovery of Amelia Bixby's manuscript and the likelihood that she was the true author of the three Andrew Bixby novels, we are proposing that the Larkspur House be refashioned as an arts retreat center and conservatory for talented up-and-coming artists of all disciplines."

Now Rose stepped in, her voice quiet as if she didn't want to take the focus away from Erin's presentation. The slide shifted to a slide showing a collection of very familiar headshots. "We are blessed with a wealth of artistic talent here in Haven Ridge. Thomas Rivas is an accomplished painter with a master's degree in fine arts and teaching experience at a major university. Liv Quinn is a well-known book editor. And Erin Parker is a talented cellist with experience at one of the largest and most respected symphonies in America."

Will's eyes flickered to his sister, who seemed to be holding her breath, waiting for his reaction. "You want to leave the symphony?"

Erin swallowed hard. "I've already left the symphony. I'm not really on a leave of absence. I put in my resignation."

Will sat back in his chair, stunned, not so much by the fact that Erin was quitting, but the fact she hadn't told him. "You kept this from me?"

"I didn't know how you would react. After all you sacrificed for me, I thought you might be . . . mad."

He just sat there silently for a long moment, mulling the revelation. He'd always known that Erin struggled, that every time she reached some measure of success, she sabotaged herself. He still didn't understand why, but it looked like this time was no different. "And this is what you want to do? You want to give up performing to teach?"

Erin threw a helpless look at Rose, and the other woman stood up. "I'm sorry. Maybe we shouldn't have sprung this on you in this format. I'm going to give you two a little time to talk."

"No." Will waved Rose back down, even though his eyes never wavered from his sister. "What's done is done. If you don't want to perform . . . then you don't want to perform. I don't have to understand it to support it. But . . . do you really want to teach? Here in Haven Ridge? You're better than that."

"Right. Not living up to my full potential and all." Erin pushed herself to standing, her expression crumpling. "You know, this was a mistake. I knew you wouldn't take me seriously. Rose can finish the presentation." And without another word, his sister turned and ran from the room.

Will stared after her, flabbergasted. When he finally managed to pull his gaze away from the door, it landed on Rose, who was looking at him with a sad look on her face. Or maybe it was disappointment. In him?

"She was hoping you'd be supportive," she said quietly. "She was afraid to tell you. She thought it might be easier if you knew that she wasn't just abandoning her music, but actually helping other people."

"I . . ." Will shook his head. "I am being supportive. She can do whatever she wants. I just think that with her talent . . ." He trailed off when he saw that Rose's expression still hadn't shifted. He was missing something big here.

"I know you want the best for her, Will, but talent isn't the only thing that matters. Heart matters. And Erin hates performing. She hates having all eyes on her, judging her. She hates the pressure of feeling like all her mistakes are on display, because she feels like she was never allowed to make mistakes."

"I never told her she couldn't make mistakes. Of course everyone makes mistakes. It's just . . . talent like hers comes around rarely and it feels like such a shame for her to waste it."

"But maybe it's her talent to 'waste.'" Rose pushed to her feet and swiveled the laptop around to face him. "Take some time to finish the presentation. Erin put a lot of work into it. The structure, the schedule, the fees . . . that was all her. All I did was make it look pretty."

Quietly, Rose left the room and shut the door behind her, sealing him in. He stared at the wooden slab, his heart sinking to his stomach.

He wasn't entirely sure how this had gone so wrong so fast. He'd never meant to make Erin feel like she had no choices. He'd supported her in everything, given up his own goals and desires to make sure that she could reach hers. He just wanted her to be happy and successful.

Somehow he'd screwed even that up.

And from the disappointed look on Rose's face, that might not be the only thing.

CHAPTER TWENTY-FIVE

ROSE HAD JUST MADE A BIG, BIG MISTAKE.

She walked away from the study with a knot in her gut and regret swirling in her chest. She'd known there were some complicated family dynamics at work here, but she hadn't realized just how complicated. Even knowing Will's concern for his sister and Erin's supposedly fragile mental state hadn't shown her the full picture.

And she wasn't blaming Will. Perhaps he hadn't been *quite* as supportive as she would have hoped, but they'd sprung the thing on him in the middle of something else. She'd even warned Erin about this course of action. But his sister had been afraid to tell him directly and thought burying it in the middle of the presentation might go over a little better.

Evidently, she'd been wrong.

Will would come around. Rose was sure of it. He just wanted the best for his sister, even if half the time he expressed it the wrong way. She was beginning to realize that he could be thoughtful and considerate, but what came out of his mouth wasn't always the most diplomatic.

In a weird way, it made her like him a little more. His gruff demeanor, his looks, and his intelligence combined would make him too intimidating if it weren't for that touch of awkwardness.

But this wasn't about Will right now, this was about Erin. Rose climbed the stairs slowly to the fourth floor and then knocked on the door. No answer. Slowly, Rose pushed it open and found the room empty. The bathroom door was closed, though.

Rose's heart jumped into her throat as she crossed the room and knocked on the bathroom door. Still no answer. She tried the handle and gingerly pushed it open.

It was empty as well.

Rose let out a breath and shook her head at the direction of her thoughts. Now Will had her doing it. She'd seen that Erin could be emotional and volatile, but she had no reason to think that something like this would push her into self-harm or worse. She was becoming just as bad as Will.

Except those few moments of fear made her understand him a little better. Why he might be walking on eggshells every time Erin seemed the least bit upset. After all, she'd shown no warning that she was disturbed enough to kill herself the first time she tried, so why would he think that he could foresee it happening a second?

Slowly, she moved back into the bedroom, and movement outside the window caught her eye. She crossed to the glass and looked down on the grounds. Just beyond the conservatory in the tangled garden, still dressed in her presentation clothes minus her blazer, Erin dead-headed rose bushes at a furious speed, the ferocious chop of the clippers clearly showing her mood.

Rose smiled. At least she was taking her irritation out on the overgrown landscaping instead of herself, even if the wooden flower that Will had carved her was going to be the only one left at Larkspur House at this rate.

She wound her way back down through the house and into the backyard. She'd barely gotten within speaking distance of the other woman when Erin bit out, "Is he mad?"

"Mad? No. He feels bad about his reaction."

Erin snipped a dead rose into a bucket and looked up, her expression surprised. "*He* feels bad?"

Rose stopped a couple of feet away. "You can't fail to see that he loves you and just wants the best for you."

She sighed and lowered the clippers. "I know he does. It's just. . . he thinks *he* knows what's best for me."

"That's an older brother for you."

"I thought you were an only child."

"I am. But I've seen the dynamic enough. Erin, you are so incredibly talented. I think he just wants to make sure you know what you're really doing. That you're not going to regret it. Some paths are hard to turn from once you're on them. What happens five years from now if you're bored with teaching and you're sorry you gave up your performing career?"

Erin straightened and dropped her clippers into the bucket. "I never wanted to leave Haven Ridge. I love it here. It's the only place I've ever felt at home. And as much as I love the cello, it's the playing I enjoy. Not the rigor or the weird schedule or the life that I've had to live in order to be 'successful.'" She made air quotes around the word. "You know how they say that the fastest way to kill your passion for art is to try to make money from it? Well, I'm there."

"Then tell him that," Rose said softly. "He'll understand."

"Will he?"

"Now I think you're not giving him enough credit. But if you don't sort this out between you—what you want versus his expectations—there will always be this distance between you that you can never close."

Erin softened, her expression turning sympathetic. "Now I know you're speaking from personal experience."

Rose sighed, recalling the strained phone conversation with her mother. "Maybe I am. And trust me. You don't want that."

"You're right. I don't." Erin handed the bucket to Rose. "I'll go do that. You can finish the roses. You know how to cut off all the blooms?"

"I grew up with them. My name isn't much of a coincidence, I guess."

Erin smiled. "Okay then. And while I'm at it, I'll do my best to convince him that you're the perfect person to help administrate the arts center."

"What?" Rose stepped back. "That wasn't—"

"Come on, Rose. I see the way you look at my brother. You don't want to leave, and from what I saw, he doesn't want you to leave either. You have the experience we need. It's a win-win, for all of us."

"Erin—"

"Can't hear you!" Erin sing-songed as she walked away. "Wish me luck."

Rose watched the other woman leave the garden and shook her head. This was what had to happen. Erin needed to take control of her destiny, show her brother that she was capable of more than he thought.

But Rose hadn't truly realized how caught up her own destiny was in this outcome as well.

* * *

After Rose left the office, Will shoved his feelings aside and clicked through the rest of the presentation.

It was . . . good.

Well thought-out, well-presented, and more than that, it honored both the history of the house and the Bixby family's legacy while acknowledging the reality of what it took to maintain a house like this over the long term. Erin's fee schedule was reasonable, and—he suspected Rose might have helped with this part—the projected revenue even after they accounted for the repairs to the house and paying the various staff would be high enough to leave the trust in the black.

Assuming they were able to book out every slot in each session.

He pulled out his own notebook and began to make notes. When the door opened again, he was fully engrossed in extrapolating utility costs under full occupancy for the budget that would need to be made before they could determine if this was feasible. He almost didn't look up, too busy mentally calculating figures. Until he heard his sister's voice.

"Will? Can we talk?"

He jerked his head up and dropped his pencil. "Hi. Yes. Of course."

Slowly, Erin crossed the room and seated herself in the chair in front of the desk. "I'm sorry for springing this on you like I did. I thought it might be easier, but clearly I was wrong."

"Erin—"

"No, could you please just let me talk for a second? I have some things I need to say."

Will stilled and dipped his head in acknowledgment.

Erin took a long, deep breath and let it out slowly. "I love the cello. I loved the cello from the first time I picked it up. Sometimes it's hard for me to express my feelings—the difficult ones—and in a way, it became my voice when I felt like I had none. I appreciate all the sacrifices that you and our grandparents made for me along the way to get me here.

"But Will . . ." Her voice cracked on his name. "I hate performing. I hate being up on stage with all eyes on me. I hate the looks I get if I make a mistake. It feels like . . . it feels like making something intimate public. It would be easier for me to stand on stage naked every day than it would be to continue performing."

Will swallowed at the raw pain in her voice. That was . . . not what he'd expected. He'd thought that perhaps Erin just couldn't cope with the usual performance jitters, that it exacerbated the anxiety that already existed. Except now he wondered if maybe the anxiety was because of performing, and they had just never listened to her closely enough to understand.

"Before you say it, I started seeing a counselor in Chicago before I left, before I considered quitting. And he helped me see that there was nothing wrong with me. That of course I feel trapped, because I'm not living my life for me. I'm living my life for you, and for my dad who I never knew, and for our grandparents. That I've been so worried about disappointing all of you that I haven't ever thought of the costs of disappointing myself."

Tears glimmered in Erin's eyes, and he felt moisture spring to his own. He had to clear his voice several times before he could speak. "Erin. I'm sorry."

"No. That's not why I told you. I don't want you to feel—"

"No, now it's my time to talk." He took a deep breath and considered his next words. He wasn't so good at expressing his emotions either. Now that he thought about it, emotions weren't really a thing in Larkspur

House growing up. Not with grandparents who for all their good qualities had had a stoic "fake it 'til you make it" mentality that they'd passed on to them. "I have only ever wanted you to be happy. I only ever wanted you to accomplish your dreams, no matter what it took. I knew from the time we were kids that you were way more talented than I would ever be, and I couldn't stand the thought that our parents' selfishness or anything else would get in the way of them."

"I know," Erin whispered with a smile. "You've always put me before yourself. But I think maybe it's time that we stop worrying about each other and start making choices for ourselves."

He swallowed and nodded. "Is this really what you want to do? And I don't mean because it's the only way to save the house. Is this what would make you happy? Help run an arts center? Teach music? Stay here in Haven Ridge?"

"Yes. All I've ever wanted was to be part of a community I can give back to. I just couldn't see how to make that happen until Rose came along."

Rose. "This was her idea then?"

Erin nodded. "She doesn't want to take credit for it. And yes, I figured out how it should work. But she was the one who could see how it all came together. How we could make it profitable, how we could market it. We need her to make this happen."

He had to ask. "And what role do you see me playing?"

Erin blinked, legitimately surprised. "As big of a role as you want. I had hoped that maybe you wanted to stay here. Especially because of . . . " She trailed off and bit back a smile. ". . . recent developments. But there's money in the budget to hire you to act as a part-time CFO. Keep an eye on the books. I think Gemma could probably put us in touch with a bookkeeper for the everyday tasks, and she can help us with the legal stuff."

"It would be a big change," he said quietly. "And one I'm not entirely sure I'd be willing to make."

Because let's face it. He'd shared two kisses—two amazing kisses—with Rose, but that didn't mean he was willing to change his whole life to stay here for her. As Erin had said, it was time to start making the decisions that were best for themselves. He wasn't yet sure what that meant for him. He loved his job. He didn't love Chicago, but then again, he had mixed feelings about Haven Ridge, too. If he stayed here to help with the arts center, would that be one more thing he was simply doing for his sister? Or would he be doing it for himself?

"Can I think about it for a bit? Of course I'll help you get set up. Between Gemma and I, we'll be able to establish the business structure. But I think this has to be your project." Sink or swim, it was time that he get out of Erin's way. He could be there for assistance, for advice, but it was time to stop trying to steer the direction of his twin's life.

"Of course you can think about it." Relief dripped from Erin's voice. "So this means you're on board? We're going to do this?"

Will tapped his notebook. "I'm still trying to figure out the numbers. We have to fix the roof and we'd have to convert some things in the house to make it usable for guests. There's still a cash flow issue, and there will be until we have money coming in. But if I can make it work . . . yeah. Let's do this."

Erin jumped up from her seat, circled the desk, and threw her arms around him. "Thank you."

"I should be the one thanking you. You were the one who figured out how to save Larkspur House."

"You're not going to be sorry, Will. You've kept the

trust afloat for years. Now we're going to make sure it lasts."

Will smiled at his sister as she backed away, excitement written all over her face. And more than that, there was a lightness about her that he wasn't sure he'd ever seen, as if a heavy weight had been lifted off her shoulders. He held the smile until she left the room and shut the door behind her.

And then blinked away the moisture that sprang to his eyes.

Because this might be a victory for her, but it also showed him just how badly he'd failed her over the years. How in his attempt to make everything right for her, to make everything perfect, he'd been harming her even more than she'd harmed herself.

He wasn't sure he could ever forgive himself for that.

He didn't know how long he sat there, staring blankly at the paneling in the study, feeling all the bad feelings he habitually pushed down and buried under pragmatism. He almost didn't notice when a knock came at the door. Absently, he answered, "Come in."

Rose pushed the door open, her expression concerned. "You okay?"

He blinked. "Yeah. Why?"

"Well, Erin came out over an hour ago, telling me that you'd agreed to the plan. But you never reappeared."

Will held up his notebook. "I was running some numbers. I told her that we'd need to look at the budget and figure out the cash flow issues for now." In reality, he'd already figured out he could make a small loan to the trust without putting himself in financial jeopardy. If their estimates checked out and they were able to book half the rooms in the first and second sessions—which they were proposing for late fall and early winter—he'd be able to justify the repair of the roof in the spring.

But Rose didn't look convinced as she moved deeper into the room. Instead of sitting across from him in the chair as she had earlier, she circled the desk and perched on the top right next to his chair. Her eyes were gentle, sympathetic even, as she looked down on him.

"Something tells me that might have been harder for you to hear than you thought. After all we've talked about."

Will shook his head and looked away. "I'm glad she told me. I finally understand. I didn't before."

"But you're still going to hold yourself responsible for things you did when you *didn't* understand?"

He chuckled, though it wasn't exactly humor he felt. "Of course I will. What reason have I given you to expect anything else?"

"That's fair." She smiled and pushed herself off the desk. "But I'm hoping that maybe you'll cut yourself a break and move on. I don't think either of you understand how lucky you are to have each other."

Will reached out and grabbed her hand before she could move away. "What about you? I haven't heard about what you think of this whole plan."

She froze and turned back to him, but she seemed to be avoiding his eyes. "I love it. I think you'll be very successful."

"You think *we'll* be very successful? You're not including yourself in that statement?"

"I don't know what I could do, Will. Between you and Erin, I think you've got it covered."

He narrowed his eyes. "What aren't you telling me?"

She flinched. "Nothing. It's just that . . . this isn't my home. And I know I might have gotten a little pushy—I prefer to call it passionate—but when it comes down to it, you don't need me."

Will tugged her back toward him as he rose from his

seat to face her. He took her other hand so she couldn't turn away. "But what if I want you?"

Her eyelashes flickered. "You're offering me a job?"

"Yes. From what I can see already, you understand how to present the idea. You already have experience on the marketing and communications and fundraising side. It was thanks to you that we even discovered the Amelia Bixby connection. I can't imagine creating the Amelia Bixby Arts Center and Conservatory without you. But more than that, I'm offering you a home. I see how much you love Haven Ridge. Could you see yourself staying here long term?"

Something sparked in her eyes, brighter than hope. "Of course I could. But there are things you should know about me. Things that would change your opinion."

He shook his head. "I find it hard to believe that anything you would tell me could change what I think about you. Say you'll stay and help us build it. I can't promise that I'll be here all the time. . . I still haven't figured out what to do about my job. But I'll be here some of the time, at least. Is that something that you could live with?"

Finally, she met his eyes. And slowly, she nodded. "I think I could."

"Good." He bent to press his lips to hers, just a brief, sweet kiss, and then straightened with a smile. "Go let Erin know the good news. And meanwhile, I'll be hard at work here trying to make these numbers work."

Rose smiled and squeezed his hand before she turned and left the room. Almost before the door closed, he was back at his desk, his attention back on his calculations.

He'd told her the truth. He didn't know what his involvement here would look like, but now he had more than one motivation for making this new dream of his sister's work.

CHAPTER TWENTY-SIX

ROSE RODE THE ELATION OF HER SUCCESS through dinner, which she cooked quickly from the disparate collection of ingredients Erin had picked up at the store. At this point, she thought the woman was just doing it to challenge her, to see what she could come up with, which was how she ended up serving pork tenderloin on a bed of roasted, shredded cabbage, broccoli, and apples. They all looked at it doubtfully until they took the first bite—and pronounced it delicious.

But after the dishes were cleaned up and they all retreated to their separate spaces, that elation plummeted, taking her mood with it. She couldn't quite explain it. It wasn't that she wasn't excited about the prospect of having a place here at Larkspur House. . . or rather, the Amelia Bixby Arts Center.

It was simply that she couldn't completely believe it was going to happen.

Because how many other times had she gotten excited about a new situation just to have it come crashing down around her? Every one of those times had involved a man.

She wasn't accepting the job because of Will. That was just a bonus. And yet. . .this all felt way too familiar. Falling in love fast, moving to a new town, taking a job that she thought she'd love, just to have it fall apart with the relationship.

It took several seconds to register the words she'd used, even if they were only in her head.

Falling in love.

Was she really falling in love with Will Parker?

It took only the sight of the carved cherrywood rose, now back on her nightstand as if by magic, to know the truth. Against all odds, against her attempts to the contrary, she was.

Maybe she wasn't all the way there, but she was getting there fast.

And then what?

"And here's the part where you try to sabotage something good because of all the bad stuff that's happened to you," she told herself wryly.

Because every single bit of this was proof. Proof that if she just stayed the course and made her own decisions, she could make her own life, without having every decision second-guessed and micromanaged. Maybe there was something to the magic of Haven Ridge. Because it had sure brought her here at the right time, just when she and the Parkers needed it most.

By the time she'd climbed in bed, she'd mostly managed to throw off the quick burst of pessimism. So what if things weren't perfect? And even if she didn't work out with Will long-term, even if it got too awkward to stay around here, she'd have some valuable experience for her resume. She had helped authenticate a manuscript and uncover a major mystery of American literature. She would have helped start an arts center and created their marketing, communications, and fundraising strategy from scratch. That alone would get her to the next level in her career. There were hundreds of nonprofits starting all over the country every day that needed someone to help them set their direction and get them launched.

She could practically make a career from start-ups like that.

Her fallback position determined, she pulled up the covers with a smile on her face and fell into a deep, dreamless sleep.

Until a knock at her door startled her awake.

Rose sat up, blinking owlishly in the bright light through her window. She could have sworn that she had just closed her eyes a few minutes ago, but a quick look at her phone said it was already nine a.m.

"Rose? Are you awake?"

She threw back the covers and stumbled to the door before she was fully conscious, then threw the door open to Will. He stood there, already dressed, a mug of coffee in his hand. He held it out to her. "Sorry to wake you. I just thought we might want to get a start before it gets too hot. It's easy to underestimate the sun at this altitude."

"I'm sorry?" She accepted the cup of coffee automatically, even though nothing else he was saying seemed to want to penetrate her brain.

"Horseback riding. Remember?"

Rose blinked. "Oh. Right. I'd totally forgotten. You still want to do that?"

Something vulnerable flickered over Will's face before it was subsumed by his usual calm expression. "We don't have to if you don't want to."

"No! I want to. I'd just thought . . . isn't there a lot of work to be done now?"

He smiled. "It can wait a few hours. We wouldn't want to disappoint the ponies, would we?"

Rose chuckled. "I guess not. Give me about twenty minutes and I'll come down to the kitchen."

"Can't wait. Make sure you put on sunscreen."

"Definitely." Rose shut the door, a smile coming to her face. Somehow she'd thought that he would have forgotten about his suggestion in the excitement of their new direction, but it seemed to be the exact opposite. She quickly dug out some skinny jeans from her suitcase and paired it with a white long-sleeved shirt that would protect most of her pale skin from the sun. After she'd washed her face, brushed her teeth, and slathered herself in SPF 50, she grabbed a pair of old cowboy boots from her larger suitcase and made her way down to the kitchen.

Will took one look at her and started laughing.

"What?" she fired back, offended. "You said we were going riding."

"Your cowboy boots. They're . . . pink."

Rose glanced down and cracked a grin. "And they have sparkles. Only thing I have with a proper heel for the stirrups."

"They're adorable," he said, and he really looked like he meant it.

Only then did she notice that he had the griddle going, a batch of pancakes bubbling on the surface. "You went all out."

"Considering it's the only thing I can cook, it's literally the least I can do." He grinned at her and dropped a couple of blueberries into the batch on the right before he flipped them. "Breakfast coming up in two minutes."

"Ooh, do I smell pancakes?" Erin pushed through the door to the kitchen with a hopeful look on her face, then clutched a hand to her chest. "I've died and gone to heaven."

"Someone woke up dramatic today," Will said, throwing a smirk over his shoulder.

Erin stuck out her tongue in return. "And someone seems to be in an awfully good mood. Does *someone* have a date today?" She glanced over at Rose. "Great boots, by the way."

"See?" Rose threw a look at Will.

He held up his hands in surrender, a spatula in one of them. "I stand corrected. They are amazing boots and the ponies will love them."

Erin plopped onto a stool next to Rose. "I thought while you guys are out riding, I would go into town and talk to Thomas and Liv about their parts in this whole venture. See what their schedules look like for the next few months, hammer out the session dates based on their schedule."

"That seems like a good idea," Will said. "I'm assuming you're going to give them first pick and you can fill in with music sessions?"

"Something like that. I also thought I might call the pianist at the symphony. He and I were relatively friendly. I think he might agree to come here on the off season to teach a piano session. Of course, we would have to figure out the whole piano thing . . . ."

Will chuckled. "Maybe we stick to strings for now. Just because the students bring their own instruments."

"That's fair. I quite like the third chair violinist . . . she might be a good option."

Rose let Will and Erin chat about potential session instructors while her mind whirred around the to-do list she should be making. There would be press releases and advertisements. Lots of phone calls. Marketing strategies. Not to mention all the things that actually were required to make a retreat center run . . . the considerations were vast. In fact, she really should be spending her morning just putting down some of these tasks on paper.

"Will, I think she might be hyperventilating."

Will set down the plate of pancakes in front of Rose, snapping her out of her sudden spiral. "You okay in there?"

"Yeah. I just. . . we have a lot of work to do."

"We certainly do. Which is why we should take advantage of a relative lull."

"But I really should—"

Will fixed her with a look. "Technically, the fact that I'm the trustee makes me your boss. So as your boss, I'm telling you to have fun horseback riding with me today. Unless of course that's weird. . . does that make it weird?"

"It makes it totally weird," Rose said, but the playfulness was bringing her out of her momentary panic. "I have lots of time. Erin hasn't even figured out the sessions yet."

"Exactly." Will slid into the seat across from her. "Lots of work, lots of time. But first, ponies."

"I never thought I'd say it, but you might have found someone whose work ethic rivals yours, Will." Erin grinned at the two of them and shoved a bite of chocolate chip pancake into her mouth.

Rose finished her meal, letting the twins' banter flow around her, and at last the tension seeped out of her. When they'd cleaned up and put all the dishes in the dishwasher, Will held out his hand toward the kitchen door. "Shall we?"

Their destination turned out not to be far from Larkspur House, just a few minutes down the highway and then back up a winding dirt road in the hills. Gradually, as they climbed in altitude, Rose saw the landscape change from the piñon and scrub oak that dominated most of Haven Ridge to a sea of evergreens. And then she looked closer. "Are those. . . Christmas trees?"

Will laughed. "That is exactly what they are." He flicked on his signal and made a left-hand turn onto another dirt road. Except this one had one of those ranch-style gates with the overhead rail. The painted sign declared it *Christmas Creek Inn.*

"What is this?"

"It's a Christmas tree farm. Technically, it's also an inn, but that's been closed for a while. Now the owner just grows and sells trees and does sleigh rides and things during the winter."

"I see," Rose said, watching with interest out the window. This dirt road was bumpier, more rutted, and narrower than the last, but it opened into a wide gravel parking lot. Several ramshackle structures, their sides open to the air, dotted the edges. From what she could tell, it was where they wrapped and tied the trees. And beyond that was a log cabin.

No, cabin didn't quite cover it, though that was clearly the style. It was a two-story log house with a wide wrap-around porch on the upper floor and a steeply pitched roof. Almost as soon as Will turned off the engine and they stepped out of the vehicle, a door on the lower floor opened and out walked a tall blond man, dressed almost laughably appropriate in a thin flannel and jeans.

"Travis!" Will greeted the man heartily and they exchanged one of those masculine hug-back-slap things. He turned to Rose. "Travis Miller, this is Rose Cameron. She's working at Larkspur House."

Rose accepted the man's outstretched hand and shook it heartily. He smiled at her, his expression open and friendly. "Welcome to the Inn at Christmas Creek, such that it is. Not really an inn anymore, but the name stuck. I hear you agreed to help me out today."

Rose threw a questioning glance at Will, who just laughed. "I told you that the ponies would be disappointed if we didn't come. It's the off season and they don't get nearly enough exercise when they're not pulling a sleigh."

"Come on, I've already brought them in from pasture." Travis gestured for them to follow and then started up a little dirt trail that wound behind the house.

A few minutes later, Rose drew to a stop. "Those are *not* ponies." The horses that stood already tied in the barn weren't the shaggy, docile little things that she'd come to associate with ponies, but full-grown horses with slender legs and glossy coats.

"Technically, they are, because they're only fourteen hands. But they're quarter ponies. Basically just small quarter horses. I rescued them from a hobby farm a few years ago in Monument. They were in bad shape, but they're doing great now." Travis ran an affectionate hand over the neck of the nearest horse. "This one here is Merry. Will, you'll be riding him."

"Merry," Rose said. "Perfect for a Christmas tree farm."

He grinned. "And this rascal here is Pippin. He'll be yours."

A surprised laugh broke out from Rose. "You named them after hobbits?"

Travis shrugged. "Seemed appropriate. Watch Pippin though. There's a reason why I named him that."

Rose grimaced. "He's going to do something stupid and dangerous that we're going to regret?"

Now Travis laughed heartily. "More like, he forgets what he's supposed to be doing and needs reminding. Gets distracted by butterflies. Tries to eat trees."

Well, that sounded better than a horse that would

take off and leave her careening through the mountains of southern Colorado. Travis showed them how to saddle the horses—Rose refused to call these creatures ponies, even though technically they were small enough to be. And then it was time to mount. She shoved her foot into the stirrup and swung her other leg over the horse's back, then searched for the other stirrup. Pippin didn't move a muscle. It was as if she wasn't even on his back.

Will looked more comfortable when he mounted; obviously, this wasn't his first time riding. Travis unhooked the tethers from the horses' bridles and made sure they had the reins before he opened the barn doors again. "Have fun, guys. Just watch for snakes."

"Snakes?" Rose threw a worried look at Will, but he and Merry were already moving out of the barn.

She clucked her tongue at Pippin and gave him a little nudge and the pony obligingly moved forward. Not fast, but at least he was moving in the right direction.

It didn't take long to realize why Travis had been so excited to see them. The ponies *were* lazy. Once they left the grounds of the tree farm and crossed the road onto another trail leading upward, they perked up a little, their pace quickening as if they were happy for the change of scenery. But it seemed pretty clear she and Will were in no danger of anything but a long, slow ride.

"See, nothing to worry about," Will called over his shoulder, grinning. That smile really should be illegal. It lit up his entire face, and her heart tugged as if it was somehow connected to the corner of his lips. He so rarely smiled that each one, especially those real and unrestrained ones, felt like a personal victory. A challenge to draw more out of him.

The trail was quiet, filled only with the buzzing of

insects and the far-off cry of birds and the soft thud of the ponies' hooves on dirt. They were following a well-worn trail through the trees, and Rose could tell when they left the tree farm and crossed into the actual forest. The evergreens here were less regular, and they towered over them, their tops swaying in a breeze that they couldn't feel down below.

For the first time in longer than Rose could remember, she actually felt relaxed. Happy. As if she didn't have the weight of the world—or maybe the weight of responsibility—on her shoulders. Instead, she lifted her face to the sky and enjoyed the warmth of the sun on her skin; she breathed deeply and noted all the scents that seemed so different from Wisconsin, dustier and drier without the ever-present humidity.

And if she were being honest, she was enjoying watching Will unnoticed. He seemed like a natural horseman—not that their mounts posed much of a challenge—his posture relaxed, one hand holding the reins loosely while the other spread on his jeans-clad thigh. His broad shoulders and back filled out his thin T-shirt nicely, giving her a view of flexing muscle as he effortlessly balanced in the saddle.

At times like this, she had a hard time believing he was an accountant. Not when he seemed so comfortable outdoors or working with his hands.

Somehow, this felt like the real Will Parker. The one who precious few got to see.

As if he felt his eyes on her, he twisted in the saddle. "What?"

Rose's thoughts had been too intrusive to voice aloud, so she went for teasing. "I'm just thinking how at home you seem here. Cowboy is a good look for you."

His flash-smile in response sent a shot of heat through her gut. "Back atcha. Pink boots and all."

Rose was so busy focusing on Will that she didn't notice the snake slithering from the underbrush onto the trail until she heard the rattle. Almost too quickly to register, Pippin reared and twisted away from the snake. Rose clutched desperately at the saddle, clenching her thighs into its sides as he did a one-eighty and then tore off down the trail the way they'd come.

"Rose!" Will shouted after her. "Rein him in!"

Except Rose had no idea how to do that, especially when he was galloping faster down the trail than she thought he was capable of running. She pulled back on the reins but nothing happened. She jostled and bounced in the saddle, clutching the reins with one hand and the saddle horn with the other, silently praying Pippin didn't stumble into a hole or put a foot wrong.

When they came up to the dirt road that they had crossed initially, though, Pippin drew up sharply and stopped in a cloud of dust, as if he had finally realized where he was and that he was out of danger. Rose sat in the saddle, shaking and sweating, but at least she wasn't moving any longer. Only a few moments later, Will approached on Merry at a sedate trot.

"Are you okay?" Will dismounted quickly, Merry's reins in hand, and grabbed Pippin's bridle. But the spooked pony seemed no more interested in running than he did in Will's presence—he was far more interested in nipping the evergreen branch that was edging into the trail.

"I'm fine," Rose said. "No damage to anything but my pride."

"Your pride is the last thing that should be damaged. You did really well."

"I just held on."

"Exactly." Now that he was sure that Pippin wasn't going to bolt again, he let go of the bridle and rested his hand on Rose's knee. "I guess now we know why Travis warned us about snakes. Pippin must have had a bad experience before."

"You think?" Rose threw back, but she wasn't really irritated. Now that the adrenaline was draining out of her, she just felt tired. "I think I'm done with riding for today. On the upside, the horses got their exercise."

Will still looked a bit concerned, but he chuckled and remounted. "That they did. I think we might have as well."

There were no further incidents on the short ride back to the farm, and Travis was waiting for them when they arrived. He took one look at Rose's face and asked, "What happened?"

"Rattlesnake."

He blanched. "I'm so sorry. Pippin has a bad history with snakes. He happened on a nest of rattlers at the old farm and got bitten several times. I give the warning, but I never really expect to see rattlesnakes at this altitude. You okay?"

"Yeah." Rose swung her leg over Pippin's back and lurched down. "I'm fine. At least I didn't fall off. I'll probably be bruised tomorrow."

"She did great," Will said, dismounting. "She got him stopped before they crossed the road."

Rose didn't tell him that the horse had done that on his own; she hadn't done much to help. But she didn't mind his solicitousness when they returned the ponies to the barn, unsaddled them, and brushed them down. His eyes kept darting to her as if to assure himself that she was really all right, and when they said their goodbyes to Travis, he rested his hand on the small of her back on the way to the SUV.

It felt nice to be taken care of for once.

When they were both safely inside the SUV, Rose let out a long breath and a shaky laugh. "So. Exciting day."

Will smiled at her, but it was regretful. "I'm really sorry. That was not quite how I expected that to go. I was hoping for a calm, relaxing ride. We didn't even make it to the creek."

"There's a creek?" Rose asked, disappointed, until she realized that the name of the inn probably should have given it away. "Is it really called Christmas Creek?"

Will laughed. "No. It's Cottonwood. Christmas Creek is just called that because of the tree farm."

"Oh. Well in that case, I'm okay that we missed it." Rose flashed him a smile. "Cottonwood Creek sounds much less magical."

"It actually is pretty magical." He flashed her a smile. "I had it all planned out. There's this boulder above a little waterfall where we would sit. And then I was going to kiss you again."

Rose felt her cheeks pink, not at the idea of kissing him—okay, maybe a little at the idea of kissing him—but the fact that he'd planned it out. Gone to some effort to be romantic. Who knew that practical Will Parker had a sentimental side?

"I don't need a waterfall for you to kiss me," she said softly.

He smiled, taking it for the invitation that it was, and leaned across the seat. But he only brushed his lips against hers briefly before he pulled back. "I had something much more private in mind." He nodded ahead of them, through the windshield where Travis was coming out of the barn. He lifted a hand in their direction.

Rose laughed through her momentary disappointment. "That's fair. Home, I guess?"

"Yes, home."

And in that moment, if she were being honest, that sounded better than anything else he could have planned.

CHAPTER TWENTY-SEVEN

THAT HAD NOT AT ALL gone the way that Will had intended.

He'd been thinking romantic trail ride, a rest at the little waterfall, unquestionably a kiss or two where they wouldn't be interrupted by his twin sister's bad timing. Instead, they'd ended up with a spooked horse and in Rose's case, a bruised behind.

And yet from the way she kept glancing at him in the car on the way home, the fact that she reached across the console to take his hand, he didn't think it was a failure.

He liked Rose. If he were being honest, it went deeper than that, to feelings that he wasn't ready to voice out loud. She was beautiful and intelligent and compassionate. Easy to be around. Made him remember a little bit of who he'd been before he'd let his concern for his sister and living up to his family's legacy take over his own hopes for the future. Had it not been for his desire to do something thoughtful for her, he never would have remembered what it was he liked about working with wood. Not that he was going to quit his accounting job and be a full-time carpenter, but it had been a long time since he had remembered that hobbies were even a thing. Even his daily run, which he'd been ignoring since he got back to Haven Ridge, had become something he did merely to stay healthy, not because it was something he enjoyed.

He wanted to do things that he actually enjoyed. With her.

When they pulled into the driveway of Larkspur House, there was an unfamiliar car in the driveway. No, scratch that. There was an *unexpected* car in the driveway. Because one look at the dark blue SUV and he knew exactly who it belonged to.

As did Rose, apparently. "What is Liv doing here?"

"No idea," Will said slowly. "My guess would be that Erin called her?"

Rose sent him a look. "Are you okay?"

He blinked. For a moment, he genuinely wasn't sure why she was asking that question, until he remembered all the history that had been following him for the last year. "Yeah," he said slowly. "I'm absolutely fine."

She smiled then, and the relief on her face hit him in the heart—not just the fact that she still felt insecure about his feelings for Liv, but the fact it mattered so much to him. He leaned over, took her face in his hands, and kissed her.

This time, it was neither brief nor light, and by the time Rose pulled away, they were both a little breathless. She looked at him, eyes wide. "Okay. Point taken."

He grinned. "Should we see what's going on?"

They climbed out of the car and headed for the front door. Just before he pushed it open, he reached back and grabbed Rose's hand. Not because he was trying to make a point to anyone inside, but because he wanted her to know that he had nothing to hide about the status of their relationship.

Which was good, because when he opened the door, he came face to face with the woman in question.

Liv stepped back, wide-eyed, and almost bumped into Erin behind her. "Oh! Hi! I was just about to leave." Her eyes flicked to their clasped hands, but rather than looking surprised, a smile came to her face.

"Hey, I'm sorry we missed you," Rose said smoothly, letting go of his hand in a way that felt completely natural and not a bit guilty. "I take it that Erin told you we managed to convince Will of our idea?"

She was good, he'd give her that. There was no indication that Rose felt at all uncomfortable, walking in with a guy who had supposedly been in love with Liv the year before. She really was going to be the perfect spokesperson for this venture, given the way she managed to make everyone feel instantaneously at ease.

Liv was fully focused on Rose now, her expression animated. "She did. And I have to tell you, I'm thrilled. More than a little bit intimidated, I'll admit. I know how to edit, and I know how to spot a good book, but I've never thought of myself as a teacher or a coach. It's going to take some time to put together my lessons."

"To be fair," Rose said, "I would think the one-on-one critique is going to be what's most appealing. How often do writers get to spend time with a seasoned editor before they get published? I bet we'll have it filled the minute we announce it. Or at least it will be once I get done hyping everyone up about it."

Liv grimaced, no doubt at the idea of being put on display, but then she laughed. "I'll leave that to you. I'm just going to show up and do the best I can." She glanced back at Erin. "Like I mentioned, I told Thomas that the arts center was on. I'm pretty sure he's already writing his lesson plans in his head."

"Once a college professor, always a college professor,"

Erin said with a grin. "He's going to be brilliant, both of you are."

Will watched the three women talk about their plans for the castle, and he couldn't help but catch their enthusiasm. He'd agreed because the numbers were sound and it offered the best chance they had to keep the Larkspur House under the control of the trust. But until now, he hadn't really spent much time thinking about what it would actually be like. There couldn't be a better place for artists to submerse themselves than a historic building that had witnessed the creation of great works, which was in itself an impressive bit of architecture.

It didn't even matter that he wasn't a part of the conversation. He understood his role. He was there to keep track of the money, make sure that they were thinking long term, all the boring things that the creatives didn't want to think about but needed to be done to make any venture work.

"Let me know when you finalize the dates. Summer really is better for me so I can have Taylor watch the store while I'm here, but I might be able to make the other ones work if I have to. Speaking of which, I need to get back." Liv smiled at the three of them, but her gaze lingered on Will the longest. Something unspoken passed between them, and then she gave him a little nod and a wink as she moved toward the door.

It could be nothing but her approval, congratulations for moving on and finding someone else.

Oddly enough, he felt like he needed it.

"One down," Erin said as the door shut behind Liv. "Thomas said he would be over later when Mallory came into the restaurant. I thought it would make sense to have him look at the rooms and decide which ones he wanted for art classrooms. The biggest spaces aren't necessarily the ones with the best light."

"Yeah, that was a good idea," Will said. "Let me know what you decide. We'll want to budget for the renovations and equipment."

"And we'll want to have those rooms already outfitted before we take the professional photographs for our brochures," Rose put in. "People will want to see the spaces they'll be working in. That doesn't even include what we'll want to do for the guest rooms." She paused, her eyes widening. "I really do need to go make some lists. And take a shower. I smell like horse."

"Pony," Will put in playfully, but he just nodded. "Lunch in an hour?"

"Sounds good." Rose smiled at the twins and then turned and dashed up the staircase, taking two at a time.

Erin watched her go, and when she was sure she was out of earshot, turned to Will. "So . . . your date. How did that go?"

"It would have been a lot more romantic without a rattlesnake and an out-of-control horse."

Erin grimaced. "Yikes. Yours or hers?"

"Hers."

"Oh good."

Will frowned at her. "Why on earth would you say that? I've ridden a fair amount. She hasn't."

"Yeah, but there's nothing that's more of a mood-killer than a man on a runaway *pony*."

Okay, his sister did have a point, though he still would have rather been the one with the tense experience. "It seems like everything is starting to come together."

There must have been something in his tone, because Erin actually looked suspicious. "But?"

"No, there's no *but*. Between you and Rose, I'm confident that you'll be able to make this work. But I'm beginning to wonder how much of this I can do remotely."

Something like hope flickered over Erin's face. "What are you saying?"

"I don't want to quit my job. I like my job. I *need* my job. But. . .maybe I could arrange it so I could work remotely. So I could be here for a couple of weeks at a time. And then—long term—if the business can support a full-time CFO, maybe I would consider coming back permanently."

Will hadn't even realized he was going to say the words until he did, even though it was all true. He didn't want to quit his job, though the fact that he hadn't even started reviewing the records for his next case didn't exactly make an argument for how productive he could be while he was at Larkspur House. Still, there was literally no difference between doing the work on his computer in the office in Illinois or in the office in Colorado. He'd have to fly back for meetings and to give testimony, but there were firms in his industry who hired out-of-state employees all the time.

And that's when he realized that in the scenario he was envisioning, his home wasn't in Chicago. It was in Haven Ridge.

Erin was watching his face as all these thoughts flew through his head, her smile growing wider every second. "Can't stand to leave her behind?"

He was all set to argue against it, but he found he couldn't. "No," he said finally. "I can't."

His sister let out a happy sigh. "Good. It's about time."

Inwardly, he was thinking the same thing, but he wasn't going to say that aloud. "I'm going to the office to review some documents while I wait for Rose to get out of the shower. She's not the only one who smells like horse."

"Pony," Erin cut in, but he just waved her off while he headed for the staircase.

He wasn't crazy, was he? This could actually work, assuming he could convince his boss that it was sustainable and wouldn't affect his output. At this point, he was the second most senior forensic accountant at the firm, as well as their most accomplished fraud investigator. Hadn't he told Rose that if he had access to someone's accounts, he would know everything there was to know about them? People might lie to your face, but income and expenditures never did.

His laptop was still waiting for him on the desk, and it only took a couple of minutes to boot it and connect it to his phone as a wireless hot spot so he could access the documents in the drive through his company VPN. There had been a number of folders and files added since he last checked, records from various employees of the company, it appeared. *Egard, Melissa. Geary, Delano. Kelly, Rose.*

His eyes snagged on the third name. He'd never met a Rose in his entire life, never seen one in a deposition either. And now two in the same month. Maybe it was something like white cars—you never realized how many of them were on the road until you bought one and then started seeing them everywhere. Idly, he clicked on the folder. Just a resume and a handful of expense reports from the look of it. Standard due-diligence sorts of records.

Until he noticed the name on the resume file: *Rose Cameron.*

A wash of heat went over him, followed by a downward rush of cold, as if all the blood in his body had left him. Surely this was just a coincidence. After all, what were the chances . . . ?

He clicked on the file, his fingers moving automatically even while his brain stuttered over the mad thoughts whirling through his head.

The resume opened, a neat and modern-looking layout with *Rose Cameron* in block letters across the top. The address was in Chapel Hill, North Carolina. Degree from Brown and an unfinished master's/PhD program at Chicago Loyola.

Will swallowed hard, still unable to believe what he was seeing. It could all still be a coincidence. Because if *this* Rose Cameron was *his* Rose Cameron, she would have told him. She would have said something, especially knowing what he did for a living. Especially knowing that they had lived less than ninety minutes away from each other.

There are things you should know about me. Things that would change your opinion. Wasn't that what she'd said when he offered her the position, asked her to stay? And idiot that he was, he thought she'd been speaking about personal matters. Had brushed her off.

Hadn't wanted anything to change his opinion of her when for the first time in his history, he was actually happy. Actually making strides toward the life that he wanted, not the one he thought he should live.

No, he wouldn't believe it without good reason, without proof.

He started flipping through files until he found the dossier for the main object of their investigation, the son of the nonprofit's founders, Jordan Kelly. And sat back in his chair, gutted by what he saw on the screen.

Spouse: Rose Cameron Kelly

The room spun around and for a moment he thought he was going to be sick. It was no mistake and it was no coincidence. Rose had been married to a man who was accused of embezzling from his family's nonprofit organization.

A knock at the door dragged his attention away from

the computer screen, and the door cracked open. Rose poked her head in. "I'm done with the shower if you want to use it."

Will just stared at her. Rose stepped inside, her brow furrowing. "Is there something wrong?"

It took Will another several seconds to get his voice to work, but when he did, even he heard the coldness in his tone.

"Why didn't you tell me you were being investigated for fraud?"

CHAPTER TWENTY-EIGHT

It was remarkable how quickly a future could come crashing down.

Rose stood in the doorway like a trapped animal, afraid to move or even breathe, as all her anticipation, all her excitement for her life here at Larkspur House came caving in on her. "How did you find out?"

"I say you're being investigated for fraud and the only thing you can ask is how I found out?" Will stared at her, his tone incredulous but his expression so cold she had to repress a shiver. This was the Will Parker she'd known was lurking underneath, the one she'd secretly somewhat feared.

Binary, Erin had said. On or off. And right now, she knew that every warm feeling he'd had for her was off.

Slowly, she approached the desk and lowered herself to the seat in front of him. "I tried, yesterday. When you offered me the job. You didn't want to hear it."

"You should have tried harder, Rose. This isn't some minor thing. You're being accused of defrauding a nonprofit just like the one you're trying to get a job at. You didn't think I would find that suspicious?"

Immediately, Rose stiffened at the accusation in his voice. "First of all," she said sharply, "*I* am not being accused of fraud. Every single person involved in this case knows I had nothing to do with it. My *ex-husband* is the one being accused of fraud. Why do you think I walked away with nothing but the clothes on my back? Why do you think I'm twenty-eight years old with a fantastic resume, but I answered an ad for a house assistant in Nowhere, Colorado? Because he ruined my life. He embezzled money, telling me it was from various investments that I didn't have access to. He lied to me for more than three years. And he made me the focus of a police investigation.

"And after all that, even the authorities could tell that I had nothing to do with it."

That seemed to cool a little bit of Will's ire. He sank back into his chair and rubbed his temples with his fingertips. "I believe you. I haven't even looked at the records, and I believe you."

She blinked. "Why?"

"Because I know you, Rose." His voice was pained, and beneath his tight expression, she dared to think she saw the slightest glimmer of the affection—perhaps even love—that she'd glimpsed over the last few days. "I know you're not capable of something like this. And judging from how few files I actually have on you, everyone else does, too."

Rose let out a long sigh of relief. "Good. Because I was starting to worry—"

"But you have to understand this changes things."

She froze, her skin prickling. "How?"

"Rose, my first responsibility is to the trust, and now to this venture, whatever it's going to be. How is it going to look if I hire someone to run the whole thing—including fundraising—when she's being investigated for embezzlement? All it would take is one person to make the connection between your maiden name and your married name—and see some news from Chicago—and it's over for us. Not a single person is going to feel secure in giving us any money. Our reputation would be ruined before we even started."

Now Rose sat back in her chair, all the fight leaving her. "I didn't do anything wrong, but now I'm being punished for it?"

"You had to know it was a potential problem or you wouldn't be using your maiden name."

"I'm using my maiden name because my husband was a criminal who lied to me from the day we met. Whose parents tried to pin this whole thing on me to get their precious baby boy out of trouble yet again. Why would I ever want to bear that name? It has brought me nothing but pain."

Will blew out his breath and rubbed his face again. "Maybe if you could wait a little while . . ."

"Wait for what? For the investigation to be finished and for me to be clear? Let's assume I did. Then what? You're the one who has to clear me. You don't think investigating a woman you're dating is a conflict of interest? Anyone who catches wind of my past is going to think that you overlooked evidence because of our relationship so you could hire me. Or worse. That you were in on the whole thing and we've just started a new scam."

Rose could tell that Will hadn't even thought that far down the line, because his expression turned a little sicker with each word.

"Let's face it," she said, her voice catching on the words through her tight throat. "I can't be within a thousand miles of this arts center without casting suspicion on it. And I was just fooling myself otherwise because I wanted it so much."

Rose swallowed hard, her throat aching and her eyes stinging. "I'm going to go now. I need to pack. And call my mom to tell her I'm coming home."

Will jumped from his seat and circled the desk in a flash. He reached out to grasp her arms before she could go. "Rose, please. Don't."

"Why should I stay? You and I both know that this is what Larkspur House needs. And you need it, don't deny it. No matter how you might feel about your childhood here, this place is part of you, and you need to save it. Erin can't do it by herself."

"And what about what I want?" he asked, his voice hoarse.

Rose looked at him. "Can you look me straight in the eye and tell me you could walk away from everything for me? Give up the trustee position? Let someone else handle the finances for the arts center? Could you back away from this case and let it go to someone else at your firm, someone who is less qualified to handle it than you?"

She took a deep breath and made her voice hard. "Could you burn down your entire life for a woman you've known for three weeks?"

Will looked stricken, each word impacting him like a blow. She saw the moment that the hope went out of his eyes, when he realized it was pointless. When he registered how much he would have to give up in order to have her.

For just the slimmest chance that whatever was between them might be real and true and lasting.

"That's what I thought," she said quietly. She stepped close and stretched up on her tiptoes to press a soft kiss to his mouth. "Thank you for reminding me that there are some honest men in this world. That alone made this all worth it."

And without another word, she turned and left the study.

CHAPTER TWENTY-NINE

Rose returned to her room, her heart heavier than even her steps. Now that she was away from Will, her brave facade crumbled and tears slipped down her face. She wasn't even sure which hurt more—the fact that she would never find out if what she had with Will could have grown to something real and special or the fact she had to leave behind the one place that had ever felt like home.

She stopped in her first room on the fourth floor— the one where she had inadvertently climbed into bed with Will the first time they'd met—thinking to retrieve the few items she'd left in the closet there. Somewhere in the time that she and Erin had been working on the presentation, Will had removed the soaked mattress and cleaned up the mess, leaving only the antique bed frame standing like a wooden skeleton in the middle of the room. She moved quickly past it, collected the shoes and the handful of blazers that were still hanging in the walk-in, and rushed just as quickly back out.

Not quickly enough, though, because Erin was waiting in the hallway when she emerged. She took one look at Rose's tear-stained face and gasped. "What happened?"

Rose couldn't bear to see the look on Erin's face when she told her, so she turned away and started down the hall. "I'm leaving."

Erin trailed after her. "What? What do you mean you're leaving?" She grabbed Rose by the arm to pull her to a stop, and one of the jackets slipped out of her hands and onto the parquet floor. "What did my brother do? I'm going to kill him—"

"It's not him," Rose said hoarsely. "It's me. I haven't been entirely truthful with either of you about why I came here."

Erin froze and slowly, her hand dropped from Rose's arm. "What do you mean?"

"You should probably ask your brother. He can explain it better than I can." Rose swallowed hard. "Please believe that I never meant to hurt either of you. I just wanted so badly for this to work. I wanted so badly to belong here that I overlooked all the reasons why I couldn't."

This time, when she turned away and headed down the hallway to her bedroom, Erin didn't follow.

Well enough. She didn't think she could face Erin when she learned that she was abandoning her to accomplish their mad, beautiful plan for Larkspur House by herself.

It took surprisingly little time to pack her things, mostly because she had so very little to her name. She'd been a struggling doctoral student when she'd met Jordan, and she'd never thought his generosity, his eagerness to provide her with the things that she couldn't afford, things she'd never even dreamed of, had been a way to hide his misdeeds. For all she knew, marrying her had been part of his grand plan.

She ground to a halt. Somehow, that possibility had never occurred to her. Jordan was scum, there was no doubt about that. But the embezzlement had started shortly before they'd met. Had he only married her to be a scapegoat? Had she been his "get out of jail free" card?

Was anything about their relationship real at all?

Why that should crush her now, seven months after she'd known the marriage was over, she didn't know, but the weight of the thought dropped her to the edge of the bed, her chest tight. Somehow, she'd deluded herself into thinking that he'd fallen in love with her despite his faults. Not that every last touch and kiss and profession of love had been cultivated to gain her trust and exploit it.

She was even stupider than she'd thought. Rose picked up her cell phone to call her mother, but she didn't have it in her to hear *I told you so*. Instead, she dialed her dad's office line. But it only went to voice mail.

She waited for the beep before she left the message, her voice cracking. "Hey Dad, it's Rose. I . . . I'm coming home. I just finished the job in Colorado and I'm not sure what I'm going to do next. I was hoping I could move back in for a few months while I find something new. It will take me a couple of days to get there, so . . . call me if that's not okay, I guess."

But that wasn't going to happen. Her relationship with her parents might be strained, but they would never tell her she couldn't move back home. There would simply be a price attached to their generosity.

Rose could see her future laid out ahead of her now. Her mother would pull strings to get her accepted into the literature doctoral program at Duke. Given Rose's discovery of the manuscript here at Larkspur House, she might even get the chance to coauthor a paper with her mother and help in the authentication of the book. She'd of course change the focus of her dissertation to the Andrew/Amelia Bixby novels. The discovery would make her name in academia and set her up with at least an assistant professor position at a decent university in the southeast.

And if she didn't want that path, there was always an editorial position for the academic line of her dad's publishing company.

She'd eventually make enough to purchase a small house ridiculously far away from the city, and maybe she would meet and fall in love with an academic or a software programmer or someone who wanted the white picket fence and a smart career-focused wife who nevertheless had the time to pick the kids up from school and make cookies for the bake sale.

And the whole thing made her want to scream.

Because what she wanted was a small town where everyone knew her name and her business. A hundred-year-old house with hand-carved flowers for cornices and creaking floors and ceiling water leaks. A man who smiled so infrequently that coaxing one from him felt like a personal victory. Who could take her from irritated to laughing to yearning for him in seconds with a single touch.

She was in love with a person and a place and a life that could never be hers, because she'd been too credulous and believed it when a smooth-talking man said he loved her.

Rose didn't even bother to pack neatly. She threw all her clothes on the bed in a pile, folded them inward on themselves, and stuffed them in whatever suitcase would fit them. She piled her shoes in boxes, including the stupid pink cowboy boots that she would most certainly never wear again. At the last minute, she remembered all her toiletries in the bathroom, which she swept into her zippered bag.

She was turning away from the counter when her eye caught a small glass spray bottle with an expensive-looking minimalist label. She lifted it to her nose and sniffed, even though she already knew it was Will's cologne. And then, because right now pain was better than the creeping numbness that was slowly overtaking her, she sprayed a little on the inside of her arm.

His scent would be with her the whole trip home, fading only when she was far enough away to accept that she would never see him again.

It took supreme effort to get her huge suitcase down the stairs to her car, and two more for the second suitcases and boxes. The whole time, she expected Will or Erin to catch her, to tell her that it had all been a mistake and she shouldn't leave, that they would find some way out of this mess. Or at least to help her pack her things up and say goodbye.

But she met no one on the stairs or in the wide, beautiful, deserted hallways. Until it was just her standing at the door of her battered three-thousand-dollar Volvo, staring up at the stone castle that for a moment she'd dared to believe could be her home.

And this time, when she finally climbed into her car and made the wide turn around the parking area, she didn't look back.

* * *

Will stared at the polished wooden shelving of the study for what could have been minutes or hours, not seeing the books or the place where the shelf needed to be repaired or the slight peeling of the wallpaper that he'd been vowing to fix for at least the last year.

He was too busy trying to figure out how to fix this mess.

He knew what he should have done. He should have told Rose that her past didn't matter, that they would find a way to clear her name, that they would figure out a way that she could stay without her husband's misdeeds casting a pall on the whole venture.

He should have told her that he'd give up the case to someone else just so there would be no question of favoritism or conflict of interest.

He should have told her that he was falling in love with her, and the chance to see where their relationship might go was more important to him than any job or trust or responsibility.

But he hadn't, because all of those doubts and responsibilities had clouded his mind and clogged his throat. The idea that if he was wrong this time, he wouldn't just be letting down his sister, but also his family's legacy and the entire town of Haven Ridge.

And because he was afraid that he would be burning down his entire life, not for a woman who loved him, but a woman who would soon find out that she didn't.

He was thirty-six years old and he hadn't had a serious relationship that had lasted more than a year. Every single time he thought he was getting close to something permanent, they'd broken up with him. Said he was too humorless, too focused, not spontaneous enough. He was a "great guy" but it just wasn't the "right relationship" for them. It was why he'd never made a move on Liv. Because he liked her company, and the chance of ruining their friendship was greater than the chances that they'd work out.

And as it turned out, he had been right. Liv had met a man who was freer, more passionate, less bound by rules and strictures and routine.

Not that he regretted it. It wasn't until he'd met Rose that he'd realized why he and Liv would never have worked out. Their relationship had been completely one-sided. Through no fault of hers, he'd given without asking anything back, taking responsibility for his best friend's wife and daughter because he thought it was the right thing to do.

No woman wanted to be merely a duty or an obligation.

Erin burst into the room, interrupting his train of thoughts. "What did you do?"

Will frowned. "What did *I* do?"

"Rose is leaving."

"I know." He swallowed. "Erin, she's my case. The one that I'm supposed to start on? She's one of the people I'm investigating."

That halted Erin in her tracks. The first kernel of doubt appeared on her face. "The embezzlement investigation?"

"Yes. Her husband—her ex-husband—is accused of defrauding contributors to the family's nonprofit."

"But she didn't do it. You know she couldn't have."

He sighed. "I won't know for sure until I start the investigation, but no, I don't think she did it."

"So then, what's the problem?"

He didn't even have the heart to go into it with his sister. "Long story short, we cannot hire an employee— or even a volunteer—who is actively being investigated for fraud. Not if we ever want to make this idea of yours work. Not if we want to save the house."

"It was her idea," Erin said, but her protest was half-hearted. She sank down into the chair in front of his desk. "What now?"

"We go on without her as planned, I suppose. Everyone is on board. We hire an administrator to help you with the details. Considering you hired Rose without consulting me, I figure you can handle that much." It was a low blow, but it didn't even seem to strike. Erin was staring at him as if he'd lost his mind.

"I'm not talking about the house or the trust. Forget that. I'm talking about you. You're in love with her."

"And after some time, I will fall out of love with her. I've had a lot of practice at that."

Erin just stared at him. "I can't believe you just said that."

Will sighed. "You know I have rotten luck with relationships."

"You just admitted that you're *in love with her*, Will. And you're still going to let her walk away from you?"

Will stared at his sister, the words' implication of the words sinking in.

Erin leaned forward, folding her arms on the top of his desk. "You've sacrificed what you wanted for long enough. For me, for this family, for this house and this trust. If you want her, go get her. Don't throw away something potentially great because you're scared of everything you'll lose. We'll be fine. We have to be fine. Because I believe everything happens for a reason, including how Rose came into our lives."

The silence stretched between them. And then Will pushed to his feet and walked out of the room without another word.

He took the steps up to Rose's room two at a time.

Where he found it clean and empty. No clothes hanging in the closet. No battered suitcase pushed into the corner. It was exactly as it had been when she came, except for the cherrywood rose sitting precisely in the center of the nightstand.

His chest squeezed as he lifted it and turned it over in his hands. She had been the one who had lied to him—or at least omitted the truth—but now he felt like the one who had committed the betrayal.

Erin came into the room behind him, breathless. "She's gone?"

He turned and held up the rose. "And left this." He brushed past his sister and broke into a run in the hallway, taking the stairs down as quickly as he dared. He burst out of the front door, certain he was going to see Rose struggling to heft her suitcase in the back like last time. He'd take it from her, set it down, and tell her in no uncertain terms that he wasn't letting her go anywhere. That they would work it out somehow, because she was important enough for him to fight for. To give up whatever he had to in order to make it work.

Because he loved her.

But when he broke out onto the front steps of Larkspur House, there was no Volvo, no Rose.

Only an empty spot where her car used to be.

CHAPTER THIRTY

IT TOOK TWO DAYS AND SIX TANKS OF GAS to drive from Haven Ridge to Chapel Hill, mostly because Rose was afraid if she stopped, she would turn back. Not just because of what she was going toward, but because of what she was leaving behind. She had to stop every three hundred miles or so to fill up the Volvo—which got only slightly better than abysmal gas mileage—use the restroom, and pick up gas station snacks that would get her through the next three hundred miles. Gradually, the scenery got greener and less desert-like, a sign that she was leaving the Midwest for good and entering the South.

She realized when she stopped in Arkansas late that night and got a motel room that was little more than a concrete box with curtains and an equally concrete-like bed that from now on she would be stopping only for gas and not for snacks. Her bank account had dwindled to an embarrassingly low balance, and with no credit card in her own name, she risked getting stuck with no way to get home. She had visions of herself washing dishes or waiting tables in some small-town Georgian diner, just to afford her last tank of gas. Because there was no way she was calling to ask her parents to transfer money into her account at the age of twenty-eight.

Unfortunately, all that driving gave her plenty of time to think about her bad decisions and what a wreck she had made of her life. She replayed the inevitable lecture she would receive when she walked through the door, hoping to inure herself to its impact by anticipating it. If she had only listened to her parents in the first place, taken the sensible route, she would already be settled in her life and her future career. True, it was a life and career she didn't want, but she couldn't say she was particularly enjoying a cross-country drive in a rust-bucket of a car with every last thing she owned packed in the trunk. She'd been so eager to escape the tedium of the life that her parents had planned for her that she had forgotten to account for her complete lack of alternatives.

Her cell phone rang just as she was climbing between scratchy sheets for the night—the iffy-looking comforter tossed across the room and her air conditioning turned on high against the southern summer humidity. She reached for the phone and her heart sank. Her mother.

"Where are you?" Elizabeth Cameron asked without preamble.

"Mountain Lake, Arkansas."

"Where in God's name is that?"

"I don't know, Mom, somewhere on Highway 40. I got tired so I got a motel for the night. I'll be home by tomorrow night. I think I've got something like eleven hours left to drive."

The line fell silent, and Rose braced herself for the incoming lecture. But her mother only said, "Okay. We have your room made up for you. Call us when you're in North Carolina so we can be sure to be home."

Because her parents were such party animals that

they'd be out on the town at nine p.m. on a weekday. But she was so grateful that her mother was holding back her opinions that she said, "I will. Thanks, Mom."

"You're welcome. Oh, and your dad says hi."

Rose chuckled at that, because she could just imagine her father putting down his book and saying, "Oh, is that Rose? Tell her I said hi." It hadn't varied in the decade since she went away to college.

The ache that the memory brought came as a complete surprise.

"Tell him I said hi too. I'll be home tomorrow one way or another."

"Good. We can't wait to see you." And then the line went dead.

Rose stared at her phone. Had her mother been abducted by aliens and returned as a pod person? Because in her entire life, she didn't think Elizabeth Cameron had ever said *can't wait to see you.*

Don't make too much noise when you come in, I have to be up early tomorrow, maybe. Or, *couldn't you have timed it to make it home for dinner? I have a lecture at eight.*

Someone had to be dying. That was the only explanation for it. Or maybe they thought *she* was dying. After all, she'd made it pretty clear that would be the only way she'd ever voluntarily move back to North Carolina after the heated argument they'd had when Rose had accepted Jordan's proposal.

Rose plugged her phone in and set it on the nightstand, then clicked off the dim bedside light, plunging her into darkness. The neon from the gas station across the street shone through the thin window curtains, casting muddy patterns across the ceiling.

Somehow the idea of dying didn't feel too far from the truth. What she'd managed to avoid thinking about on the long drive while she practiced her responses to her mom's snarky comments was the hollow in her chest. She'd always thought that the association of the heart with love—metonymy, her English degree reminded her—was an ancient conceit, from the times when they also thought that a person's soul resided in the liver. But now, she realized heartbreak felt like a physical thing—a constriction in her ribs, an ache in her chest that was most definitely not symbolic.

She remembered the way that Will had kissed her in the car, held her hand when they'd walked into the house, claiming her publicly as his own. A mere hour before he'd rejected her in favor of his responsibilities. It didn't even matter that it wasn't fair, that she'd brought it on herself by not being honest from the start. Those had been the happiest moments of her life, not just because of him but because she'd actually believed that things would work out for a change. That she'd finally found a place—and the person—that felt like home.

Rose tormented herself with memories until the early hours, replaying every interaction she'd ever had with Will. She tried to linger on the ones where he'd been gruff and dismissive, but those were fading already. Instead, she could only remember how he'd kissed her in the library, sweet and restrained until he hadn't been, just beginning to hint at a passion that he kept so carefully hidden, that she would now never get to uncover.

When she woke, sunshine streamed through the thin curtains, splashing across her face. She pushed herself up and jolted at the bright red numbers on the digital alarm clock on the nightstand. 10:05. She hadn't even started her day and she was already behind.

She jumped out of bed, took the quickest shower of her life—helped along by the grimy tile that reminded her not to linger—and dragged her small suitcase out of the room and back to her car. A quick trip to the vending machine—oatmeal cookies and pistachios counted as breakfast, didn't it?—and she was back on the road, heading for a life that she didn't want.

It was the most tedious day she could remember. She had just enough money for the gas to get home, so she made the cookies last as long as she could and filled up her water bottle at the next station, counting on a stomach full of liquid as a substitute for food. It didn't work. If she'd been smart, she would have asked for her wages, meager as they were, before she went, but she'd been too crushed to think of it and probably too proud to do it even if she had.

By the time she crossed the border into North Carolina, she was tired, hungry, irritated, and still so heartsick she almost didn't care about the other things.

A little less than four hours later, she pulled up at the curb of the Chapel Hill house she'd grown up in. Almost as if the car itself had a sense of irony, the gas light flicked on. Rose chuckled wearily and killed the engine, even as a single tear slid down her face. Then she swiped it away, grabbed her purse, and staggered up the driveway.

The porch light was on. She realized at the last minute that she no longer had a key and lifted her hand to knock, but before she could, the door jerked open.

Her mother stood in the doorway in a silky robe. "You're home," she said, stepping back to let Rose in. "How was the drive?"

Rose hung her purse on the coat tree by the doorway. "Long. If you don't mind, I think I'd like to grab something to eat and go to bed."

Elizabeth swallowed hard and nodded. "Of course. Your bed is made up."

"Thanks," Rose murmured with a wan smile, intending to move around her mom to the kitchen.

And then, unexpectedly, Elizabeth reached out and pulled her into a tight hug. "I'm so glad you're back," she whispered. "I've been worried about you."

Rose was so surprised, it took a couple of seconds to return the embrace, and the proper words never came. But when she pulled away, she saw legitimate concern on her mother's face.

For the first time in longer than she could remember, she saw her actual mom. Not the tenured professor Elizabeth Cameron, but the woman who had played Barbies on the floor with her, who had read *The Very Hungry Caterpillar* to her at least a million times, who had greeted her after school with cookies when she knew she'd had a big test or a bad day. The realization unlocked something inside her so deep she'd forgotten it was there. Rose started to cry.

And once she started, she couldn't stop.

CHAPTER THIRTY-ONE

ROSE AWOKE TO THE SMELL OF BREAKFAST the next morning. For a long moment, she thought she was back at Larkspur House, even though the smell of Will's cooking had never drifted all the way up to the fourth floor in the morning. And then she rolled over and took in the sight of her childhood room, complete with framed awards on the wall and trophies on the shelves and it all came rushing back.

What she had left behind. The utter ruins of her life. The shame of moving back home with no plans for the future, an incomplete degree and a divorce behind her.

The fact that she had fallen in love with a man who, purely because of circumstance, she could never have.

It was enough to make her want to pull the covers over her head and go back to sleep, but the cooking made her curious enough to instead swing her legs over the side of the bed and push herself to her feet. Wearily, she followed the hallway to the kitchen and paused in the doorway, blinking at the image before her.

Her mother stood at the stove in sweatpants and an old Duke T-shirt, flipping slices of French toast on the griddle as if this were something she did every day.

"What are you doing, Mom?"

Elizabeth twisted to take in her daughter for a second, but her expression never wavered. "Making breakfast, what does it look like I'm doing?" She gestured to the kitchen table with her spatula. "Have a seat. You'll want to eat these while they're warm."

Rose sat down automatically in front of one of the plates that had already been set at the scarred oak. "I meant, don't you have a lecture this morning?"

"I called my TA. He'll teach it."

Now she knew she had walked back into some sort of alternate reality. Her mother was of the opinion that students went to college—especially Duke—to be taught by the person with the doctorate, not their graduate students.

"Are you dying?" Rose blurted.

Elizabeth let out a choked laugh as she stacked French toast slices onto a plate and then brought the whole thing over to the table. "What a thing to ask! Why would you say something like that?"

"Because in my entire life, I can think of two times when you made me French toast. It was always Dad. Or we went out to breakfast."

Her mom pulled out the other chair and seated herself across from her. "And there have been perhaps two times that my daughter had a broken heart."

Rose went still. That was true, wasn't it? The first time had been at age twelve when she'd broken her leg right before her ballet recital and couldn't perform her solo. The second time had been after her high school boyfriend dumped her for another girl the day before prom.

"Mom, Jordan didn't break my heart. Made me question my judgment, my sanity, and every choice I'd made up until that point, but I think I always knew something was off. I just didn't want to believe that I'd made a mistake."

"I'm not talking about Jordan. I'm talking about this other guy. Will, was it?"

Rose stilled with the syrup above her French toast, then jerked when she realized she was flooding her plate. What exactly had she said last night? She remembered pouring out the details to her mom, but she knew for certain that she hadn't said anything about being in love with Will. "Why would you say that?"

Elizabeth fixed her with a reproving look. "Darling, I'm not stupid. Why else would you be so upset about a temporary job not working out?"

"Because he was investigating me for fraud?"

"You didn't do it, right?"

Rose gaped. "Of course not."

"Then there's no reason to be upset about that, either. Time will prove that you're innocent. But that's not why you come running back home and break down the minute you get back. You, my dear, are not a crier."

It was true, though it was more out of necessity than a lack of emotion. There had never been much room for emotion in this house when problems could be solved by logic and reason. "Don't cry about it," her mother had always said. "Think through it."

How she had hated that when she was a child. She'd been convinced that her parents were cruel and unfeeling. But now she realized they just hadn't wanted her to think of herself as a victim. Bad things happened. It was what you did afterward that mattered.

Almost as if she knew the direction of Rose's thoughts, Elizabeth asked, "So what do you plan on doing now?"

Rose cut a piece of her toast with her fork and chewed the bite slowly to give herself time to think. No, to give herself courage for the groveling that had to come next. "I thought I might see if I could finish my PhD program. I know I would have to start from scratch, but I'd change my dissertation topic anyway. It doesn't make any sense not to study the Bixby books and this new manuscript, particularly since I was the one who found it. What are the chances I would get into Duke's program the second time around?"

"Considering I have to accept the candidates, not good."

Rose stilled, shocked by her mother's blunt statement. "You don't think I can hack it? Or is it that you simply don't want me there?" She should have known that the kind and caring mother was just a facade. Now she was going to get the lecture that she'd been bracing herself for since she left Colorado.

"I'm sure you can hack it. I just don't think you want it. If your PhD had been really important to you, you would have finished it in the first place."

"I got married!"

Elizabeth fixed her with a reproving look. "And you're telling me that you couldn't have delayed the wedding a year? That you couldn't have told him that you needed to live somewhere between Milwaukee and Chicago until you finished your program?"

Well, when she put it that way . . .

But that didn't matter now. "There are other schools then, if you won't have me. UNC Chapel Hill, NCSU . . . Or maybe I'll just take that junior editor position that Dad has been pushing me toward for the last ten years."

"They're not hiring."

Now Rose set down her fork with a clank. "Mom, what's going on here? You have been on me about my education for as long as I can remember, and Dad has made it clear that he wanted me to take over the family business someday. And now that I'm back and I'm saying that you're right, that I'll do it, you don't want me anymore?"

Elizabeth pushed away her untouched plate and folded her hands on the table, leaning over them. "Tell me why."

"Tell you why what?"

"Tell me why you love academia. Why you love publishing."

Rose opened her mouth, but nothing came out.

"That's why. It has nothing to do with us not wanting you. It has to do with you not wanting this life. Rose, do you think we ever wanted to push you into something you hated? Of course not. You were just always so . . . enthusiastic. Right up until the time you rebelled by quitting school and marrying a man that I think we all knew wasn't right for you."

"That's what you thought that was? Rebellion?"

"Wasn't it?"

Rose opened her mouth to say *No, absolutely not,* but she found she couldn't. Maybe she hadn't recognized it as such at the time—she'd truly thought she was in love, swept away by Jordan's intelligence and passion and sophistication—but hadn't it been more about rejecting the plans that her parents had for her than what she wanted for herself? She'd truly loved working at the literacy nonprofit, but if she were being honest with herself, it hadn't been the literacy part that got her excited. It had been the administration, the fundraising, the challenge of working with so many moving parts and different personalities to make a worthwhile endeavor function. In her day-to-day life, books and literature had been the backdrop but not the focus of her work.

She could have done that anywhere.

But giving it all up for love was more acceptable than quitting everything she worked for because she didn't want it anymore. Had never wanted it.

"That's what I thought," Elizabeth said softly.

Rose tunneled her hands through her hair and hung her head over her half-eaten breakfast. "So what do I do now?"

"What do you want to do?"

"What I want to do is go back to Haven Ridge and help Will and Erin start an arts center," she muttered.

"Then what's stopping you?"

"The fact they won't hire me because of my connection to Jordan?"

"That sounds like self-pity. Use your logic, my dear. If you really want to help them with their endeavor, I imagine you can find ways to do it that won't cast doubt on its credibility."

Rose fell silent, thinking. She supposed that was true. Perhaps as an independent contractor who had no access to the money. Someone who wasn't on the board of directors, staff, or administration. A consultant perhaps.

Except there was still the problem that Will was investigating her. He was too straight-laced to ever consider anything that might harm their family trust or put this new endeavor at risk.

"Or is it the man you really want?" Elizabeth asked softly.

Rose jerked her head up. "Why can't I have both?"

"Because sometimes life doesn't work that way. You need to ask yourself, which is more important to you? What you think might be your life's purpose or who you think might be your life's partner?" Her mother's gaze was steady but sympathetic, as if she knew what a difficult choice it was.

It really wasn't all that difficult of a choice, even though Rose knew it should be. Even though she knew it was far more complicated than her mother made it out to be. But even if she were to voice it out loud, she had no real idea how to make it come true.

* * *

Will spent days staring at the list of files in his company database without opening them. Normally, numbers were his refuge. It might sound ridiculous to those around him, but they had always been his way to ignore the messiness that he couldn't or didn't want to deal with, a place where there was only one right answer to every problem and everything made sense.

Right now, nothing made sense.

For a moment, he'd almost been tempted to believe in the magic town nonsense. Because how else could he explain the perfect timing that had been Rose coming to Haven Ridge? They were a tiny town in the middle of nowhere, and suddenly someone showed up just when his sister needed help, who had the exact skills they needed to help them save the house. Who had discovered a family secret and somehow turned that into a sense of purpose for Erin when she was so sorely lacking direction.

Who had unlocked his heart when he thought that he might never love anyone again.

It all felt like it had to have been for some sort of purpose, too coincidental to be mere chance.

Yet by that same coincidence, by that same stupid chance, she had been someone that he was supposed to be investigating. And now it didn't matter what he did. The well was poisoned—or at least that's what they would say in court if this ever went to trial. An expert witness with a personal relationship with one of the parties in the case was easily discredited.

Which was why he hadn't opened any of the files again. Because the minute he did, he was committed.

He could go forward with the case. Yes, he'd had contact with one of the people he was investigating, but he hadn't known it at the time. The chances of anyone ever finding out the connection was slim, and now that Rose was gone for good, it would probably never find its way back to him. He was aware that it wasn't one hundred percent honest, but there had been times when he'd had personal knowledge—if not quite as intimate—of a person of interest in a case and it turned out not to be a problem.

Not only was this a fascinating case, but he was fairly certain just from his initial perusal that Jordan Kelly had embezzled a lot more money than the organization thought. It would bring him immense personal satisfaction to nail the creep, particularly if he got to get on the stand and stare at him while he did it.

Except there was always the chance that his lawyers would try to argue that Rose had been behind it, and no doubt they would uncover at some point the three weeks that she had spent in Haven Ridge. They might subpoena witnesses to make statements that he and Rose had been seen engaging in a personal relationship. No one here would willingly give them up, but he also knew they weren't going to lie under oath. Not that he would ever ask them to.

Which made the decision painfully clear.

Will picked up the phone and dialed the owner of the company, Arlene Vance. She answered her cell phone immediately. "Good morning, Will. I imagine you're calling to tell me you're well under way on the Accelerate Lit case?"

"Not quite. I have bad news for you . . ."

He went on to explain an abbreviated version of the situation—that he had temporarily employed one of the nonprofit members they were investigating before he had looked at any of the documentation, and he was worried about a conflict of interest.

"Hmm. That's a strange coincidence. Still, I don't think it's necessarily a problem. You said it was your sister who hired her, she was there for three weeks, and you let her go as soon as you found out the connection. If anything, it looks worse for her than it does for you. You could always testify to it should it come up . . ."

"There's more," Will said quietly. "She and I were . . . involved."

"Oh." A long silence stretched. "I don't have any choice then. I have to take you off the case. If this goes to court and someone can claim that you were unduly influenced in your investigation by your personal relationship . . ."

"I know."

Arlene heaved a sigh. "It's a blow. This is a complicated case, Will, and you're the best I have. But I think Dana could probably handle it. I've been impressed with her work since you hired her."

"Dana would be excellent," Will said immediately, irrationally pleased that Arlene hadn't made a bigger deal out of it than she had. "And I haven't spoken with Dana at all about it. No one can say I tried to influence the outcome of her investigation."

"I'm not concerned about that," Arlene said. "I'm in the process of closing another big client right now. Money laundering. Mob ties. The FBI says they don't have enough evidence for an indictment, so the client has hired us to find it. It'll be wrapped up by the time you get back to Chicago. When do you think you'll be back in the office?"

Will almost laughed. Erin would be thrilled. All this time and he was finally getting the sort of case that she'd always insisted he should be working. And then his amusement faded. "About that . . ."

"Oh no, Will, don't tell me you're quitting on me."

"Not exactly."

By the time he hung up the phone, Will felt wrung out. Arlene hadn't exactly been pleased with his request, but she also knew that it was easier to accommodate him than hire someone else with his expertise. He'd been counting on it. As soon as he hung up the phone, he went in search of Erin and found her in the conservatory, tapping away at the laptop resting on her knees.

"So, good news."

Erin perked up and shoved aside her laptop. "You got Rose back?"

The words knifed him in the heart. "No. But I did get Arlene to agree to a remote schedule. Working from Haven Ridge three weeks a month. One week a month in the office, and of course, whenever I need to come back for court."

"That's great!" Erin jumped up and threw her arms around his neck. "But are you sure? You always said you would never come back to Haven Ridge permanently."

"I don't know if it's permanent," he said. "But at least until we get the center up and running. It would just be too hard to do it from afar, and I believe in your vision."

Erin smiled at him, but it was a wary smile. "Will, I know you're doing the right thing here, but is a case really worth giving up Rose over?"

He shook his head. "It's not about the case. I had to give that up anyway. There's just too much potential for it to go wrong if anyone's lawyers dig up the connection between us."

"Then it's settled! Call her back, tell her you made a huge mistake, that you love her and you want her to come back."

Will faltered. "I . . . what?"

Erin cast him a reproving look. "Come on, Will. I saw the way you looked at her. I've seen the way you've been moping around the house since she left. Are you telling me that you don't love Rose Cameron?"

"I . . ." He broke off. He had fallen *in* love with her, sure, but that was different. That was infatuation. But real, deep, true love? Surely three weeks was too soon to feel something of that depth. Love took longer. It was built on weeks, months, years of friendship and intimacy . . .

Like Liv, his inner voice prompted skeptically. *You thought you loved her from afar for years, but you never did anything about it. You missed your chance.*

No, he hadn't missed his chance; he'd never wanted to take it. Because deep down, he'd known that what he'd felt for her wasn't entirely romantic. He'd been attracted to her, he'd cared for her, but he couldn't imagine them having a life together. He wouldn't have found it so easy to be apart from her for months at a time if it had actually been love.

Rose had been gone for six days and already he felt like he was being torn apart by her absence. As if he'd done something that he'd never be able to reverse by letting her go, something that he'd always regret.

Maybe it was a romantic notion, but he felt like he *knew* her in a way that he'd never known another woman besides his sister. He might not know the details of her past—who her first grade teacher was, what condiments she liked on her burgers, whether or not she could sing—but he knew that right now, she was at home with her parents, trying to fit back into an old life that was too small for her. Probably looking for a new PhD program and preparing to go back to work at a job that satisfied her family.

And—maybe this was just wishful thinking—missing him. Wishing that it hadn't ended this way. And quite probably, hating him for not being able to answer the only question that mattered.

Could you burn down your entire life for a woman you've known for three weeks?

Now that she was gone, he knew the truth.

Yes. Absolutely.

Because the only future he was interested in was one that involved her. Where she was here with him—and yes, Erin—working to make the plan she'd so effortlessly devised to save Larkspur House a reality. Where he could see her every day. Kiss her and hold her and make her smile.

He pushed to his feet and Erin just stared at him, baffled. "Where are you going?"

"To get some help."

"For what?"

"Fixing it so Rose can come back."

Erin's face split into a wide smile. "Can I help?"

Will smiled down at his sister. "I'm counting on it."

CHAPTER THIRTY-TWO

IF ROSE THOUGHT THAT HER REALIZATION would give her an instant sense of purpose and direction, she was sadly disappointed. Days passed at her parents' house without any idea of what she wanted to do next or how she should proceed. She cooked breakfast, lunch, and dinner. She cleaned out her childhood room, tossing sheaves of paper that contained half-finished stories and very poor sketches.

And she missed Will.

Not just Will, either. She missed Erin and Larkspur House and Haven Ridge. She missed being able to run over to the Brick House Cafe for a burger or a salad and catch up on the town gossip. Chat with Mallory and Thomas. Stop for cookies at the Broken Hearts Bakery and a paperback novel at the Beacon Street Bookshop. Haven Ridge had felt like home in a way that no other place, not even the city she had grown up in, had felt.

It was enough to make her get in her car and drive straight back there, whatever happened with Will notwithstanding. Except she knew that it would be torture to see him and know that she couldn't have him.

Who says you'd even see him? that inner voice said. *He was going back to Chicago. You wouldn't have him, but you'd have Haven Ridge.*

But was that settling? Was that pathetic? Was that her just trying to justify the choices she'd made now that her parents had made it clear that she didn't have the fall-back options she thought she'd had in North Carolina?

She needed help. She needed a second opinion. And oddly, she knew exactly who she needed to call.

Rose checked her phone for the time. One o'clock, which meant that it would be eleven in the morning back in Colorado. Perfect timing. A quick internet search brought up the number she was looking for, and she clicked the number to dial.

The line picked up on the second ring. "Beacon Street Bookshop, Liv speaking."

"Liv. Hi. It's Rose Cameron."

"Rose!" Liv's tone was welcoming, pleased, but Rose didn't think she imagined the surprise in her voice. "I was sorry that I missed you before you left! I wish you had come to say goodbye."

"It was a last-minute decision to go back to North Carolina. I'm sorry. I really did want to say goodbye."

Liv didn't say anything, as if she was waiting for Rose to go on.

"I need some advice and you were the only person I could think of to ask."

"That's a new one," Liv said wryly. "Would this have anything to do with Will Parker?"

Rose grimaced. "Is it that obvious?"

"That there was something going on between you two? Yeah. For someone like Will, holding your hand in public is practically announcing his engagement."

Rose's stomach clenched with guilt at the same time

that her hopes rose. But she knew Will had feelings for her. That hadn't been in question. It was simply that those feelings didn't trump his responsibility.

"Did he tell you what happened? About the case he was working on?"

"Will? No. He's been close-lipped about the whole thing, which is not much of a surprise if you know him. But Erin told me that he had been assigned to conduct the forensic investigation on your ex-husband."

Rose opened her mouth, then shut it quickly. Maybe it was just that she had spent too much of her time analyzing every word of literature, but. . . "*Had been* assigned?"

Now she could hear a tinge of amusement in Liv's voice. "He had to quit the case because of his connection to you. He didn't want to invalidate his findings should they constitute a conflict of interest. To quote Erin, 'Her ex is a real piece of work who stole a lot more money than anyone knows and Will wants him to pay for it.'"

Despite the fact that it was clearly Erin's wording, the sentiment seemed straight out of Will's mouth, and Rose smiled. "He is and he should."

"So. . . not that I don't love hearing from you, Rose, but what can I do for you? I know you didn't just call to chat."

Right. To the point. "I want to come back to Haven Ridge and I was hoping you could help me figure out a way to make it happen."

"Why me?"

Because you have experience in awkward situations with Will in town, Rose thought, but she couldn't say that aloud. "I don't know. Because I feel like we have something in common, being book people. Because you've been there just as long as anyone?"

"Because I know Will the best out of anyone you know and you want to know how awkward it's going to be?"

Liv didn't mince words, so neither did Rose. "Yeah."

"It's not going to be awkward for anyone else. Everyone loves you, Rose. If you live in a small town long enough, you realize that sometimes relationships don't work out. And unless we're blood-related to them, we generally try not to take sides. Things happen." Liv paused. "The bigger question is, how guilty are you going to feel when you see Will around town?"

Rose frowned. "What?"

"I mean, I don't know you, but the fact you're even calling me means that you don't want to hurt him, even if you don't want to be with him."

Now she felt like she'd entered an alternate reality. "I don't?"

Now Liv stumbled. "I . . . it was my impression since you left that you had broken things off with him."

"No! He broke things off with me."

"That . . . doesn't make any sense."

"Why doesn't it?"

"Because, Rose . . . he looks miserable. I mean, he's trying to hide it, but it's clear that he misses you. I've known the man for years. He might not wear his heart on his sleeve, but when he feels something, he feels it deeply."

Rose's thoughts whirled. "I don't understand. He essentially told me that he wasn't willing to give up any of the things he'd have to give up for me. Which is why I left." But he hadn't, had he? She'd asked him if he could burn his life down for her, and he'd just stared at her with that shocked, pained look.

She hadn't really given him any time to think about it or consider his answer.

Was she the villain in this story?

"What's he still doing in Haven Ridge? I thought he had to go back to Chicago."

"He negotiated a remote position with his company so he can be here three weeks a month to help Erin get the arts center going." Liv fell silent and then asked quietly, "Rose, why don't you just call him?"

It was a good question. It was the adult thing to do, rather than talk to one of his friends like they were in high school and she was gathering information on a boy she liked. But she knew the answer, even if she didn't say it out loud.

His first rejection had hurt so much that she wasn't sure she could take a second one. Somehow, it felt too much like begging, and she was done with begging a man to love her. To put her first. Either he could or he couldn't, but she'd already made too many decisions based on who loved her or who didn't. It was time to make a decision based on what she wanted.

And she wanted to make a home in Haven Ridge.

It might kill her to see Will and not have him, but how much worse would it be to know that he was the reason that she had walked away from the one place she thought she could be happy? She knew it didn't make any sense, but she'd known it from the first moment that she'd set foot in the town.

"I don't suppose you know anyone who's hiring in Haven Ridge?" Rose asked hopefully.

"Well, it's funny you should say that . . ."

Twenty minutes later, Rose hung up with Liv with a notepad full of notes and finally a sense of direction. She scrolled through her contact list and hit the one named *Mom - Office,* hoping she wasn't too late to catch her before she headed to her next class.

"Rose! Hi!"

Rose took a deep breath. "I hate to ask you this, but can I borrow three hundred dollars? I'm going back to Colorado."

* * *

Will could hand it to Haven Ridge. It might be a small town, but its people were well connected. Forget six degrees of separation. It took exactly two degrees to find the person he needed to make this whole mad idea of his work.

It turned out that Gregory, the owner of the Koffee Kabin, was friends with a Colorado-based artisan coffee roaster, whose wife just happened to have the exact skills that he needed. Which was how Will found himself driving the farm truck two-and-a-half hours northwest to a small cafe in the center of Denver.

He squeezed himself into narrow on-street parking and then strode up to the glass door of the corner bakery. Even at two p.m. on a Tuesday, the place was buzzing with conversation, a line forming from the register in front of a glass case and winding out the door. Will stood in line patiently until he got to the register.

"Welcome to Bittersweet Cafe," the male barista said with a friendly smile. "What can I get you?"

"Just a drip coffee and an eclair, please. For here."

"Coming right up." He swiveled away to serve up Will's coffee in a ceramic cup and saucer and then placed an eclair on a pretty patterned plate.

Will paid at the register and then nabbed a small two-person table in the corner where he could watch the door for Gregory's contact. Though how he was going to figure out who she was in this buzzing place with its constant flow of people in and out, he had no idea.

Turned out that it wasn't all that difficult. He caught

sight of the petite Asian woman the minute she stepped through the door, her stylish business suit and high heels standing out among the Colorado casual attire of the rest of the patrons. He must have been equally easy to clock, because after a quick scan of the interior, her eyes landed on him and she smiled.

She marched right over to him, her heels clicking on the tile floor, and he rose as she approached. She held out her hand. "Will Parker, right? I'm Analyn Shaw. But you can call me Ana."

Will shook her hand with a smile. "Thanks for meeting with me."

Ana pulled out her chair and seated herself across from him. "It's my pleasure. Greg told my husband, Bryan, that you have a crisis publicity situation with a nonprofit?"

"Sort of." Slowly, Will unraveled the entire situation for Ana, what they were building, and the problem of having a founding member who was under investigation for fraud. She listened attentively, her gaze never wavering from his face.

"Right," she said. "And you're absolutely sure that she's innocent?"

"One hundred percent. I'd bet my life on it."

Ana nodded thoughtfully. "In that case, I have a few ideas. In my experience, transparency is the best approach when you're dealing with something tangential to a crime. Supporters don't get upset when someone's been caught up in a situation beyond their control; they get upset when they think you've been hiding it from them."

"So you can help?"

His hope must have shown on his face, because she sighed. "Can I ask you a question?"

"Of course."

"Why do you have to employ Rose Cameron? Why not give her some sort of compensation for her contributions and just move on without her?"

Will swallowed and opened his mouth to explain, but it seemed that his feelings were plain on his face because Ana smiled. "I see. You don't need to elaborate. Yes, my firm can help you. Let me do a little research on the media coverage of the case. Put me in touch with Rose's attorney if she has one. And then I can give you a quote for my retainer."

The word *retainer* made him cringe, but he'd known it was going to be costly. Ana was right. If Rose was just some person, it would be easier and less expensive to compensate her and move on. But she wasn't. Both he and Erin had agreed that this had been her vision and it didn't feel right to move forward without her. If this was what he needed to do to make it work, he would do it.

Will rose and offered his hand, and Ana followed. "Thank you for your time. I appreciate it."

"Again, it's truly my pleasure. Don't worry, I've dealt with far worse situations than this one. All things considered, this is an easy fix."

Will watched the publicist go, his hopes lifting for the first time since Rose had walked away from Larkspur House. From the research he'd done, he'd learned that Ana Shaw owned one of the most-respected crisis publicity firms in Colorado, and she worked with everyone from professional athletes to politicians to billionaire real estate developers. If she said that their situation was an easy fix, it was.

He let out a long, unsteady breath and sank back into his chair in front of his untouched coffee and pastry. That was one big hurdle out of the way. Now he had the biggest one yet to go.

Getting Rose to forgive him.

CHAPTER THIRTY-THREE

ONE OF THESE DAYS, Rose would roll into town with money in her pocket and a full tank of gas, but today was not that day. To her mother's credit, not only had she lent her the money, but she'd given her more than she'd asked for with no pressure to pay it back. Rose would, of course, after she settled into her new jobs—plural—but she knew that it might take a while to get situated in her new life in Haven Ridge.

At least this time, she knew it was different. This time it was a coming home story.

Rose navigated the pitted streets of Haven Ridge, her heart lifting with every familiar sight. How was it she had only been here for three weeks and already it felt like she had spent a lifetime here? For all their Southern charm, the familiar streets of Chapel Hill had felt dull and uninspiring to her when in her heart she yearned for mountain views and stunning sunsets.

Up ahead, she saw the jauntily bobbing gray-and-blue head of Granny Pearl as she strode down the sidewalk in her jean jacket and Air Jordans. Rose rolled down her window and raised her hand as she passed.

Granny Pearl beamed at her. "Welcome back, Rose!" she yelled, her voice following her down the street.

Rose took a deep breath and let the smile that had been threatening all afternoon rise to her face.

She pulled into a spot in front of the Brick House Cafe and climbed out of her car, inhaling the hot, dry air and lifting her face to the summer sunshine that already beat down with surprising intensity. When she stepped into the cafe, Thomas immediately looked up from behind the counter and smiled. "Mallory is waiting for you. Go on up. All the way to the top."

Rose gave him a little wave and moved through the cafe to the back, noting the smiles that got sent her way. She might have only been here for a few weeks, but people knew who she was, knew what it meant that she was back. Her heart swelled.

She slipped into the back and then up the stairs that led to the third floor of the building. She raised her hand to knock at the door before she realized that it was already slightly ajar. Slowly, she pushed the door open. "Mallory?"

"Rose!" came a voice from deep in the apartment. "Come in! I'll be right there!"

Rose stepped inside and closed the door behind her, then drew in her breath. She'd already seen the Rivases' charming apartment, but she hadn't expected the vacant space above to be an equally lovely time capsule with parquet floors and Victorian furniture. She was so absorbed in her examination of her new home that she almost didn't notice Mallory as she came out of the other room, her arms full of linens.

"I just put fresh sheets on the bed for you," the woman said. "There's a laundromat down the street when you need to wash everything again."

Rose turned to her, tears pricking her eyes. "Mallory,

thank you. You have no idea how much this means to me."

"I think I do," Mallory said softly. "You know, our stories aren't all that different. In fact, they're shockingly similar. I stayed in this apartment when I was trying to figure out what to do next with my life, so it feels appropriate that it does the same for you."

Impulsively, Rose reached out and hugged the woman around her armful of sheets, and Mallory laughed. "Okay, okay. I'll let you get settled. Let us know if you need anything. Obviously there's just a hot plate and a microwave here, but you know there's plenty of places to eat in town. Oh, and there's a spot out back for your car. It's better if you don't park on the street."

"Thank you." Rose opened the door for Mallory with one more smile, then closed it softly behind her. She needed to go down and get her suitcases and her boxes of books—she was hoping she could talk Thomas into helping her bring up the heavy ones—but right now she just wanted to look around at her new place. She explored every corner of the small apartment—the red-upholstered settee, the antique table and original fireplace, and in the bedroom, a four-poster bed heaped with a luxurious comforter so soft she wanted to heave herself into the middle of it. A tiny bathroom with a shower was attached to the room, as was a closet just big enough to hold her daily wardrobe.

It might be temporary while she looked for an apartment, but it was still lovely.

It just wasn't Larkspur House.

Rose shoved the thought away, knowing that the sudden stab in her chest wasn't about the house anyway. Beautiful as it was, as much as she'd loved her short time living there, it hadn't been the grandeur that mattered to her. It had been the people.

She breathed in slowly through her nose, held her breath for a few seconds, and then let it out through her mouth, feeling her jitters subside and her pulse stabilize. Whatever happened next with Will was okay. She'd learn to see him on the street and in the cafe, and gradually, this pain and this yearning would go away. She would forget what it felt like to be in his arms and have his lips on hers. Those three weeks would fade into the background like a lovely dream, and eventually she'd be able to smile and chat with him.

As impossible as it seemed, she might even be friends with whoever he chose to settle down with.

Because Will *would* settle down now that he was back in Haven Ridge. There were too few eligible bachelors in a town this small to go unattached for long. What woman wouldn't look at a man that handsome, smart, talented, and stable and want to lock him down?

Yes, someday she'd be able to be gracious about the woman in his life. Right now, though, she was pretty sure she would hate her.

Rose let out a watery laugh at how quickly her imagination had spiraled and shoved the thoughts down. Today was a day to celebrate the start of her new life, what might be, and not mourn what could have been.

She grabbed her keys out of her purse and made her way back down through the building and out the front door of the cafe, where she moved her car around to the back. Then she popped the trunk of the aging sedan and wrestled one of her suitcases out.

Three trips later, she'd gotten all her clothes up to the top floor, but the book boxes were too heavy to even get out of the trunk. Maybe her dad hadn't been teasing when he put them in the trunk and said she'd permanently crippled him. Still, she was going to get these upstairs one way or another, even if she had to unpack them by the armful and take them up in another twenty trips.

"Need some help?"

Rose froze with her arms wrapped around the cardboard box, the back of her neck prickling. Surely this was just her imagination playing tricks on her. Slowly, she straightened and turned to see Will standing behind her, a slight smile on his lips.

Her heart lurched at the sight of him, and all of her earlier convictions flew out the window. How had she thought she could do this? Face him like he didn't matter? Pretend that every fiber in her body didn't stretch toward him when he was near?

Because no matter what she told herself, she loved him.

Will didn't seem to be bothered by her lack of response. He just gently nudged her out of the way and lifted the box easily. "All the way upstairs?"

Rose cleared her throat. "Ah, yes, please."

She followed him up the stairs to her apartment where she opened the door for him. He deposited the box on the floor with a sigh and straightened slowly. Maybe it hadn't been quite as easy as he'd made it look.

"Cute place," he said. "I've never been up here."

"Yeah, it's just temporary," Rose said. "I need to find an apartment, but I don't have the money for the deposit yet. I'm going to be working part time at the bookstore and the bakery."

A faint smile came to Will's lips. "I heard. You'll love working with Liv and Gemma. They're both great."

"I'm not entirely sure they didn't hire me out of pity," Rose admitted. "I don't really think they need the help."

"They don't," Will said quietly. "But we all knew you wouldn't come back unless you had something lined up."

Rose stilled, something fluttering in her chest. "What does that mean?"

Will gestured toward the old-fashioned settee. "Let's sit."

"No, I'd rather stand. What do you mean *we*?"

Will cringed and rubbed a hand over the back of his neck, a sure sign he was uncomfortable. "This is not how I meant to do this."

"Do what?" Rose's heart fluttered. "Will, you're scaring me."

Horror washed over his face. "No, Rose, I'm so sorry, I just . . . suck at this."

"Can you just tell me? Because right now, it feels like I've walked into a really creepy set-up and I don't know what to think."

"Fine. I'm . . . .I'm just going to say it." He took a deep breath. "I love you, Rose, and I want you to come back to Larkspur House. Help us build the arts center."

Hearing it all so plainly rocked her back. "I think I am going to take that seat now." She stumbled to the sofa and sank down onto it, wide-eyed.

Will sat down beside her and took her hand. "Rose, from the first day, we started off wrong. I constantly put my foot in my mouth, much like I'm doing right now. But the truth is this. You asked me if I could burn my entire life down for you. And I didn't answer you, because all I could think about in that moment was what I had to lose."

He took a deep breath, his eyes connecting with hers. "But then I realized I don't want any of it if I can't have you."

"But what about the investigation? What about the fact you can't be associated with me if you're running the center? If you're going to be fundraising?"

"I hired someone," he said simply. "And she's going to

take care of it. Rose, this was your vision, your dream. There is no arts center without you."

Rose blinked, her head spinning. "And Liv and Gemma knew about all this?"

Will grimaced. "Don't be mad at them. They were just trying to help. And if after all this, you don't want anything to do with me, if you don't want anything to do with Larkspur House, you still have jobs with them until you figure out what else you want to do. I would understand."

"Are you crazy?" Rose whispered.

Will nodded slowly, then began to rise. "I can't say I blame you."

Rose grabbed his hand and pulled him back down beside her. "Don't be stupid." And she kissed him.

It seemed to take a moment for Will to register what was happening, the rapid switch between what he'd been sure was a rejection to what was most certainly not a rejection. And then he was pulling her closer, his hand sliding behind her neck to angle her head, kissing her until there was no room for thinking, just feeling.

When he pulled back, Rose felt breathless and dizzy and so happy that she almost didn't trust it. Because Will might struggle with the right words at times, but there was no mistaking the emotion in his kiss. "You could have just led with that."

Will laughed, but that light was back in his eyes. "Does this mean I haven't screwed things up completely?"

"No, not completely."

"Then what do you say?"

"To what? I don't remember a question."

His grin flashed, unrestrained, at the playful lilt in her words. But his reply held a formal cast, as if he were asking her something of gravest importance. "Will you take me back even after I was foolish enough to let you go the first time? And will you come help us build the Amelia Bixby Arts Center and Conservatory?"

"I would be delighted to," she replied, equally formally. And then she laughed as he swept her up again and kissed her.

"I really wish you would've agreed before I moved that box of books up here," he murmured in her ear, and she laughed.

"It's not a waste. I'm still going to stay here for a bit while we work out all the details of my employment." Rose pulled back and smiled up at him. "After all, there's got to be some ground rules if I'm dating my boss, right?"

"You're probably right. What type of rules were you thinking? No kissing between the hours of nine and five?"

Rose looked at him in mock horror. "What's the point in dating my boss if there's no kissing on company time?"

Will laughed and pressed one more kiss to her lips before he pulled her to her feet. "What do you say we go tell Erin the good news? She told me I couldn't come back unless I brought you with me."

Rose laughed, the weight of a thousand bad decisions lifting off her, as she let Will lead her out of the apartment down the stairs. She wasn't foolish enough to believe in uncomplicated happily-ever-afters. There were still details to be considered and negotiations to be made and the simple fact that she was in love with a man who it would take a lifetime to fully know. Who said the wrong thing, even though he always did the right thing. Who was willing to risk everything important to him—not so he could have her, but so she could have everything she wanted, everything she needed.

Who felt, inexplicably, like home.

EPILOGUE

Four months later

SNOWFLAKES FELL SOFTLY from the flat gray sky, blanketing Larkspur House and grounds in a thin veil of white and covering the property with a hushed whisper. The first snow of the year was late this year, falling this second week of November, but Rose couldn't be more delighted.

For one, it hid the still-unfinished landscaping and the fact that while the repairs might be done on the house, there were still plenty of cosmetic touches to be completed.

For another, their first batch of guests were from all over the southern United States, mostly from places that didn't get snow. They were going to lose their minds.

Almost as if she'd conjured them with the thought, the rumble of an engine caught Rose's attention amidst the crunch of gravel outside the house. Moments later, the door opened and Will burst in, covered in snow and beaming.

"No problems?" Rose inquired, rising from behind the table they'd installed to act as a welcome desk.

"A little slippery, but the plows are out." He moved to her side and bent to drop a quick kiss on her lips just before their guests burst in—five women and two men—all smiling and chatting among themselves, their cheeks red from the cold and puffing from the weight of their suitcases and instruments in the unaccustomed altitude.

Rose straightened from behind the desk, a welcoming smile coming to her face without effort. "Welcome to Larkspur House. We're happy to have you for our inaugural music session."

To say the last four months had been a whirlwind would be an understatement. Between Will and Gemma, the business structure of the arts center had been put together quickly, but Erin and Rose had been working nonstop on all the administrative and creative tasks necessary to make the endeavor into a real, legitimate retreat center. She didn't think she'd gotten more than five hours of sleep in a night since she'd come back to Haven Ridge, but she was so blindingly happy that it didn't matter.

This is what she was made for.

In the end, they hadn't needed to worry. As soon as they'd begun their marketing campaign to build awareness of their intensive retreat sessions, they'd been flooded with far more interest than they could manage. It seemed that Erin's reputation spread further than she thought, helped along by the bios and videos they'd posted of her on their website as the master instructor for the cello program. All seven slots for both Erin's sessions had been booked by the end of the week and they were already scrambling to see how they could expand capacity for the following ones.

Rose pulled her mind back to the task at hand and greeted the students one by one as she presented them with their room keys and the welcome packets containing information on the house and their schedule for the next two weeks. In the end, they'd decided to reserve the fourth floor for family and instructors, the third floor for guest rooms, and the first two floors for classrooms and work spaces. The house that had felt so cavernous and empty to her now felt pleasantly full and friendly. Homey.

"Okay, if you'll follow me, I'll take you to your rooms on the third floor and then I'll show you your classroom and rehearsal spaces. And the kitchen and dining room, of course. I expect you'll be spending plenty of time in there."

Nervous laughter rang out around her, and Rose caught Will's quick smile before she led them up the staircase to their rooms. As they bumped up the stairs under their heavy loads, she made a note that they really needed to move up the elevator project as soon as they had the funds. It was one thing for staff to go up and down the stairs multiple times a day; quite another to expect guests to haul up suitcases and cellos without it causing some wear and tear on the house. Rose could just imagine Will's sigh at the thought of another expense, but like always, he would simply write it down and start figuring out how to make it work.

Rose got everyone settled into their rooms on the third floor, though two of the students quickly decided to swap since one wanted to be near the restroom and the other wanted to be as far away from it as possible. She stood in the hall, watching and listening in bemusement. Their guests were all adults, ranging in age from twenty-two to fifty, but now they seemed like excited children away at sleepaway camp for the first time. Which was really what this was—an intensive, very expensive, luxurious sleepaway camp.

"What do we think?" Erin materialized beside Rose, pitching her voice low.

"They seem like a good-natured group," Rose whispered back. "They all get along well so far."

"Good. I tried to pick people I thought would be a good match." They'd had so many applications from talented musicians who wanted the chance to study underneath an accomplished cellist that it had been hard to narrow them down. Erin had finally chosen her top fourteen candidates and then sorted them into two sessions based on their compatibility; the second session would start just after Thanksgiving.

The guests began to emerge from the rooms into the hallway now, and Rose smiled at them. "Everyone, I'd like to introduce you to your master instructor, Erin Parker."

Erin stepped forward, smiling warmly. She might have hated to be on display on stage, but here she seemed perfectly comfortable, confident. "Welcome, everyone. We are so pleased to have you here for our first cello session at the Amelia Bixby Arts Center and Conservatory. You were each chosen because I saw something special in your application videos. I'm so looking forward to working with you over the next two weeks. Now if you'll follow me, I'll show you to the classroom and rehearsal spaces we'll be using during the session . . ."

The group shuffled off after Erin, back down the stairs, and Rose followed them at a distance, continuing down to the second floor where Will was waiting for her, a smile on his face.

"Big day," he said. "You did it."

"*We* did it," Rose corrected, but warmth spread in her

chest from his praise. "It was a team effort and we couldn't have done it without the three of us working together."

But Will was still looking at her, smiling.

She frowned. "What?"

"I heard from Ben."

Rose's eyes widened. Ben Levine was the literary agent who had taken on the unpublished Bixby manuscript as soon as her mother had confirmed that she did indeed believe it and the three other books published under Andrew's name had been written by Amelia Bixby. The last she'd heard, he was in intense talks with several publishers who rightfully saw the potential for long-term sales to academic institutions.

"And?" Rose prompted.

"He has several offers for us to consider."

Rose's heart rose into her throat and a smile trembled at the corners of her mouth. She was almost afraid to ask. "How much?"

"He's advising us not to take the highest offer. Another press offered a smaller up-front advance but superior royalty rates. Ben is confident it will earn out, given the number of universities who already want to teach the book as part of their core literature curriculum, sight unseen."

"Which is?"

A slow smile spread over Will's face. "Five hundred thousand dollars."

Rose stared at him. "We expected half of that."

"You didn't ask who the publisher was."

She froze. "Who?"

"Coriolanus Press, Durham, North Carolina."

Rose's mouth dropped open. "My dad's company? I didn't even know they were bidding. He didn't tell me."

"Probably didn't want to get your hopes up. They

weren't even close on the cash they could bring to the
table, but their royalty offer was aggressive. And long
term . . ."

". . . it's enough to keep the center operational and
the trust solvent." A smile spread over her face. "That's
amazing."

"And it's all because of you." Will slid his arms
around her waist and pulled her close, so she had no
choice but to look up at him. "Had you not pushed, had
you not been so determined to find out the truth, it
might never have come to be. For that matter, one of
literature's biggest mysteries might never have been
solved."

She wanted to brush it off; praise still made her
uneasy. But Will looked so pleased she didn't have the
heart to argue. He was always going to think she was
more amazing than she was, and he'd never believe
differently. So she lifted her face for his kiss and sank
into the warmth of it, the safety and love that was
present in every touch.

"There's one more thing," he murmured.

"One more?"

"I told you it was a big day. Arlene called me on the
way back from the airport. The investigation is
complete. They have officially found that you were in
no way involved and that you never profited from
Jordan's fraud. The police are pursuing criminal charges
against him, and the nonprofit's biggest donors are
filing a civil lawsuit not just against him, but against his
parents as well. They're not getting away with it, Rose."

It was almost too much on top of everything else
he'd told her. But as she considered what it meant, the
ever-present knot of anxiety unraveled inside her. She'd
known it would happen—she was innocent, after all—
and the publicist, Analyn Shaw, had done a remarkable

job in their initial publicity for the center, painting her as a crusader for arts and literature despite her tangential involvement with a criminal. But hearing that the investigation against her was closed, that the world would see Jordan for who he was, that that chapter of her life was officially over . . . it was as if the last tangled threads holding her to her old self and her old life unraveled.

"Thank you," she said softly, looking into Will's eyes.

"For what?"

"For believing in me. For helping me believe in myself. For being willing to risk it all for me."

He pulled her close and rested his chin on top of her head; she could hear his heartbeat beneath her ear, as strong and steady and reliable as he was. "You know, I never believed any of it."

"Any of what?"

"The magic of Haven Ridge. I thought that all there was to this world was what we could see and touch. The lives that we've made for ourselves. But it has all fit together too well to be an accident. You coming here just when we needed you and you needed us. Everything that's happened. What do you suppose it means?"

Rose pulled back to look into his eyes. "I don't know. Maybe there really is something bigger than us out there. But whatever it is, whoever it is, I'm grateful. Because without it, without you and Erin, I'd never have understood what I was missing."

What it felt like to be exactly where she needed to be, doing exactly what she was meant to do. Being loved by a man who showed her his love not with pretty words, but through actions.

And a place that showed her what it meant to be home.

WANT MORE HAVEN RIDGE?

READ THE PREQUEL NOVELLA

THE BRICK HOUSE CAFE

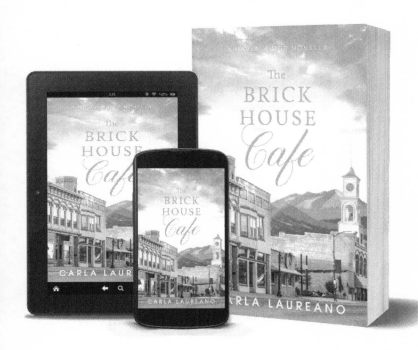

ABOUT THE AUTHOR

Carla Laureano could never decide what she wanted to be when she grew up, so she decided to become a novelist—and she must be kinda okay at it because she's won two RWA RITA® Awards. When she's not writing, she can be found cooking and trying to read through her TBR shelf, which she estimates will be finished in 2054. She currently lives in Denver, Colorado with her husband, two teen sons, and an opinionated cat named Willow.

Made in the USA
Las Vegas, NV
08 August 2024

93570537R00203